Secret Transgressions

The Whistling Girls & Crowing Hens Series
Book 3

Jan Anthony

Secret Transgressions is a creative work of historical stories. Names, characters, places and incidents are products of the author's imagination, and media articles are used as fiction and are not to be construed as real. Any resemblances to actual events, locales, organizations or persons, living or dead, is coincidental.

Copyright © *Jan Anthony*, 2024 All Rights Reserved
This book is subject to the condition that no part of this book is to be reproduced, transmitted in any form or means; electronic or mechanical, stored in a retrieval system, photocopied, recorded, scanned, or otherwise. Any of these actions require the proper written permission of the author.

Published by Mother Courage Press

ISBN: 979-8-3302-3623-7
Library of Congress Preassigned
Control Number 2024911928

Secret Transgressions

The Whistling Girls & Crowing Hens Series
Book 3
*A creative memoir based on letters,
prose, poetry, journals, diaries and imagination*

Jan Anthony

Mother Courage Press
Publisher, Jeanne Arnold

The Whistling Girls & Crowing Hens Series

Two straight married women risk families and careers, leave society's compulsory heterosexuality in 1972, and boldly thrive in an unchartered, intimate relationship. Jan and Bea experience historic events in the women's movement and gay/lesbian world in their 39 years together. Each book presents deeper levels on major topics and adventures.

The stand-alone books in this Whistling Girls & Crowing Hens Series will appeal to:

- readers to experience straight and lesbian lives,
- young adults to appreciate what has come before them,
- adults and elders to remember what they've survived and
- women-loving-women who've defied society's rules.

DEDICATION

Dedicated to the women in my life,
especially Bea for her love, her poems
and journals,
and to those who love her and them

Possessed by demons,
whipped by wicked witches
with their tainted messages,
driven almost to madness
by other value systems,
a teeming tropical sea
dreaming oneself a desert.
The nightmare vanished
one morning when I woke up
and fell in love with myself.
by Bea

Prologue

Jan's Intensive Journal on May 7, 1977
Dialogue with Work

Story: I am a story that must be told. I am bursting to be expressed. The pressures are great. I want it to be a universal experience for all human beings. I want Jan to write me.

Jan: But you're too great a risk. You demand all my energy and I don't have time.

S: You must take the time to finish me now before someone else does it and takes away your rightful claim to immortality.

J: Immortality. Shit. No one will want to bother with you. Only Bea gives me any encouragement to finish and that's because she loves me.

S: Well then get it written only for you, and anything that happens after that, let it happen. Besides you really can't write anything else until you know what I'll need first. I'm your real priority.

J: Yes, you bastard. You get me into tough problems with my lover, my husband, kids and my career. I could be a real pro at work and get a bigger salary if you weren't behind my head demanding my time and energy, my dream. You're only a phantom dream.

S: Phantom, true, because you need me to get those specters out of your head. You've been planning to use this means for release for years. You've capitalized on this. You even use your lover, family and friends for characters.

J: Write what you know best, they say.

S: Besides, you're using me as an excuse to live your own lifestyle. Who else gets away with what you do and isn't demolished by society and/or friends/relatives? You keep this up, you're not only going to lose me and what I have to offer, but you're going to lose them and end up alone.

J: If it weren't for you and all you stand for—my creativity—I wouldn't be as frustrated and discontented as I am today.

S: You have always been discontented with limits. When you finish me, you'll set new goals. Part of your frustration is because you've put me aside for so long to take care of your lover and children. You wanted to do that too, remember?

J: I've wanted to do a hundred great things, and I've done many already.

S: And that's why now you're impatient. It's getting time for you to complete that primary responsibility and be confronted with the reality of proving whether you're good enough to complete me.

CHAPTER 1

Jan on January 3, 1976

"Lust" is the first of Dante's seven deadly sins in his moralistic *Divine Comedy.* Maybe I should read Dante someday to learn what hell I will endure after I die. Yet who am I to disagree with this ancient moralist who defines lust as attempting to fill the deep emptiness in one's life? Who am I to have the power to redefine, to decide what is right and wrong? "Lust is no lady" is another cliché. Lust is negatively defined as being out of control and self-centered, primarily in sexual behavior, and certainly not ladylike. But what about being womanly? To give to another, to abandon one's self, to be pleased with the satisfaction of another and, in the process, to be pleased and satisfied with oneself.

Maybe I should read Kinsey someday in my spare time? I am a woman who lusts in the broad definition encompassing joy, play, people, career, courage, laughter, and making angels in the snow: a lusting for love and happiness. However, when my concept of lust, desire and pleasure is condemned by society, how can I escape negative stress and emotional turmoil?

And in emotional turmoil, decisions that could produce creative results may end up becoming grievously poor judgment.

Be careful.

Jan on January 21, 1976

During some free time to shop Downtown, I stopped my car in front of the well-known, established Marquette Apartments four blocks north from my home with my job at Lakeshore Med only two blocks in between.

Curious? Why not ask if there are any vacancies?

"Sorry. No. There's even a waiting list."

"I need space to write." And his eyes lit up with a chance to rent the little room that had been a maid's sleeping room for one of the tenants, now deceased. When he showed it to me, I decided it was perfect for my needs.

It's about the area of two double bed mattresses laid flat on the floor. The height of the floor to the ceiling seems larger than the room itself. A chipped old washbasin lavatory hangs in the corner next to a window. Another door opens to a bathroom big enough for a toilet and a tiny tub. The closet's in a hall alcove outside the room.

The rent is $60 a month. I can afford that. "I'll get back to you," I said.

Alex and the kids managed well without me when I stayed at my dad's house to be company for his damn dog while he spent a couple weeks in the hospital. Then I worked long hours every day during the six-week strike at Lakeshore Medical Center and then Bea and I spent three weeks together in Europe. Yes, three weeks with my lover in Europe.

And Alex knows that I love Bea and want to be with her.

Alex also knows about my strange project of writing a gender-free novel and he barely tolerates that idea too. Last evening I showed him what I'd written and how hard it was to concentrate on getting the work finished. Somehow I persuaded him to let me have a "sabbatical" of three-month's time away from home to work on my life's goal to finish my novel. I surprised him when I said I had a place to stay and I would begin my sabbatical on the morning after Matt's 17th birthday supper on February 2.

I will have what Virginia Woolf had: a tiny "room of one's own."

Jan on January 30, 1976

When I was a homemaker with time to read, I chose enlightening biographies and non-fiction books that stimulated my liberal tendencies. However, if I were happy in my marriage, books like Nena and George O'Neill's *Open Marriage* wouldn't interest me. The book that described more revolutionary models was Nigel Nicolson's *Portrait of a Marriage* about his mother, Vita Sackville-West who had several women lovers. Ha! She even ran away to Europe with her lover Violet. And Vita and Virginia Woolf were tender friends and lovers.

My trip to Europe with my lover may have been my dream since I learned about Vita's trip tryst with Violet. I became an English Bloomsbury groupie via British movies of the era and my hero Virginia Woolf who graced her lover Vita with a celebration of *Orlando*, Virginia's androgynous story. Vita's free and open sexual and intellectual life was possible because her husband played the same game.

Of course, my husband couldn't and wouldn't think of that and is constantly threatened by my behavior. Who wouldn't be? Lakeshore Med's strike lasted for forty days and then I left with my Bea for Europe. And now I want a "sabbatical" to write my androgynous novel. Who do I think I am, Vita Sackville-West? Well, Alex's certainly not the stoic, accepting bi-sexual man like Vita's husband.

And he's trying to save our marriage.

<<<>>>

It's been a heavy day with Alex after he and Matt set up our children's oak bunk bed in my room. The lower bunk with a shelf for my record player and books will be my "living room couch" and the upper bunk will be where I sleep.

Because of my bad back, Marge and Bea helped me move the rest. We placed my mother's old Smith Corona portable on the typewriter table with the phone next to the bed. The door crashes into the table when I open it completely. I bought a small, second or third-hand refrigerator and had it delivered. An electric cooking plate sits on the file cabinet that holds all my writing. I'll eat breakfast and lunch at the hospital. Instead of seeing the lake and the sun and the moon rising in the east, my view is now two garbage cans on a worn wooden porch with a green slate roof beyond. To compensate for my lost view, Bea and Marge painted a mural on the white bathroom wall of flowers growing from the floorboards, birch trees that I love to hug, green leaves and ivy vines, and an inspiring red apple hanging from those vines. The Garden of Eden? Do I take a bite of the apple? Haven't I done that already?

When Marge's nine-year-old Tommy came to see my mini-mural, he said that I certainly wouldn't be having any folk dance parties here. It will be my space during February, March and April, the duration of my temporary home to write my book, get my life together and maybe even heal my back.

Alex wants promises I cannot make. Of course he must know that. He said he wants to cry. My scar tissue from past arguments thickens. He knows I have the courage to find what I need. The velvet chains of acceptable middle class values will finally break when I complete my responsibility to my teenage children.

When Nick Dixon asked me to work for Lakeshore Medical Center, he was confident that he hired an intelligent, liberal-thinking woman, a good writer, faithful wife, dedicated mother and a calm and compassionate person. I was all those things and, for the most part, I still am, yet he didn't know what lay behind that. Nor did I.

I found the person, a woman, to fill those needs, to love me. I also found in loving her how much I respect myself as a woman, as a mother, as a daughter, as a whole person filled with goodness and with life.

Jan on February 3, 1976

Yesterday started with severe pelvic pain in the morning before work while I prepared the main course, my German recipe for roulade for Matt's delicious birthday dinner. It will simmer in the Nesco while I'm at work. I picked up the chocolate cake I ordered on my way home from Lakeshore Med. Our dinner was pleasant with family, Alex's sister Var and niece Sona and my dad.

Matt remarked, "I guess this will be our last good meal for a while."

Bea on February 8, 1976

Jan is free to be with me.

With intense joy, we drove to the Wisconsin Women in the Arts Conference at the University of Wisconsin-Green Bay campus. Being away together is like the three passionate weeks touring Europe. This exhilarating reunion seems free and bold starting on Friday night with cocktails in our tacky, grape-colored motel room, then weaving our way in abandoned and boozy euphoria to the steakhouse across the street. We devoured what steak we could for nourishment and took our leftovers for breakfast—washing it down with our wine in a room without coffee service.

We nourished ourselves in every way among the starched sheets and thin blankets on a hard, flat mattress.

<<<>>>

The conference theme, "Women Together: A Moving Mosaic," featured Kate Millett, a scholar, an artist and radical feminist author, and Judy Chicago, a scholar, a feminist writer and an unconventional, revolutionary artist.

On Saturday morning, Kate Millett's overpowering presence, her courage, strength and intelligence became engraved upon my psyche. Millett's book, *Sexual Politics*, forced her out of a bi-sexual closet into a lesbian locker. Undaunted, she then created a media blitz greater than Betty Friedan's book, *The Feminine Mystique*. Friedan's book gave new life to our current women's movement after Friedan feared the "Lesbian Menace" by citing "guilt by association" because of the many lesbians who helped push feminism's political and social agenda forward. Millett's courage demanded women's equality—emphasizing equality and sexual freedom.

The conference women in the auditorium stood and cheered Millett and her bold ideas. Both of us, with our brains and our spirits united, burst with an affirming rush of commitment.

Inspiring workshops led by unique artistic women followed as we made our way among several hundred feminists. Many of them seemed to be lesbians, but we couldn't be sure about that. How could you be sure? We aren't even sure of that label for ourselves. I know I'm not a lesbian. I've been married for twenty-one years and have four children. I happen to love someone who happens to be a woman among other active, creative, and confident women surrounding us.

At Saturday evening's banquet, we danced together in the midst of all of them. What a liberating contrast to our initial scary yet curious descent into our first women's bar in Milwaukee several months before. At Milwaukee's seedy-looking Sugar Stop's exterior, we stepped furtively between motorcycles parked in a slanted row and slipped silently into the dark tavern, its back bar mirror illuminated by the Pabst Blue Ribbon Beer neon logo. The patrons, clad basically in black, either leather vests or t-shirts and jeans, blended into the smokey background. Our pastel polyester leisure pantsuits worn earlier to the evening's theater date made us seem strange to them—too conventional and straight.

The thrill of our dancing that night overcame the tension of our first daring venture into a lesbian bar that advertised in a gay newsletter that Jan picked up in our first visit to Sister Moon, Milwaukee's feminist bookstore. Being together in a lesbian bookstore or a bar, realizing you belong to a hidden culture, finding others out there who are somewhat like you and your lover may be empowering or frightening or both.

"Our first dance together in public," Jan whispered in my ear. "I'll always remember it." And we embraced and swayed as one, two women on the small dance floor in Milwaukee under the reflected colored swirl of the mirrored mosaic globe above us while women at the bar, their secret den, watched and speculated about us.

But this Saturday at the UW-Green Bay campus, everyone danced and I found myself in the center of a circle of observers with Jan leading me on. I shifted into overdrive as I had done when I danced at teenage parties after I lost my weight and my inhibitions while striving to be like Diana Rigg's Emma Peel.

Here, now, with one hand on my belt buckle and the other hand held high with bracelets jingling and rings sparkling about my head, I gyrated from the waist, pulsing toward my lover. My heeled boots accented the pounding rhythm of "Funky Town" with Jan clapping and yelping in encouraging admiration. Always aware of the people around her, she stepped back and made room for other women watching in the ring around me, making room for others to dance with me. I found myself in step and, in turn, first dancing with Kate Millett, then Judy Chicago, then others from the celebrating feminist circle.

I actually danced with Judy Chicago and Kate Millett!

Wah Hoo! What a night!

And what a Sunday morning!

At dawn, a gentle mouth touched my shoulder to wake me and I kissed her back. "You turn me on again, Bea."

"You didn't get enough?"

" Remember my motto: 'I want one more!'"

"But we must hear Judy Chicago. And have some breakfast, especially after all our strenuous exercise."

"Yes. I guess so, but it's important that we're physical. It's not just the orgasm, it's the intimacy, the closeness. It's warmth and comfort, skin and lips—and all that may follow."

"Yes, dear. But I think it's time for a shower."

"Let's shower together!"

Starting with a stunning and startling illustrated lecture by Judy Chicago, she described her monumental *The Dinner Party* project by first introducing us to her published *Through the Flower* book using passages and illustrations on new ways of making women-centered art to better understand, collaborate and create alternative art outside of male domination and dogma.

Power, energy and genius exploded from Judy Chicago's small frame topped by her bursting black halo of tight curls. Her slide images honored menstruation, birth and breasts with newer creations from her *Dinner Party* project: vaginas as ceramic sculptures celebrating the rising power and influence of our feminist foremothers. Her ideas challenged us to demand equality in a peaceful world because of women's values.

How could we aspire to more? Well, Jan found out. She won a writing award for her "Nightmare" submission. The reviewer described Jan's winning submission as raw, but funding must be found to publish the work.

Then came the Women's Kitchen Band of playful seniors who filled the stage with joy, laughter and clever arrangements of kazoos, washboards, strainers, peelers, toy instruments and a piano. The audience would not let these witty, white-haired kitchen musicians stop and, after being encouraged to join in a dance on the stage, women of all ages, nuns, dykes, weird-looking women, barefoot teens and fabric artists in hand-crafted outfits kicked up their heels and started a line dance that encircled the auditorium while the rest of us stomped, clapped and sang: truly a moving mosaic.

Finally, exhausted and inspired, we tumbled out into the cold but sunny February afternoon to return to Jan's room and celebrate another significant event in our lives with sweet, quiet loving on soft, smooth sheets without blankets on top of an oak bunk bed mattress and being careful not to topple off.

<<<>>>

Jan on February 12, 1976

I've played around with the concept of androgyny and the use of gender-free pronouns since I was captivated by the concept presented in Carolyn Heilbrun's *Toward a Recognition of Androgyny: the realization of man in woman and woman in man*. I was entranced with her analysis of Virginia Woolf and her *Orlando* novel inspired by Virginia's beloved Vita Sackville West. These ideas inspired me to advance this concept as a new way toward equality.

Many persons indicate exactly what pronouns they prefer on emails, stationery, name tags, etc. It's amazing! And if you make a mistake, they may think you're inconsiderate.

Ms. Magazine's article described the use of neutral pronouns and I tried to write my androgynous novel and hide behind gender-free characters. I was determined to tell the world about my loving another woman and if I used neutral pronouns, I would keep everyone guessing and, at the same time, save the world from the degenerative power of gender-bias and the denigration of women.

I titled my work "being." It was to describe what it's like to be a human being—not a man nor a woman—but a human being. I used the neutral pronouns tey, ter and tem which creates androgynous characters in a contemporary time and place. My six major characters would interact and the reader never knows who is what gender, but it doesn't matter. These characters are human beings searching for universal truths: finding meaning in life, experiencing loneliness and separation, having dependencies and fears while looking for love and acceptance.

My neutral pronoun is also used for unborn babies and God. It may help to resolve the he/she and him/her language hang-up. And even more importantly, it may desex Christian's and most religions of the maleness of God that, by tradition, subordinates the female half of the population.

My main character Andy is a liberal minister who's married to Chris. In ter (his/her) openness to others, risks a sexual affair with Bernie and later falls in love with Jamie. Andy realizes that each person is ultimately alone and tey (he/she) frees temself (him/her/them) toward self-determination.

Here's a sample.

Andy's capacity for love seems infinite; ter hunger for it too. Being an only child, it's important to be aware of what it takes to please others and replace ter loss of your loved ones. Perhaps that's why tey chose a helping profession. And the liberal ministry was surely that. Compared to the bureaucracy of social work, the disciplinary requirements of teaching, the rigid discipline of medicine, ter rebellion from the restraints of fundamental Protestantism, and ter need to communicate with others at a spiritual level made the liberal ministry a natural choice.

All Andy had to do was report to the board and committees, prepare an intellectually satisfying and emotionally inspiring Sunday service and meet all the needs of each person in the congregation who thinks each is as worthy as tey. It's a challenging, delightful and inspiring tightrope-walking profession dealing with life and death, turmoil and love. Yet despite of the intellectual standards set by divinity school, the denomination and the congregation, Andy's faith was basic, simple and positive.

I believe in the goodness of people. If you're going to love your neighbor as yourself, you better love yourself.

Tey knew that persons were not born good or bad—original sin be damned. When persons are free from fear of doing wrong and are encouraged to love themselves, they can open up to let the sun shine in, and they, in turn, are able to let their suns shine out.

I believe that this life is good. If you live the best life you can now, you need not fear the future. It will take care of itself while you appreciate each day.

Why settle for promises, promises, promises when Paradise can be here now. Why put up with, cope with, endure—for the better life after death. The joy tey felt watching the last scene of Thornton Wilder's *Our Town* never left tem. When Wilder's Emily came back from the grave, she said to the stage manager, "I didn't realize. All that was going on and we never noticed . . . Oh earth, you are too wonderful for anybody to realize you."

Then she asks the stage manager through her tears. "Do human beings ever realize life while they live it?—Every, every minute?

He answered, "No." And paused, "The saints and poets, maybe they do some."

Andy contemplated, "Which would I be? A poet, certainly not a saint." So tey threw out all the "nays" in ter life and Andy celebrated children and other people, trees, spring, kissing and hugging, fresh air, folk dancing, skinny dipping, dogs, peanuts, peace, quiet times, fun, wind, rain and making angels in the snow.

I believe in the mystery and glory of this earth and this universe. How many stars are there? Yes, they found that humankind can live in space. But how big is the universe? And how does a seed in the earth know how to grow into the plant it will be?

Andy threw away the need to know the answers to all things and trusted in deeper thoughts: feeling confident with all the uncertainties, celebrating each day, and learning to live happily with vast unknowns. From Edna St. Vincent Millay, tey caught the mad intensity of this security in not knowing all, yet feeling all: "God, I can push the grass apart and lay my finger on Thy heart!"

The search for truth is more important than finding it.
"What is God like, Andy?" asked a child.

"I don't know what Tey is like, but I do know that exchanging ideas and feelings about big questions like yours lets us learn more new things and care for others more deeply. I guess I believe in thinking and wondering."

"But what happens when we don't have an answer?"

"We will be content in this atmosphere with others that help us grow naturally toward our own faith in what we can understand and an open mind to wonder about what we cannot comprehend."

We need not follow only one voice or one teacher; we when learn from many and add our voice to the lessons, we can choose what has most meaning for each of us.

Though ideas were formed from the past, we need to adapt them to understand the present. Moses, Jesus, Mohammed, Confucius, Copernicus, Darwin—even before them. How far back? How did cave dwellers celebrate new life each spring? Once the past was now. There are universal concepts that unify all cultures and all ages.

"What is God like? And if we think we know, how can we be sure? And what may be sure for me may not be sure for you. Is there anything great enough for the answer? We can discover within ourselves a wellspring of wisdom, strength and beauty within our own minds and hearts that frees us to trust ourselves without another's set of rules. We need no set beliefs because we will not be restrained in our belief.

I believe we can try to make the most of our lives so that people and the earth will be glad that we have lived.

And making people happy gave Andy great joy.

Lots of luck pulling all that together. Family, job responsibilities and Bea called and I answered. And writing is hard work.

Bea on March 2, 1976

During her first month in her room, we spent almost every night together, or at least some part of the day at her place or mine, but now she says she has to work on her novel to get enough done to justify her absence from home. Yesterday she confessed her fears to me while we were still in bed. She visualized Alex crashing through my door, finding us in bed and brutalizing both of us. I don't think so, but then that's what fuels a creative imagination.

We'd swim and shower at the YMCA and she loves to have a massage for her bad back, her sore stomach and her tense nerves, but that's expensive. She talked me into having a massage and I couldn't stand having another person handle me like that, even if it is a woman. The treatment was to be a gift from Jan, and we lay under the sunlamp together after, but my body was not as happy and relaxed as hers.

She's been going home for suppers and plays games and stays with Jenny when Alex and Matt are away. So much for that time with her. And there are problems with the Lakeshore Med neighbors protesting the hospital's expansion plans so she's spending more time turning shit into sunshine, which she does so well at her PR job. And we could use more sunshine.

I hate March and always have since I was housebound when my husband was dead to me. I used to have to beg him for it. I needed sex and/or I needed love. I think my kids loved me, and now I miss my kids!

It's such a long and dreary month at the end of winter. When will winter ever end.

It's bad enough thinking about another weekend with Marge and Charlie, but when Jan invited Marge to join us for a movie date that I'd planned for us, I got angry. Good thing I still have my drinking buddies. That's more relaxing than a massage. I went home after supper at Greek Feasts to fall asleep, as usual. Jan phoned, was angry with me and cancelled our plans. Then she spent all day Saturday writing. I got pissed and had a real binge all day. And to top the whole thing, after being on the nod all day Saturday, the doorbell rang at 2 a.m. It was Charlie after coming from Marge's. He stayed with me and snored until 8 a.m.

Jan on March 10, 1976

About four years ago, Randy King became the hospital administrative intern and moved into my humble basement office of my then part-time job. Like other interns, I expected him to move on and earn big bucks at a huge hospital in a warmer climate. But he's stayed around. We shared—that is, he shared and I asked questions and listened to him volunteer personal details of his life. That's what I did to restart my career holding down two part-time jobs as a newspaper feature reporter and a part-time hospital public/employee publications writer.

Randy reported to work full time after finishing his post graduate work. Polite, quiet and extremely handsome, like a soft-spoken Montgomery Clift bachelor guy, Randy comes across as vulnerable and sensitive, considerate and cool.

He must think I'm cool too, maybe because I'm older and more liberal than most. I think he respects older women like Marge, and Bea too, when Randy first met them in November of '73.

That's when I read *I'm OK–You're OK*, a book about Transactional Analysis by psychiatrist Thomas Anthony Harris, attended a TA session, wrote a newspaper feature article about it and convinced our church to sponsor a TA marathon weekend at our Emerson Hall. We needed more participants to cover the fees so I convinced Randy to join us.

I was convinced he needed someone else to hear his stories.

"But I avoid serious conversations, Jan, except maybe for you. I don't talk about how I feel. I play the piano at parties so I don't have to talk."

"I understand. You're a budding young executive who might have to be hiring or—" I proposed as a joke, "—firing any of us."

"That won't happen because of me. I like Unitarians. You do

things together, with your family and with your church. Unlike you liberals, my parents were strict. Other than my family, I had only a few friends in school. I made them like me by being clever and by playing the piano at parties and in dance bands. Everyone picked up that the music was cool and then I was cool."

"This is interesting. It's quiet today; the phone's not even ringing. We can talk some more."

"Well Jan, when I knew that girls liked me, my best friend was Brian. We could talk about everything. Horse around and wrestle in the leaves, shoot baskets together and laugh."

"It's good to have a friend who shared those days."

"Brian shot himself late one night."

"Oh, how awful for everyone. What a shock."

"Yes. I guess so. No one talked about why he did it but I thought a lot about it. I still do. I even considered going to seminary but the idea of a hospital career was more appealing."

"That makes sense. You have compassion; that's rare in business. Hospital management is a good match for you."

"I'm happy you're interested in me as a person, and that we share this office when I'm not at college. We see most issues from similar values. I like talking with you. I trust you, Jan."

At our TA marathon, Randy chose to be an observer in contrast to my wrestling with marriage issues. Marge struggled about being a newly divorced unemployed woman with two sons. He said he remembered Bea crying about being an unemployed divorced mother of four teenagers and, as a new college grad unsuccessfully competing against an oversupply of younger education majors looking to start their careers.

And I remember her transitioning from a demanding diet and exercise regimen that gave her the slim new body and spirit yearning to be like Diana Rigg in "The Avengers."

<<<>>>

Bea on March 16, 1976

Friction started up between Jan and me. I can't win; our relationship always depends on her time and place. It may seem petty to her but not to me. When she called me the other night, she didn't want to talk about our relationship, she said. Alex makes them work on theirs all the time and she hung up saying, "No matter how much I do, it's not enough." I didn't care and went to bed.

> To Jan,
> At your pleasure, I'm at your pleasure
> While I sit on the shelf and wait
> 'til you need me, 'til you want me,
> 'til you can fit me in.
> I am at your pleasure when you can
> Fit me in to your full life.
> I'm at your pleasure. I wait for your pleasure.
> When, when do I be me—at my pleasure?

    Good thing I have Marge, my other drinking pals and church friends, including our women's rap group. Marge and I finished leading our "Employing Your Total Self" classes at church on a high note. I think we've helped most of the group to analyze their life goals and get motivated. I think we've made an impact on all of the women in the class who have either been newly divorced and/or signed up to finish their college education, like our buddy Betty Willing and Betty's newly divorced friend Carolyn Schafer who has two daughters and four sons to support.
    The Rev. Dr. Tony Logan, our new Unitarian Universalist minister right out of seminary, and I, the director of religious education at our church, are getting along quite well. Alex and his committee searched for months and found a perfect minister for our little congregation so now Alex is home a lot more.
    I work many hours at our church's Emerson House. That house,

adapted to classroom and office space, is critically important to Jan and my relationship since we signed up for two weekend marathon sessions with School Psychologist and Transactional Analysis Counselor Rachael Sandler. It changed our lives for sure. Jan recruited enough participants to make the weekend possible and that included Randy King who came because of their friendship and, after we agonized with the group over each of our traumas, he passed when it was his turn and went home rather than stay overnight with us at Emerson House.

Randy and our TA leader Rachael went their separate ways for the evening, and when she got back on Saturday morning, Rachael gave all "Stroke Cards" and what to wear. We listed our most precious gifts in the upper right. Marge wrote on hers: "myself, my children, participating in life, my friends." At the bottom right in a place of honor, she printed "Jan C." (That's me.) Her top left listed high points in life: "giving birth," and "discovering that people like me." In the lower left, the "pit" part of the card, she printed "ex-husband."

After more Saturday sessions ended, three of us stayed to prepare Emerson House for Sunday School. I showed Bea and Marge a curious TA "stroke" on my card, "Please save a night for me." Then Bea showed us hers: "Very tempted to get your phone. Dig your body. Sincerely." I told Bea that her comment and mine were Randy King's handwriting.

CHAPTER 2

Bea on March 19, 1976

Jan was working harder at Lakeshore Med doing an eight-hour job in six hours so that we'd have two hours left over each day to see each other. I pick her up in the hospital's loading dock and head for Emerson House or church or at any and every place where we could comfort and talk with each other. Then I'd drop her off at her corner when it was time to get home to make supper for Alex and her kids.

And now we can meet in her little room too.
Ironically, two other homemaker friends with husbands use her room when naive Jan offered it to them after they hinted broadly that each desperately needed to meet her male friend during his extended lunch break. One of her friends picked up Jan's key at the hospital reception desk to meet her lover for the initial sexual encounter of their affair, and they ate a Snickers bar together for nourishment. Then she met Jan for coffee in the hospital cafeteria to return the key. A bit disheveled, she confessed, "Jan, I'm a fallen woman."
Join the crowd!

Jan on March 20, 1976

Alex is meeting with Bea for cocktails and dinner and I'm alone in my room fearfully fantasizing over what's going to happen. Those two are jousting for my life and time as if they could determine my future for me. And I'm as concerned for Bea's safety as I've been for mine.

Scared, I waited for over five hours, when she finally called me at 9:30. "I'm broken, bruised and bleeding—emotionally. I think I gave us away, but I have to have some time to make some notes. Give me time before you come to me.

An hour later we met to share her notes of her evening with Alex.

He: I married Jan because I needed her extroversion—her joie de vivre—her love of life. We belong together. This is leading nowhere but shit for all of us. He's intimating that I'm responsible for the shit. I told him about TA intensive workshop where you beat the pillow in ferocious anger at him, fell against me and cried.

He: "I wish I had that release. I have no safety valve. Except for you two and some half-brained psychologists, I've no one to talk with about this."

Me: Understanding his feeling, how he's been cuckolded. Understanding his anger and frustration. Not blaming him. He has every right. Trying at times to be objective, uninvolved, sympathetic and viable to anger, aware of his threats and interdictions? Daring him. Trusting him but not able to trust him. I'm strong, unafraid, cautious, but not cautious? I did not waver."

He: "I find myself beginning to like you."

We: "This is absurd."

Me: Alex's power, Jan's fear.

He: "You have power over her. A lot of power."

Me: "You think, 'Heh. Heh, Jan is in your power. Under your spell, you evil woman.'"

He: "Remember when I came to Emerson House? Are you

afraid?"
Me: "Yes." And he reached over and took my hand—
He: "You needn't be."

Looking up from her notes, Bea told Jan, "We went to Greek Feasts, Jan, after 6:30. He ordered two Greek salads and one gyros sandwich cut in half to share. I'll never share half a gyro again! We finished eating. Drank a whole bottle of roditis. Everyone else was out of the dining room. We stayed in the far corner intent in conversation. The waitress kept coming back, apologetically asking if everything was all right?"

Me: "Leave me alone, Alex. I've given you what you need to know. Then he told me his dream—to retire to a Greek island. Sounds like Zorba or like Pete when he's dancing like Anthony Quinn in *Never on Sunday.* I remembered my traumatic incident with Pete that was nothing for me. It was like sneezing."
He: "Pete is my significant other—like your Marge or Anna."
Me: Thinking that he imagines what Jan is doing with me while she's out of his presence or control. "What if she had affair with a man? She will. It is a sure thing."
He: "How do you know?"
Me: "Because of things she has said. Because I know she wants to experience everything in life. I don't threaten you. If I were a man I could take Jan away in every sense. I don't threaten you in that sense."
He: "You threaten me emotionally."
Me: Talking of differences between men, women. "A man isn't able to fake orgasm like a woman can."
He: "A man is sensitive to that. A man would know. Sometimes I want to hold her down. Use all my strength and weight and pin her down. Hold her immobile and talk to her. She always gets angry. We can't talk without her getting angry."
Me: "She hates to be restrained. This thing between us just happened."
He: "An accident?"

Me: "Yes. If I were to have picked someone to fall in love with, it certainly wouldn't have been Jan. I would never have chosen her. Time's wasting. She has ideas to write. How can she do that unless she works—works at it? She'll have to write that novel in three months. I don't think she can do it."

He: "Has she started writing yet?"

I said yes.

He: "I'm worried about Jenny. At 3:30 in the afternoon she's in her pajamas watching TV when she should be outside playing. She can't face friends? Doesn't want to talk about it? She misses Jan's presence. The house is empty without her. And I resent Marge's influence and I resent yours. You both are bad for Jan."

Marge on March 21, 1976

Bea admitted the next day that she was a mess. She felt like she had the flu, a cold and a crying hangover so she wanted to stay home tonight. Jan went to take care of her by warming up a can of chicken soup. When I called Bea's place, no one was there. Then I called Jan and found them in her room. I accepted Jan's invitation to join them and we sipped our wine and sat perched on the lower bunk like three cranes in a nest with our knees folded up to our chins while hearing everything that transpired when Alex and Bea met the night before.

"Alex said it was the most intimate conversation he's ever had," Bea concluded.

Jan said he called her today and she told him to leave Bea alone. She doesn't want scar tissue ripped open again.

I feel sorry for him. I guess we all do. Bea moved to sit on Jan's typing chair. As we drank our jug wine, I started to get angry at their sharing every detail and commiserating with each other. "Jesus Christ, Jan. How can you keep on trying to use the people you supposedly love. Make up your mind. Shit or get off the pot. But why am I starting to rail on like this? You two don't care what I think!"

"How can you say that! You are like a sister to me, Marge."

"And I'm your best buddy, Marge. I listen to you and you listen to me all the time. We talk together for hours at your kitchen table. We even share guys together, for Christ sake."

"So you say. But you two cling together. You think you're superior beings with your suffering and courage and all that, and you put me down for being straight! I'm disappointed in you both. This so-called sexual revolution is driving us all nuts, and it's opening doors that some of us are not prepared to pass through. You'll see! Your big secret can't be hidden forever. Everyone knows what mighty feminists you claim to be. Soon they're going to find out that you're lesbians too—and I'll be judged guilty by association."

"I'm not a lesbian," Bea evoked in hushed tones, her teeth clenched for emphasis, "just because I love Jan! I've been a married woman for twenty-one years and I have four children. I am not a lesbian!"

I don't remember if Jan responded at all. Crawling out of her bunk-bed sofa, I set my half-empty glass on her windowsill, put on my coat and left. My footsteps echoed down the stairwell and I exited into the long, winter-dead courtyard. I felt as if everyone in the three floors of apartments on each side were watching me as I paced the cold and lonely gauntlet to my car.

Somehow the next day, Bea gathered my Tommy, Jenny, her Jan, my mom and me to go to see Burt Reynolds in *Lucky Lady* tonight. I wonder if the kids and my mom recognized the plot's menage-a-trois. Ye Gods! What do they know? Afterwards we drank martinis in my kitchen, ate the fried chicken that we brought home, clowned about and laughed.

Bea on March 21, 1976

Jan and I had brunch before she went to her room to write and I went home. Then Tony phoned me. He said he wanted to talk with me. God! What's that about! Here it comes! I drove right over to church. It was such great weather that we took a long walk together, and I took the opportunity to tell him about my relationship with Jan. Maybe it was too late, but I didn't want him to hear it from anyone else and if it bothered him, I would offer to resign.

He's a good listener. Then he said that he was happy to hear about us and he said it was wonderful to have so much love that's shared. But he had already heard about us because Alex asked him to come to talk at his house. That's when Alex told him that his wife was in love with the director of religious education.

"You're kidding. Is that how he said it?"

"I don't know what he wanted me to do about it. Maybe he believed I would work toward having you resign. I personally thought to myself that it was cool about you and Jan—because, Bea, I want to tell you that I'm gay myself."

"Tony! You have to be careful. I don't think the congregation is ready for that news."

"I hate being closeted about this, but I know they're not prepared for the stigma that will come to our church by having an openly gay minister. So, I spend most of my free time out of Lakeshore Bay. I don't drink, but I don't want to give up the fun and excitement of dancing and meeting new guys. And I'm certainly not ready to be monogamous—yet."

"My brother was gay, Tony. After my father disowned him and my mother was treated for depression with electric shock as a mental patient, he committed suicide. He jumped in Lake Michigan four years ago this month, in March. I hate March."

"I'm so sorry, Bea. But I'd never think of doing anything like that. I'm having too much fun and I'm beginning to work towards a fulfilling and long life."

Tony and I let out our souls to each other. We did not pass judgment nor hold back. We each had a chance to release a lot of pressure with our honesty and laughter at our individual boldness.

"But Tony, you have to be careful. I don't think Lakeshore Bay is ready for you to come out, let alone some of our members. I think you should get yourself a girlfriend. Do you have a woman friend you can ask to go along with this charade until you think the time is ripe for you to let others know about your orientation?"

"I think some members already suspect. And yes, I do have a

friend that I stay with sometimes when I stay overnight in Milwaukee. I think I can ask her, but I'll be guarded in naming our relationship. I don't want to be dishonest, but I don't want to lose what I've gained. The world isn't quite ready for us to be completely open and free."

"Our lives are so complex, Tony. I've enough to handle without taking on the world."

We had circled back to the front of our humble yet historic old church building, Tony hugged me and whispered, "I'm so happy to have someone here to talk with, Bea."

"Thank, Tony. Maybe I should be ordained?"

Jan on April 2, 1976

Last night after our anniversary date, we sat on her couch and I told her of my hidden fears of isolation similar to what I experienced with my father during World War II and each time my mother was hospitalized for month and now—forever. Bea listened to my honest expression of what I want to do with her and for her but also of "I'm afraid" feelings and those of "I'm responsible again."

We covered our laps with her afghan. "It's also been tough remembering and writing about my mother again for my novel. In a flash of peaceful insight, I realized a significant factor in my life. I've never identified the prolonged and eroded loss of my mother and, therefore, I've never grieved."

Bea nodded and remembered, "I never cried when my mother died. I don't know why."

"And my mother is still living, but what kind of life. Still living, but I've never resolved that loss through grieving. I've always sublimated this with activity, to achieve more goals, to excel, to feel almost omnipotent in my ability to protect myself and others with my love in my childlike fantasy."

"Until you met me."

"Yes. Until I met you. Until now though, I can't remember admitting to anger at my loss. I've only made up for my loss with resignation and Pollyanna concepts. To me, the cup is half full rather than half empty."

"And you tell me that I think the cup is half empty."

"Sometimes, yes. You do. Now don't look at me that way."

"I don't know what to think or how to feel being an extension of your mother."

"That's not what I'm saying. I love you for yourself. At least I don't think that's what it is. I love you so much and I don't want to lose you. Yet the loss of my mother, though she is still alive, is real and has been for thirty-five years. If she had died, I would have been forced to confront it and it would be finished. I think, instead that it's been eroding away at my life. She vanished in another place away from me, those years of having her taken away from me again, yet she always returns yet now, each time she returns, I dread what she'll do when she's with me. If I never identify being deprived of her, I'll never confront the grief. Never confront the grief, I'll never resolved the loss."

"I don't know what you can do about that. My brother and mother are dead and I think I've dealt with that, but now my kids are off without me and I know I'm grieving for that—and it isn't over yet.

"That's the truth. You've taught me many lessons. My unconscious self knew what I needed and I searched for a significant other while my conscious self worked hard to achieve other recognition. Except for my kids, my husband and family have failed to fill that task. They absorb my love rather than fill my loss. There was safety and security in my home, but it was not the kind of creative environment that I missed from my mother. I needed more to resolve this loss so deep, and I finally found you, dear Bea. After searching so long to find intimacy and love, I found it in your genius. Only your qualities can replace the qualities of my first significant person."

"Well, that's a lot to think about. And I hear you. But I'd rather hold you now. Enough of all this analysis for a while. It's too heavy."

"I brought your last poem with me. I carry it with me to read and reread. May I read it to you again?"

"Of course."

> Take me with you into the corridors of your body.
> Lead me down through passages of delight.
> Let me descend stairways as I shed each chain
> that binds me to convention—
> as I free myself from the tight bands
> of restrictive mental discipline.
> Lead me through and into and down
> so that I may become encompassed,
> encircled, entranced by your love.
> Take me to the place where I can give you
> everything I am—without reservation—
> without unnecessary reserve
> with the greatest tenderness and gentleness.
> Take me with you—Lead me—
> and I will take you with me and lead you
> through passages of the intimate, infinite me
> that reflects you and is you and yet is me.
> One and one makes one.

Jan on April 3, 1976

After two years of being totally involved with Bea in a primary love relationship with the gamut of behavior and emotions, I can at least put grief aside. I can put my fear of losing her aside, fear that was based on my past of consistently losing pieces of my mother. I can put that loss aside because I've realized the deep, gaping hole in my life is filled with love for someone that is returned in the greatest magnitude.

I feel at peace.

I can understand why I'm so determined not to stop our relationship. It goes beyond the love of another person; it touches the frantic desperation of my filling a loss so great that I never want to go through it again. I can understand why I was so patient with Bea in working through what would have seemed like insurmountable problems and terrifying possibilities. I understand my acceptance of the fear of violence from my husband. Many of these tumultuous feelings are endured again as they once were with my mother's slipping away from me in my youth and early maturity, and I'm not going to let Bea, my significant person, slip away from me now.

We are both strong. She is even stronger now than I am because she has worked her way through the grief of losing her home and family. I still have my losses to live through and more grief to endure; yet the losses that await me are determined not as much by me but by individuals free to choose their own paths.

These are not irreversible, definite losses—like death.

Yet I'm risking all to maintain what I need now and what I've needed all my life: someone to love me more than anyone else in the world as the most important person who has accepted unconditionally, totally, with celebration, someone who compares in breadth of intelligence and range of emotions and love of life and fun and joy.

And I have found that person and she has found me.

At my birth, my mother almost died; yet she made it through her own desperate grief of a lost son as she glanced at me wanting to be fondled and held. I could not, at age zero, replace the loss of her eight-year-old son. No matter how hard I tried, I could not fill that space in her shaky life.

Some will say that I'm passing on the lost parent relationship to my own children and that it's selfish to put myself first before them. Yet what would they have to deal with if I were to continue to turn away from the realities of my own unresolved loss—a continually searching woman desperate for acceptance and a love grand enough to drive that unfulfilled quest into anger and depression; a woman taking greater risk with each desperate move—trying for peace and satisfaction, for the resolution of the emptiness that has been driving me toward greater heights of achievement and danger.

I must resolve my own grief before I can help another.

As I left my little room this spring morning, my heart was full of love. The future is uncertain but I'm ready for what is to happen.

> I just was anointed by a drop from a roof
> as I stepped from a shadow into the spring sunlight.
> The morning sun melted the dormant winter snow,
> and I was refreshed, renewed and confirmed
> when the cool drop blessed me as I walked briskly in the light.

Jan on April 30, 1976

My three months in my room were healing, healthful and positive for me. I had so much fun being my own person that I only wrote one-third of what I'd started out to do. I was with Bea as much as possible. My schedule was completely unpredictable and I felt young like an adolescent, a happy one.

But tensions were still high as I tried to balance my commitments, and Alex was shocked and surprised that I didn't even want to see him during those three months. I did so when I had to or when I wanted to see Matt and Jenny. They learned to wash clothes, cook and do the survival chores they'd taken for granted.

I did resume my wifely duties to my husband when I returned. It was OK. I was fine. But my backaches flared up again and I anticipated needing a hysterectomy because of ovarian pain.

Fantasies filled my imaginings. Catastrophes were easy to conjure. My pain continued to increase and I finally made an appointment to be examined by the most influential woman obstetrician on Lakeshore Med's staff to determine if I needed gynecological surgery.

Dr. Josephine Ross, a strong, sinewy woman, strides through the hospital corridors in her blouse and skirt, wearing white socks and flat, comfortable shoes that she'd change to scrubs for surgical procedures. Her sharp features reflect her resolve. Her face is framed with cropped hair with a wave in the flapper style of the 1920s. She was raised and educated in the masculine medical school structure.

I knew women she knew who, I imagined, had long-term relationships with other women. She mentored my old friend Dr. Gloria Stevens to move beyond nursing and to become an obstetrician and a renowned genetics researcher. Dr. Ross is unmarried and she marches through life holding definitive power over hundreds of women patients' gynecological and obstetrical experiences. She is respected by all who know her, including other physicians and hospital administrators.

I broke down crying when she told me that there was nothing wrong with my reproductive organs. I should see an orthopedic surgeon and get my back situation analyzed, she said. When I cried, she dismissed her nurse from the room and I put my life on the line—and my career at Lakeshore Med—and told her of my relationship with another woman. She asked me if I had children and then shook her head and chided me by saying that I shouldn't compromise myself, that I should know better and know what I needed to do. I didn't get any affirmation, but I was relieved. Someone in medicine in Lakeshore Bay knew about my life and would protect me as a patient if that were required in the future. Perhaps her authority would allow Bea to see me if I were hospitalized, in intensive care or dying.

I was in better shape when I returned home. The transition was cool; my family seemed happy to have me return. I didn't want to go back to Alex, but I did so want to return to my children and to my home. As a safety valve, I kept my little room of my own that's served me well. It was better than a psychiatrist as far as having a safe place to be when and if I wanted it. The $60 a month rent plus telephone was the cheapest counseling place I could go to with even better results.

Jan on May 5, 1976

Matt and I had our first blow-up fight after Matt's expectations for winning the state high school track meet came up short because of a coach's misstep. I finally blew my stack after living and feeding a temperamental athlete for another long track season. He's under so much tension. And when Alex is away, Matt is impossible. He assumes his father's traits. In the midst of the hurtful words, I called time-out and gave him paper and a pencil and told him to express his anger in writing.

"And now you're back! Hey Dad! Jenny! She's comin' back. Good! I hope this is it! She wants to keep the room? What? It's over? No, she still has the room."

He's drawn a small ax in the middle of the page.

"Be good or she'll go back. Pick up towels or she'll go back. Don't fight or she'll go back. Do the work or she'll go back. The room. The room! She's still got it. When is she going to let go of it so she can come back for good."

He's drawn a heavier hatchet. On the next page, "Unitarianism is close. If I'm anything, I'm Unitarian. Unitarian is freedom, responsibility, truth."

He's drawn a flying dove with an olive branch in its beak. "But! If Unitarianism is going to lead to the downfall of this family, I want out! Be good to her friends, even though they cause the mess."

And a huge cleaver is drawn larger with deeper lines filling in for contrast with a hefty handle. "Your UU friends scare me. You're trying to be like them, unhappy, rebellious."

On a new page, "Does Unitarianism include practicing this?" with an even larger hatchet. Do the laundry so she'll stay," is on the next page, and following that is another page with "get rid of the room" next to another small ax, "and I'll help this family move through time with the least friction as possible."

And he signed his name and added a final page. "I'm sorry the state meet came. It's just that state meets were being held before I was conceived. I should get upset, screaming inside, the night before. Choke. Pull up. Quit. I'm sorry. I worked so hard."

I left work to pick up Alex at the airport. When we got home I showed him what Matt had written. He looked at the letter. "I don't see much wrong with it. Matt's wanting to split."

"You've failed me again, Alex. When will you ever comfort me or understand me and say that it must have hurt me terribly to have Matt write that to you?"

They want me home but they can't stand my doing anything else but care for them. It's the same dumb program going around again and again. Except that I feel closer to my stronger self than before. I'll return and begin writing my book again. Even though I haven't touched my manuscript for six weeks, I've not stopped living it. And I'll continue to love people, even with the fear of being hurt again. I will be more wary, but what I will be primarily wary of is feeling responsible for those who expect me to make them feel good. They must be responsible for that.

I made supper and fell asleep on the family room sofa while Alex sat at the table and wrote checks to pay the bills. "Aren't you ever going to pay the bills again?" he asked.

Bea on May 26, 1976

How do I feel about aging? It scares me silly. I'm forty-six years old. I was frightened by my approaching fortieth birthday into losing fifty-seven pounds, writing a novel, trying to get a grip on my life, going back to college to get my degree in 1972 and trying to organize the rest of my life. When I interviewed for a teaching position in Sheboygan, which I didn't get, they asked me a question at the beginning of the session. I was placed at the apex of a square of tables around which sat nine principals and the assistant superintendent of schools. The first thing they asked me was, "Identify yourself, Mrs. Lindberg." And I said without hesitation, "I'm the mother of four children." In 1972 that was my only identity after twenty years. Mother of four children. What else? Why didn't I say I was an artist, a writer and a musician? Perhaps because I whistle in the dark with those titles. I've never been successful at anything. I dabble and piddle and do nothing.

I'm forty-six years old. What am I going to do? I'm alone. All alone. I'm my sole support, no benefits, no nothing. I see myself going into a bitter poor age. No one to help me, no one to comfort me or to keep me company—a bitter old woman living alone. There'll never be another chance for me. I had enough trouble finding a man to marry when I was twenty-four-years old. No one wanted me. Anyone who had any brains or any class wouldn't look twice at me. I was klutzy and unattractive, a smart ass, and too damned intelligent to be marketable, too independent for my own good, too masculine, too bitchy. I still am, only more so.

No man will ever look twice at me except for a one-night stand, a lay, and probably not good at that either. I'm scared enough to still think that I need some man to support me, to shelter me under his benefits and his pension plan, to keep me company, to help me when I get sick and old and ugly. I had one, but he bored me to tears. He drove me to distraction. I walked out. I lost my old-age benefits, my security I'd earned as the mother of his children. I walked into independence—and I'm scared silly.

What can I do? How can I live? Who can I turn to? What do I do? I colored my hair three months ago. It was getting terribly gray. I was in a bar with Marge one night fooling around. We were talking to some drunk. First he asked us if we were sisters, which we denied. Then later in the conversation he asked me if I was her mother. That did it! I made an appointment and had my hair colored. I watch my weight every day. I go on crash diets. I must stay thin at all costs. My hair is colored and I weigh less now than when I was married, but I seem to be gaining again, more than I'd dare to. I'm getting bags under the eyes and wrinkles. I'm getting old. OLD! OLD!

I'm not equipped to be on my own resources. I've never lived alone in all my forty-six years except now. A year of being alone, on my own. How have I lived it? Scared. Stupefied by drinking too much. Trying not to think about it. Suffering from culture shock. Suffering from a weight of guilt so big and so high that it smashes me into the ground daily, if I let it.

And I'm forty-six years old. And there is nothing ahead but

bleakness. Loneliness. Emptiness.

If I can't teach, what will I do? Wait tables. Work in a store? Work in an office? I'm too old. It's too late. I've never been successful at anything. I've been rejected and failed at so many things. The rejection of getting old and being alone is the ultimate. Aging is what I'm doing every day. Aging is what I am.

And I'm scared. And alone. And I'll be alone.

Bea on August 4, 1976

I'd renewed my teaching certificate and applied for positions when teaching became a trendy career for young college graduates competing with older housewives like I'd been. Meanwhile I get a pittance of an alimony check that my daughter writes because her father is too incompetent to handle his own checking account. Then there's the small salary for directing our church school program.

Then Betty Hannamen told me of an opening at a private school for children with learning disabilities. She also told the school about my abilities—and after my interview they hired me. I love the stimulating teaching techniques with autonomy in the classroom to add my own techniques.

I was so nervous with the inspector observing me that I couldn't spell "mansion" on the board so I wrote "big house" and then, Damn, I couldn't spell "limousine" so I erased that and wrote "big car." The kids loved it and understood more about their learning issues. The inspector said it was like TV's *Welcome Back, Kotter* with my innovative skills.

Bea on November 3, 1977

I worry about my teaching career at The Learning Center. I'm rehired at $8,500 a year, but only for four months; the school and its funding will stop at the end of December. The children will be mainstreamed into the public school system.

So now what? My father died so I have a little money for a while. I put $16,000 in the bank with more coming, thank God.

Jan's convinced the hospital that she needs an assistant and that I'd be the perfect candidate because I had all the talents required for the job. I have mixed feelings. We're having this torrid relationship and she's still married.

Marge plus a couple other women and I have picked up a lot of guys together. I've had relationships with several men during this era of The Sexual Revolution. It's fun, but it's Jan I truly love. I'm only fooling around with the guys, I guess because maybe I'm trying to prove that I'm not a lesbian. What does Jan think about them? It doesn't seem to bother her. Jan isn't jealous because she knows that I love her. I'm having sex with Jan at the same time. Lots of orgasms. We're always turned on. And she has sex with Alex, although she says it's difficult for him now after two-and-a-half years of his imagining what we two do together. She's lucky he doesn't strangle her when he's on top of her.

It's a stupid idea for us to work closely together. Yet it's exciting to be in public relations: a lot of photography, writing a newsletter and putting out a magazine. It's so exciting to think about—a lot more interesting than a teaching job.

CHAPTER 3

Jan on January 5, 1977

How careful were you to suggest that Bea join you to create the best two-person PR team for your hospital? Why not, when you trust the people you work for. How careful are you to push your husband to his limits? He has not made the final ultimatum—yet. I think he's afraid to. Besides, I am working more than full time now. I've been given a well-earned raise, making $10,250 a year. I can make it on my own if I have to. I'm independently productive.

And what about my Bea living alone and without a job since her private school will close? She continues to be lonely, depressed, fearful about her future. If I withhold from her this opportunity of a new position being created for my department, I'm unfair to her. What a team we'd make! And I'd see her every day, all day. We'd work happily and productively together in an environment that I feel deep dedication—and affection. Plus, I could help her with work suitable for her many talents. Both our lives could be smoother, even though I continue my double-life now on a full time basis. Perhaps our intense and lusty desires will moderate with more normal schedules.

<<◇>>

To get Marge off the hook and save her credibility at work because of her knowing about Bea and me, I dared to tell Randy, our friend who is now my boss, about our relationship before he decides to hire Bea.

Randy had his chance to tell me it would be impossible to have her work with me. I put it all "on the table" in his new office next to Marge's. He was surprised, he said but, old friend that he is, he didn't seem to care and he decided to work with us and help us set up the expanded program and improve our hospital publications.

Randy and I determined, against Nick Dixon's remark about her being abrasive, that Bea was the "best of the lot." I had worked up a four-page document on the goals and communications needs for my new PR department and included everything from close relationships with almost everyone in the hospital and community to every kind of communications options from varied periodicals to audio-visual posters and TV programming. I even included an employee recreation program to prove I needed an assistant and that assistant could only be filled by Bea, who with me, has all the qualifications to do the work of an entire outside PR and marketing agency.

Of course, Alex is so angry that his jaw could turn to steel while he grinds his teeth. I can imagine his wanting to call out to everyone that his wife was a lesbian and will be working with her lover. During one of our arguments, I found out that he had seen an attorney who told him what it would cost him and what a divorce would be like. I assumed he chose not to press the issue on those grounds.

Bea on January 10, 1977

I got the job! I'm numb, so excited.

I had pulled the plug on the phones this morning and Jan came at 10—had been trying to call. This waiting is just too much. She stayed about an hour, then she came back again at 6:30 to tell me she found out that it was yes before she left work. Tomorrow I am to come in to fill out the forms and get a blood test, then to Jan's office for a bit of orientation. I am to create a Wonder Woman nurse recruitment flyer plus about six other projects, including organizing an employee recreation program. The whole thing will be fun.

Jan. You throw all of my inhibitions into the wind and turn my ambition into possibility.

Jan on January 11, 1977

Bea started her new career at Lakeshore Med today, earning $9,000. We began an expanded employee relations program and communications effort. I am now the director of communications. Working closely with me, Bea joins Marge in our close comradery.

Lean, sexy, brilliant and creatively multi-talented, Bea *is* the best of the lot and I am breathless when I see her sitting next to me at the drafting table or across our tiny office at her desk.

Jan on January 15, 1977

A Friday-night sleepover at Emerson House kept the UU teens busy with Tony Logan, Bea, and a few other chaperones on this freezing January night, so Diana and Nick asked Alex and me over for a little supper and to play some bridge.

As supreme hosts on all occasions, Nick mixed several rounds of martinis and Diana set our supper table with delectable Italian salami, cheeses, breads, pasta with garlicky sauces and lightly dressed varieties of salad greens with exotic olives and garnishes. We lingered long over the generous feast, including sampling and drinking several bottles of homemade wines and bottles from Italy. One of my favorite tastes, cannoli, was served for dessert.

We were a bit fuzzy when it came time to play cards. In fact, the game of bridge had been so removed from my mind for so long that I asked them how many cards do I deal. The whole deck, of course. And don't you ever keep score. Fortunately, it was not a cutthroat game and we talked more than we played.

The teachers' strike brought concerns for our kids and when they'd go back to school. The tactics of this strike followed the Lakeshore Med pattern and caused as much bitterness in the community as did the sub-zero winds. Several of our teacher friends were now on the freezing picket lines and some were troubled about what they were doing. Others were dogmatically positive that they were on the side of truth and justice. Of course, we relived the frantic battles we encountered during Lakeshore Med's strike, which probably bored Alex and Diana having to hear that all again. Nick told us what he could about the hospital's continuing legal actions being pursued by Ray Schuster and his comrades. As the time went on, we stopped playing cards, put our elbows on the table and talked and laughed and drank more wine.

We talked about our Door County properties and our dreams for that precious space of open land, about Queen Anne's lace, tree species, campfire stories, insects and animals. Nick remembered his sister being mortified when outdoors and perhaps near any snake. He laughed about how sadistic he was when they were kids. With a grass snake in his hand, he sneaked up behind his sister and threw it around her neck. She shrieked and ran wildly through the backyards of his Chicago neighborhood until someone finally caught her and removed the startled reptile from his sister's quaking body.

I remembered earlier stories of how much Nick admired his bachelor uncle, how kind he was and what how good he could cook. Everyone in his family wanted him to get married, but he resisted; and all were shocked when they discovered that he was a homosexual. Nick said he still loved his uncle and his friends. That information was stored in my memory as a reminder that Nick also had compassion for homosexuals.

In sharing more stories, especially on this ice-crackly night with moon rays riding on broken ice floating on Lake Michigan's surface, Nick and Diana bantered on about how they were snowbound for days in their more humble Chicago apartment when their kids were small and Nick was finishing his college degree. As a nurse, Diana kept a part-time job to help support them. Regrettably, she had broken her leg and had been in a cast for several weeks. She couldn't stand not being able to soak her body in a tub for a proper bath, she said, and with everyone at home on a Sunday afternoon she decided to have Nick help her get in a hot tub with her heavy plaster-casted leg propped up and out of the water. What a relief, she recalled with a sigh.

But when Nick and the kids heard the snowplows making their way down their street narrowed by parallel lanes filled with mounds of snow-covered cars, Nick and the kids quickly bundled up to help shovel and free themselves from the elements. They were having so much fun that they helped their neighbors, made snowmen and forts, even angels in the snow. Then one of them remembered their mother, stuck naked in now chilly bathwater, helpless but able to keep warm by her increasing anger at being ignored and forgotten.

"And remember the time you left me standing in the rain in front of the Congress Hotel while you bailed the car from the lot and drove almost home before you realized you left me alone back at the hotel!"

We laughed at our couples' stories, affirming theirs. But when Alex laughed, he only expressed garbled waves of uneven air from his slightly opened smile. As long as the wine was flowing, we let Nick and Diana control the performance. Alex sat back in his customary silent mode so he wouldn't have to take a turn. And I wasn't going to encourage any tales about our mishaps together that could explode into deeper confessions, especially with Bea starting to work with me at Lakeshore Med this week. What a story that would be for Alex to reveal if he wanted to play "Can you top this."

Nick started into another tale when the phone rang and Diana went into the kitchen to answer the call. "Bring in another bottle of wine when you come back," he ordered.

Come back she did, but empty handed and gaunt, holding her stomach as if she were to vomit. Shocked at her sudden change and imagining what disaster could have happened, we waited until she could breathe.

"Diana! What happened?"

She gasped and inhaled again.

"Is it one of the kids?"

She nodded no. With a blank, gray look she finally spoke. "Maddy committed suicide. They found her. She hanged herself in the garage."

"For Christ sake, Diana," Nick shouted. "And you just spoke with her. Didn't you pick up on anything when she called? What the hell kind of a friend are you anyway!"

Diana looked at her sadistic husband as if he had bashed her with the gun butt. "Why are you attacking me?"

"She's one of your best friends!"

"I'm not to blame for not knowing what she had on her mind."

"You should have known something was up!"

Diana started crying and slumped to her chair.

I knew who Maddy was. I worked with her husband at the newspaper. He was a good guy; they and their kids had some problems that we knew about when they were our neighbors, but they had moved and started a new life. She was also a schoolteacher for Lakeshore Bay Unified. What a waste. What a shock. What a shock to find her.

Images of possibly finding my mother in the same way inflamed me and my old fears of being responsible for what I would have found.

I stood up and said, "What you've just said is the most cruel, chauvinistic language I have ever witnessed! Why do you blame Diana? No one is to blame for someone's decision to do that! Fuck you, Nick! Why pick on Diana?"

Each of them was shocked at what I had said. I never use that word. And now I laid the F-word on my boss! Burning with anger at him—and at losing control of myself, I put on my coat, swept my scarf around my neck and walked out into the night on the slick sidewalk to unlock my front door and enter a safe haven.

I had to cool down, and when I did, I realized the grievous and angry jury of his peers that I'd left behind could turn into a venue for Alex to release his fury at me and at Lakeshore Med for hiring

Bea. Everyone was weak from this horrible suicide; perhaps he'll chose this time to tell them how crazy insane his wife is for loving another woman, for that woman to be working with her, and for Nick allowing it to happen.

Feeling as if I'd broadsided myself by leaving, I put my coat on again and stepped across the crunching snow back to Dixon's and let myself in the front door. "Finally," I thought, "it's my *Who's Afraid of Virginia Woolf* night. I'll lose everything I've worked for, and Bea could lose her job too." But unlike Elizabeth Taylor as Martha, I humbled myself and apologized to Nick for what I had said. Diana looked at me with eyes that told me what she has to put up with in her marriage. Alex only looked at me. I guess he hadn't had time, perhaps not even the intent, to tell them anything about me. There would be no quarrelsome trial tonight, no showdown. I asked Alex to come home with me, and I told Nick that I would see him on Saturday morning at work to apologize again when we were in a calmer mood.

That night we walked home silently, except for our footfalls in the snow.

"I'm cold," I said.

"It's late."

"Yes. The night is still."

"It will get better, Jan."

"I don't know."

The house was warm and without more words, we went to bed.

I waited long enough to think Nick had left home for his office and on my way to the hospital this morning, I stopped and opened Dixon's front door and called loudly to check on Diana who was still in bed but awake. She called me to come up to their bedroom where, with her blond hair uncombed and no make-up, she looked completely drained and drawn sitting on the edge of the bed in the midst of their crumpled sheets. Looking into her sadly compliant eyes, I could see her anticipation of long years of conformity in this emotionally abusive marriage without escape. An intelligent woman, perhaps ambitious, but where could she go without constantly being Mrs. Future Hospital Administrator Dixon and mother of their children.

January's late-rising sun reflected off the blinding whiteness of the lake and poured into their room through the half-raised window blinds. She would be obliged to respond to her dead friend's family and help where she could. She told me that I'm not the first person to call her husband a fucker to his face. She also told me I'd better watch out because if I left Alex, Marge would go after him. I said I didn't care.

I comforted her in her sorrow and mustered up my courage to meet her husband in his office. Nick instructed me to write a formal apology for my poor judgment, which would be placed in my work file. I'm sure he never understood his part in what caused it. Oh well. I did what he asked, left it in his office in-box and went home.

So it goes.

Bea on January 24, 1977

I began the employee newsletter on my first Monday with beginner's problems plus a last minute breakdown on the copy machine on Thursday. Everybody wants to approve the newsletter before it gets printed and each one has last minute corrections. Jan's used to that, but I'm not. But it got in the distribution boxes before employees were to pick up their checks and punch out at 3:30.

Jan came after lunch on Saturday and stayed only for two hours. Me—I'm wild and came fast two times. Skyrockets! I had to make her leave because I went for a Learning Place staff cocktail reunion and then to a church supper club gathering. As the religious education director, I get invited to as many supper clubs as I can and then build good friendships with our church families. I get wine and a gourmet meal as well.

Jan on January 26, 1977
"New Spaces Appear as Expansion Progresses"

Bea's lead newsletter paragraph read, "The iron fingers of the front loader's shovel reached toward the first house to be leveled or removed for space for Lakeshore Med's expansion and parking needs. It took less than an hour to flatten the fragile frame structure. The tinderbox wood emitted clouds of dust at each chop of the shovel as new horizons appeared in the neighborhood to fill the empty space."

What a team we are! We both can take credit for our productions, for her photos and darkroom processing, for mine, our writing and editing and mutual inspiration as we energize each other.

Ha! Yes! She's come up with a dazzling word for the title of our new 16-page hospital magazine—"*synergy*." Where did that word come from? "The action of two or more substances, organs, or organisms to achieve an effect of which each is individually incapable." That's us! What a winner! What fun! What an adventure to create our own magazine!

Bea on February 22, 1977

My apartment neighbors are driving me crazy. On one side they shout at their toddler to stop terrorizing their new baby and on the other, they play their records with the bass tones at top frequency. The guy below is a ham operator and his voice interferes with my phone. I bought myself some earphones and a long cord so I could drown out their sounds, but then I decided I'd invest in one of those new electronic pianos and play that with my earphones—a more productive option.

This month has flown by and I often have to cover the office work on my own. Jan came in late after attending a City Council meeting. I was depressed, trying to write the newsletter again. Whew! They make so many last-minute changes. And there's always some new project that comes in the door before I get to finish the one I'm working on. Jan says she gets depressed some too, and I am trying to shake it off like she seems to do.

It's been a long time since Jan and I have been together, and when she does come and then leaves, I am so lonely.

Now that Randy is her boss, Marge is very careful about what she says at work and keeps a low profile relative to us. She doesn't eat with us and her office schedule caused her to change her break times, she said.

A raw, new kid joined the administrative staff as another hospital administrative resident. Chuck McCarthy, wearing his glen-plaid beige suit jacket, vest and tight pants, follows Randy around. Nick and Randy like him because of his untapped potential, as if Nick must mentor this receptive, not too intellectual male mind. Perhaps Chuck reminds Nick of his younger days as a virile stud. Maybe Randy sees him as an alter ego. Chuck knows he's not all that bright and has a sense of humor about it. He sure is rugged-looking with his brown wooly-bear hair combed back off his forehead. Add to that his dense, bushy eyebrows and a bristle of a moustache. He looks like a future movie actor in the rough. And together, Chuck and Randy certainly are female magnets who attract turned-on young women—and some older ones too.

I know that Jan is pleased at what I'd accomplished. We're generating excitement in the newsletter about our recreational and team-building effort for Lakeshore Med employees.

Our joy in work was obvious and our synergistically created *synergy,* a first-rate hospital magazine for our hospital.

Jan on March 17, 1977

When Bea passed her probation period at work, she promptly wrote her resignation as religious education director. Marge, a church board member, took it to her meeting that night. The letter read, "To the UU Board of Directors and the Religious Education Committee:

I am resigning my position as Director of Religious Education. The resignation to take effect on my replacement by a new director or at the end of the fiscal year, whichever comes first. In view of the church's current financial state, I would request that my salary cease, effective immediately. I will continue to do the director's job on a volunteer basis for these few months."

I worry about Bea. She has back pain and is "dizzy as usual," she said. She's been coming to work though, and got her pay raise after her probation ended. A week ago, the maintenance men completed her closet-size dark room and she set up all her equipment and chemicals and felt good turning out excellent prints from her negatives. The closet, which was a little toilet room off a hallway, is pretty close with poor ventilation. The chemicals could be affecting her. She's seen various hospital physicians, had ex-rays, smears, etc., but is meeting our deadlines and writing articles for our magazine. I give her the scientific topics that I don't like to do and am not good writing those complicated subjects.

A major deadline loomed: creating and setting up a new hospital wellness display table with accompanying brochures and flyers at UW-Oshkosh's Weekend College during its spring break. While they were giving their small group talks on sexual matters to women, I staffed the booth during the two-day event. I couldn't help but remember my first Weekend College in 1974 when Bea and I advanced the progress of our love affair when we shared intellectual understanding at some classes and our first self-restrained and exciting loving when we skipped other classes.

This year Pam Holmen offered an innovative class called "Vaginal Health" and no one came.

Bea surprised me by taking Saturday workshops on "Self-Confidence Comes from Within" and "Taking Charge of Your Feelings."

Jan on April 1, 1977

We spent our anniversary at two overnights in Oshkosh attending the Hospital Public Relations of Wisconsin seminar with Randy meeting us there. Bea joined me as a professional member of the group. We started the conference with Wednesday night on our own and other early arrivals with cocktails and dinner and later, Randy accompanied us to our room for conversation and drinks.

All in attendance learn a lot and, even though there is competition among different hospital circles, the networking among us PR types in the state is valuable.

When we went to our room together, Randy stayed at the edge of the pool with his legs in the water and conversed with a young woman from Madison. Randy said to us as we waved good night, "We're all consenting adults."

On Friday morning I regaled my colleagues with the confusion and conflict of our hospital's six-week strike. I covered the walls of the room with full pages of newspaper articles, set out samples of my newsletters and used the chalkboard to try to illustrate the two union factions with Lakeshore Med patients and employees in the middle of the chaos. Often they would cringe or laugh at the absurdity of situations that occurred.

I told them I felt as if I were holding by a thread a mix of information and the fear of litigation: the responsibility of tearing the whole fabric by one's misquote or another's evaluation while knowing strike leaders, government and media people would judge as I heard, wrote, read and anticipated that all could be jeopardized. I was told many times that my daily newsletters helped unify the team inside the hospital who would know of events before the media reported it. It was in contrast to the confusion on the picket line and within the union ranks.

"It would be good to say we planned our responses. But much of what occurred from our communications efforts was an immediate and intuitive response to what was needed. The entire hospital supported my needs for information to inform them and the community. People in the mail room moved over immediately to let me print on our Xerox 9200. Accountants and various records personnel stopped their work immediately to give me facts and statistical records. Administration responded instantly to whatever was needed. Our legal consultants were seconds away by phone. Hospital employees were aware of news tips and sent them on to me. They too wanted to know—everyday."

Our PR members empathized with all our efforts and several suggested that I organize my materials and submit it for an award from ASHPR, the American Society of Hospital Public Relations. I decided I would call it "A Year of Union Militancy Challenges a Century of Caring" and when I finished it, I would also submit copies of it to our public library and historical society. Perhaps my workshop is the reason Randy came. He probably came to see if I said anything out of line or something that could be used in court battles over the union suing the hospital for back pay for strike leaders. I guess I did all right because he didn't add or correct anything in my talk after I introduced him to the group.

On Friday night after the evening dinner and speakers, several met again at the pool and were diving off the board. Each one, including Bea as the only woman, tried to outdo the other until about 2 a.m. The pool was glorious, she said, with a perfect temperature. She did back dives and flips off the board. I stayed in the whirlpool with the saner crowd. Plenty of liquor came out to the poolside tables from all the rooms. Bea was terrific, the best of all, but she stopped when she whispered to me that she'd hurt her back.

Bea on April 17, 1977

Jan comes to see me at home or in her room after work as often as she can, yet sometimes we can be volatile there and at work. In the first place, she's now my boss. That irks me when she takes the boss role instead of being my lover. Sometimes we argue away from the office over personal stuff and when she has to be away from me, like over Easter.

Just before that holiday, Randy came to talk with me when Jan wasn't in the office. He pissed me off again so I came home and drank, but I'm strong. Jan came to the apartment and we had a terrible blow-up. I exploded and screamed at her—ventilated all again.

Marge and I went for a Saturday night on the town, but same-old, same-old stuff.

Yesterday I was tired and we knocked off work early and Jan came home with me for a terrific afternoon. Last night was Lakeshore Med's Goodwill kick-off family night at the Y and it was a success with volleyball, bingo and singing with me and my guitar from the gym's stage. That felt good. After it was over, several of us women went to Marge's and celebrated in her kitchen with lots of laughs and treats until 3 a.m. We were full of joy after our great accomplishment bringing Lakeshore Med people with their families together to affirm that old wounds from last year's strike have been healed.

I woke up laughing this morning.

Bea on May 27, 1977

I processed about fifty photos in the darkroom with pressure deadlines. Once I farted in there and nearly killed myself. No wonder I am fighting off dizzy spells. I've been checked out with x-rays and by my gynecologist too. Jan drove me there and home and gave me a pleasant back rub. Writing stories and getting out the newsletter demands my concentration and that helps me overcome how I feel.

Our working together has not been ideal. She is the final authority and when I disagree with her, she thinks I'm just being temperamental. Then she changes her mind and we end up doing what I suggested in the first place. Then having the newsletter reviewed by Randy King before printing rankles me. I resent that bandied-legged bastard who has power over me and Jan—and even Marge. And his criticisms are often petty and contrived.

But somehow the end results are successful, even if the job is mixed with frustration and joy.

For my birthday present, Jan gave me a silver-gray, pewter mermaid letter opener. A small substitute for her presence. I was ticked off at this token after I held it in my hand. My smart-ass idea registered and I said it out loud. I told her I would not be drowned. Why I said that? I don't know. But I guess I do know because my mother often told my brother Cal to go jump in the lake, and when my father disowned him after Cal came out to him that he was gay, that's what he did—he jumped in Lake Michigan in March 1962. I still can't get over that, I guess, especially when I'm leading a secret life as another woman's mistress.

Jan left with hurt feelings, rejected again. But she'll get over it. She always does. I guess a peaceful resolution to our double lives is not possible.

Jan on May 31, 1977

Wow! I spoke of something I haven't talked of for years. It's our Memorial Day weekend on our Door County land and conditions were just right in our barn to share with Jenny the loss of our infant son, her brother.

Alex and Matt were fishing while Jenny and Matt's girlfriend Ellie sat in the sunlight that struggled to break through the flyspecked windows of our barn. We had picked flowers and put them in a vase on the folksy oilcloth table covering. A stew was simmering on the Coleman stove.

Ellie was telling Jenny and me about her childhood. She remembered going to relatives because her mother had to stay in bed to save the life of her expected baby and to save, perhaps, her own life.

"I can't imagine my mother being pregnant," said Jenny.

"You don't remember, Jenny, but I was pregnant when you were two years old. Matt doesn't remember either. I never had the right time to tell you, so I never mentioned it until now. But we lost a baby, a baby boy. He'd be thirteen now if he were alive. On February 10, 1964, and only seven months pregnant, I gave birth to a son who died several hours later."

After a long pause, "I still grieve the loss of our son, yet his living could have created a completely different life for us all. It was a difficult pregnancy and who knows in what condition his life would have been if he lived. I never saw him and we didn't name him. I didn't want to be hurt each time I heard that name. It would have been strong male name like your brother's name. I was 33 and your dad was 34."

Jenny was quiet, not knowing what to ask. She saw that I was moved to tears, tears that still come. It's OK to cry still. I just told my daughter that she has lost a brother she never knew she had and she's quiet.

"Hmmm," said Jenny pensively. "Really?"

That was all she said. Perhaps we'll talk about it again someday, if she brings it up. Now all I'll have to do is tell Matt about the loss of this secret family member, his brother.

If this has been such a deep secret for all these years, how do I tell my children about my secret life with Bea?

Jan on June 12, 1977

A chaotic church campout came to pass. All our major characters from church were chilling out around the campfire, drinking, singing, talking close to the warmth, except for Bea. She huddled in her tent sleeping off the afternoon's drinking which was to give her courage to face up to Alex's arrival after he finished working.

The teens were swarming in their energy field. Youngsters spun back and forth about the campfire, chasing fireflies in the bushes.

When Bea finally came to the campfire, displaying her most

joyful heterosexual self, she hugged her friends totally and when some church men friends joined the group, she embraced them. Nick Dixon, seeing this, beckoned her to come to where he was sitting, wrestled her to kneel down to hear him and he actually chided her. "Behave yourself! Remember that you are now a Lakeshore Med employee and your behavior reflects on the hospital."

He obviously forgot when he would grab me and pull me on his lap during one of our early visits to his Door County land— his behavior that made Alex so angry he said if Nick didn't stop, he would tell me to tell him to take my job and stuff it.

And he surely must have heard the gossip about all the women Randy is said to have used to satisfy his appetite.

When Bea began to play her guitar and sing the campfire songs so many enjoy. Alex, burning in his own energy field of anger, walked away. In constant fear of Alex telling Dixon about Bea and me, I obeyed and went to sleep with him in our camper.

Imagine then Sunday's service in the peaceful field under shade trees; most, if not all of us, in the "spirit of fellowship" worshipping together. I was an emotional open sore from pulling and tugging at the leash that was around my neck, a long leash, true, but one that kept me from being free and open.

As part of the service, Bea sang "Mother Earth," her song to me as an anthem to the earth, but with two meanings, one for others and one for the two of us. When she sang it, some cried.

> Mother Earth. Mother Earth. Nurture me for I love thee.
> Lake and hill, can't get my fill of your sweet land,
> Your sea and sand, your trees and sky, your mountains high.
> I love them all, your spring and fall, your warmth and snow.
> All these I know are mine, my Mother Earth.
>
> Mother Earth. Mother Earth. I in turn will nurture thee
> To keep you free for all to see for all to share
> Preserve with care, my precious Mother Earth.
> My precious Mother Earth.
> My precious Mother Earth.

Bea on June 13, 1977

Because Alex was away again, Jan planned a big birthday party at our house for Marge and Diana. In the midst of our laughter, Adele McEwin spoke out and said, "I am observing tendrils of smoke rising from behind you, Marge." Sure enough. When Marge jumped up and I pulled off one of the loose pillows, tendrils of smoke were rising upward and a small burning circle glowed from the sofa lining. I took immediate action and poured my martini on the superficial singe. I was sorry to have wasted the vodka, but it did put out the fire, as far as we could tell. I hate to admit it, but an ash from my cigarette must have fallen behind Marge's cushion while I was making a grand gesture and put my arm behind her with the cigarette between my fingers.

Uncertain of the fabric's chemical component of the massive couch, and in case fire would flair up again, we women, like Amazon woman pallbearers, lifted the couch out of the living room, down the front hall, maneuvered around a tight corner to get out the front door, marched in tandem under the covered porch and down the steps, and we finally set it down away from the house on the front lawn. Jan poured some more water on the spot and we returned to the house, ate our earthy supper, drank birthday champagne and remembered to carry the couch back to its space before Betty Hannamen's husband came to pick her up and wonder why the living room sofa was on the front lawn.

CHAPTER 4

Jan on June 18, 1977

Alex: As you've watched your computer programs speed up and bear fruit from your intelligence, I've written scores of articles and documents for my journals and for my careers and watched it spew out of the copy machine. We have something in common besides our children. It is our individual drive to produce and achieve—yet why do you suffer when it's your turn to stop work, come home and produce a supper for our family and be the martyred one who assumes some of the work I have done for years before I achieved equal status in this world.

Why do I punch the clock at home when my job allows me freedom to come and go as I please?

Jan on July 5, 1977

Our work at Lakeshore Med continues, but life's not too peaceful here when I have to be the final authority in our teamwork relationship. Bea's very touchy about suggestions and I'm intimated about that aspect of her personality.

Somehow working through our mix of temperaments, we

published our first dynamic *synergy* magazine together, five thousand copies. Its publication gave the hospital a new look even before its construction renovation began. Clean, fresh, educational, entertaining, together we created every photo and every word. Bea describes it as "our baby."

Yet, my days are with Bea, my nights are with Alex, and my family and my life are in shreds.

Bea's drinking more; I'm drinking more at home more. I was haunted by fear of what would happen to her under this stress and by fear of what would happen to me living as I am.

Randy King on July 28, 1977

After hearing Jan tell me about some of the Ira Progoff Intensive Journal techniques she uses in her journaling, I'm brainstorming a list of my so-called "work stepping stones."

1. I went to college to become a hospital administrator, but Nick teaches me what the real world of hospital administration is like.

2. So many openly gay men attended my university and I was confused. It was the first time I'd seen guys flaunting their gayness. It's dangerous. They could get kicked out of the dorms and out of school. Their reputations would be ruined. We were still rebounding from the McCarthy era of suppression of Communists and homosexuals. If you had goals to work in government, being a homosexual could cause you to be blackmailed, even to jeopardize national security. How could guys be so open and be happy as homosexuals, even if it's only with other gay guys.

3. In addition to Jan, another person sharing our office was Gregory who was there before me and I think he's jealous about my advancing so quickly. It was good when he left to work elsewhere. There were tensions between us. We'd bicker a lot, but I was only helping him see all the options when we were assigned to present projects and solutions. It was better that I point out flaws than have other do so. Often, Jan would leave the office when we argued.

4. For a while, I lived in the male nurses dorm where the gay old hospital chaplain also lives. He's about as far "out" as you can be in these days. His favorite Bible stories are about David and Jonathan. The chaplain drove me up the wall with his attentions but I enjoyed living in that old house, except that it was cold all the time. I liked talking with the guys about their studies and about what they knew about hospital gossip. I became friends with one of the residents and we double-dated a couple of women student nurses together.

5. Jan and I are close friends from the start of sharing our office. Then the whole hospital and community became embroiled in the strike. We worked closely together and she was a key person in keeping all informed and motivated to keep going during the six weeks. I admire her dedication and quality of her work. Just after the strike ended, Jan and her friend Bea left for a three-week trip to Europe together. Bea had a son in the Army in Germany and Jan went along to keep her company.

6. When I was promoted to be the new human relations director and moved into my own space with her best friend Marge as my assistant, Jan told me and Marge that the hospital finally found someone who could put human relations into personnel.

7. I took on an intern myself. Chuck McCarthy is a full-bodied, dark-haired college grad with a lot of vitality—not a scholar but a diamond in the rough from working class parents. We work and study together. I guess I'm his mentor.

8. Our hospital needed more PR work when the strike ended so, upon her recommendation and my judgment, I hired Bea as her assistant. Marge has qualms about hiring Bea. We talked together and gave Bea a tough course to hurdle to prove her worth before I decided to hire her. It was then that Jan told me that Bea and she were lovers. I knew Jan's marriage was shaky, but having Jan tell me about her love for another woman made me admire her even more for her courage and honesty by telling me about their relationship rather than trying to keep it hidden.

9. When someone at work asked me, "What makes those two so happy?" I answered, "They made a good team." I think only

Marge and I know about their true relationship. In a bold balancing act, Jan claims they can work together and she can maintain her marriage.

10. I watch Jan and Bea and I worry about them. Jan is having a full life as a bi-sexual—full of tension. Her husband's away from home a lot on business. He seems to hate Marge and Bea and the friends who take Jan away. He likes Nick and Diana and is friendly to me and other Lakeshore Med people, but I'm glad he doesn't confide in me because I wouldn't know what to say.

11. Marge told me when we have our little personal talks together in my office that Bea is alone a lot when she's not out with other women looking for men, hitting the bars and playing at being femme fatales.

12. Bea is giving our student intern a back-to-school party in her apartment tonight before he returns to complete his graduate degree.

But enough writing about these other people. When I have more time, I'll get back to write the details my life instead of being preoccupied by theirs. Writing personal stepping stones and stories can get addictive. I have business to finish before I go to Bea's apartment tonight for a farewell party for Tom's returning to college.

.

CHAPTER 5

Bea on July 29, 1977

I woke up at ten, stared about my room, then realized what happened and called Jan at work. "My God, Jan. I can't believe it! I'm sorry that I'm late for work, but I just woke up and realized what I've done."

"Bea, I've been worried about you. Are you all right? I just returned from a meeting and you weren't here. I was picking up the phone to call you. What happened? Do you need me?"

"Ooh, Jan. I can't believe it."

I took a long breath and slow-motion images flashed through my brain: the farewell party in my apartment to send Tom back to school; everyone leaving except Jan helping to clean up; Randy playing on my electric piano while I strummed my guitar; Jan leaving after 1 a.m., saying she can't stay any longer and had to go home; Randy outlasting everyone else as I continued drinking to calm my nerves at his presence.

"Jan, I can't come to work today. I may have to quit my job."

"For Christ sake, Bea! What's wrong?"

"Jan. I had sex with Randy after you left."

"Oh no!"

"He asked me if I wanted to and I said why not. God. I was drunk. I had to be to let him do that to me. He's our boss. But yet I am flattered that he actually wanted to have sex *with me*. So, we went and did it, just did it, no foreplay or anything, but I think I remember him saying, 'God, Bea. Hold on. I'm having two orgasms.' Maybe I could only have been imaging that, but I don't think so. I was so wiped out. I can't remember. And I'm so sick about what I've done. Damn it all. And I'm so hung-over too."

"I'm sick, too. How could he have done that? How could you have given in? I tried to stay with you until everyone left, but he kept hanging around playing on your piano. But you can't quit this job. You have to face up to this. You can't let him fuck you over the second time by quitting!"

"I'm devastated, Jan. I can't come to work today and face him."

"And if I see him, I'll choke him right then and there. And kick him in the balls. But I can't come to you now. I have to go home and get everything packed and ready to leave at 2 p.m. to drive to be with Matt at his camp. And you have to cover the office on Monday and Tuesday while I'm gone."

"I guess I'll be all right. I have to be. This isn't the first time someone has done this to me, you know."

"Yes. I definitely know. Please, please take care of yourself while I am gone. I love you so much and I don't want you to be hurt anymore."

"I love you too, Jan. But I'm alone again. Oh well. Good for old Dandy Randy. I'll try to forget it. I don't remember much anyway."

"I'll call you when I get home. I must go with Jenny and Alex to pick up Matt. I'll see you on Wednesday at work. I have to go."

"OK. Yes. Go."

I called Marge's office and asked her if Randy was at work. She told me he had called and said he wouldn't be in until after eleven. "Well, never mind," I said. "Don't leave a message. I have to leave for my long weekend. I only wanted you to know that the office will be closed soon. You can reach me at home until 2. Bea will be back on Monday. Nothing serious. Just too much partying on a weeknight, I guess. You don't have to tell anyone else. I'll put a sign on the office door."

"Yah. I know what you mean. I have a bit of a stinger myself. See you when you get back. Have fun!"

Then I called Tony Logan and asked him to give Bea a call soon during the five days while I'm gone to see if she's all right. He said he would think of an excuse to call. I didn't tell him why I needed him to attend to Bea. And he didn't ask.

After checking all the office details, I rushed home to pack our camper van for our long drive to spend time in a cabin in Trego, our northern Wisconsin headquarters for our visit and to bring my son's girlfriend with us to see him.

While we filled the van with food and travel gear, my mind was confused and my heart was broken. How could she have done this to herself, to me, to us! What will Randy do now? What a prick! And he knows about us. What is he trying to prove?

For the first lap of the journey to visit Matt, the four of us stayed overnight in a motel with a pool and, after picking him up and settling in a cabin the following noon, I prepared lunch and then encouraged them all to go fishing while I cleaned up and rested. But rather than rest, I paced through the north woods, obsessed with what happened. Could Randy fire her somehow; protect himself from our telling others about his abuse of a drunken employee almost twenty years older than he is. If we confront him in any way, Bea will lose. And what about me?

I walked up the road and found a lonely pay telephone booth across from a seedy hunters' bar that sold fish bait from rusty 7-Up coolers leaning against the run-down saloon. Phone! Yes. I'll phone to see if she's all right. My hands went for my jeans pockets, but I could find no change. I'd left my wallet at the cabin. Frustrated and deeply upset, I tried to get through to an operator to place a collect call but misread the directions several times and hung up in more confusion and distress. Venturing past the Tombstone Pizza sign nailed under the high, narrow window, I didn't even consider walking through the patched screen door into the bar and ask to make a collect call from their phone.

Turning on the dusty shoulder of the road, I plodded in my grief back to the cabin. Bea and I will each have to deal with this individually until I return.

The three of our young people, arm in arm, walked away from us. Jenny was the sister and the observer, loving both of them and both of us. After they decided Matt needed a haircut, they returned. We watched them groom this young hero, the focus of our adoration. He loved it.

Then Alex and I retired to the cold sheets and thin blankets of our room. I heard Jenny crawling into the double bed on the other side of the shared log wall of our rooms. We could hear the couple in the main room whisper, then leave in the VW van. They returned much later. He slept on the hide-abed. She crawled in the bed with Jenny, spoke softly to her and started crying.

I could hear the young women's muffled voices comforting each other. Bea and I will comfort each other when I return. We'll plan on what to do next. We must not let our anger over her abuse create chaos; we have to be silent and hope for a secure and sane future.

Bea on August 6, 1977

Hectic! That's what it's been being alone in the office. So, what's new! I've had a chance to see Randy from a distance and he disappeared. He checked my newsletter copy via his secretary. After Thursday's fiasco with Randy, I vowed to stop drinking. I'm sucking in too much alcohol. And on Monday, alone in the office, boy, did I have the shakes. It was a wild day with one project on the copy machine and then the dark room plus working on my Lakeshore Medical Center's Auxiliary slide show.

When Jan came back from up north on Wednesday, I showed

her the slide show. She made some changes and then, all of a sudden, it became her production. That made us testy at work and did I get pissed at Jan for changing my newsletter. Then she showed me the fine things she said about me and my work on my job evaluation form and explained why she wrote some insightful points that could have pissed me off, but they were tactfully said and I could live with that.

Last night she banged on my door saying she wanted to have a pillow fight with me. What the Hell! What is that woman thinking! God! She said it would burn off some anger and maybe we would end up laughing. Ha! I think not. She probably read about that in one of the psychobabble magazines that she subscribes to. That's some joke, huh! I suggested we hit tennis balls at my school wall instead, which we did, and after working up a sweat doing that, we had to bathe together, oil one another and then we started making love. But the scene went bad. She stopped and backed away for a while, and I said, "What a terrific way to get even." She got dressed and cut out. I spent Saturday finishing my reading Kate Millet's *Sita* and drank.

I was crabby as hell and mad at the world. But I cooled off when I found out that I was given a good raise, and so did Jan with Randy writing on *my* new pay slip about delegating more responsibility for our department.

Who said Unitarians don't need a savior to sustain us as we heal our deep wounds. We sustain our faith without using a savior. Perhaps more like a phoenix who flies toward the fire that lights up our lives, a phoenix that survives from the ashes to relight our spirit.

And to excite us again with our healing, loving passion.

Jan on August 7, 1977

"I wish I could describe what my body goes through when I'm with you." And with her gentle motivation, I wrote this poem for her.

> A secret lives inside of me
> that grows with care and love
> to be so grand in scope and great in size

that when my outside touches yours—
when my eyes dwell in yours again
reflecting secrets I can see,
my inside secret swells so large, demanding to be free.

It pulls away from nurturing cells,
its warm, soft placenta place
that held with care and love and grace
this essence rising, self-contained
amid the flesh and muscle and blood and heartbeats
pounding fresh new life into love restrained too long.

Past constricted lungs, through choking throat,
this secret searches to belong and to become united
with its other self, to be reborn, rejoined, revealed
in humanness unadorned.
This secret life shouts from my mouth
and jars my brain—rejoicing, free, in oneness now—
in love—alive again.

Jan on August 30, 1977

Lakeshore Med hired a psychologist to evaluate and/or help the staff solve some of their work-related issues. After researching about to trust him, I made an appointment. We finally met and I danced about verbally, finally speaking the truth about Bea's sexual harassment. I unloaded my grief, but I avoided any use of feminine references in speaking of our relationship and why her issues cause me such pain. Of course, that tipped him off right away and he asked me if the person I was speaking about was a woman. Perhaps he knew all about this before I even started to meet with him. The dam broke for me and after I could stop my tears, I was able to feel that I found a confidant, a helper. I don't know if his job was to report confidential information to administration that paid his fee—but he disappeared from Lakeshore Med's scene.

CHAPTER 6

Jan on September 5, 1977

We've left Matt at this depressing little college in South Dakota that seems not much bigger than one of our local high schools. But they compete nationally in cross-country and track, and Matt keeps reminding me that he didn't pick the school solely on its hunting and fishing possibilities.

We decided not to have him drive the old VW to South Dakota, so we hit the road in Alex's Mercury sedan pulling a little trailer filled with our camping equipment and Matt's fishing and hunting gear, books, clothes, etc., on a family "rite of passage." We couldn't leave earlier because Matt just returned from his eight-weeks of being a camp counselor and Jenny wanted to be back to start her junior year on the day after Labor Day. Her class is going on a two-week annual field and camping trip to Galena, Illinois, and north to circle through Wisconsin's geographical and historical sites.

On the way back home, Jenny also couldn't understand how or why her parents would be so edgy and fight over trivial details like how to tie the flapping corners of the canvas cover on the empty trailer, but she felt our emotional tensions on the long, dull trip home. The minutes ticked by as we finally headed east with time challenging my unspoken scheduling options.

The drive was grim. All the Mercury's open windows let

blowing, blistering hot wind from across America's Heartland to dry away some of our sweat. The view across endless miles of corn, wheat and cattle grazing lands offered no surprises other than an occasional cowboy or two waving their hats at us or a gas station with a few groceries, sodas and snacks.

The vision of Lake Michigan revived me when I wasn't thinking about the love that I will receive when I returned.

We arrived at home with time to unpack. I helped unload the car like a compulsive stevedore and announced to Alex that I was going to work. I shocked him, I guess. Perhaps he had an agenda of his own to unload on me, but I rushed out of the house and into the van like a horny sailor on leave after months at sea.

I did go to work, but only to kidnap Bea from our office to fulfill the empty hours thinking about my return—to shower, to embrace, to laugh.

I made it back to her after driving 1,100 miles in two days.

Jan on September 7, 1977

I said goodbye to Jenny on the bus for her Thoreau High School field trip,

I called Tony for his advice about an attorney who would be sympathetic to my leaving my children—after falling in love with another woman. He's checking out a Conrad Sanders who's a friend of our church. I told Tony my plans to rent a small apartment for myself and then maybe a home for us together. I was pretty calm when I discussed this with him. Good practice for the future.

Our office continued to function as it had when I was away. Bea did a good job without me. She told me that several people commented that must be really lonesome in our office. Little do they know how lonesome it can be—yet maybe they do. It's grand having them see us as the team we are."

Our friend who uses my rented room to be with her lover called to "cheer me up," Bea grumbled, "She wanted to talk, but I begged off her visit, because she only wanted to talk about herself and her lover who's leaving her. It was a nice gesture though."

Jan on September 10, 1977

This morning Alex sat in his chair in the corner of the family room and stopped me while I was rushing about with my Saturday chores.

"Jan. Stop scurrying around and sit down. I want to talk to you." He put his hands together after he had stroked each side of his head, face and chin whiskers with his fingers. "I don't want to plan for any 25th wedding anniversary and a trip with us being in a three-way deal. You'll have to make up your mind to either stop or we'll have to separate. It's too hard to keep this up. I can't stand it."

He finally gave me an ultimatum. He can't stand it anymore. I am being let go, unless I come back as the wife he wants for himself. "Alex, I am so tired of 'working on our relationship' and 'trying to try harder' to keep our house together. Is being together where we really want to be?"

"It is for me."

"I can't say that I want to be with you for the rest of my life. There is no joy between us. I can't remember when we laughed out loud and enjoyed each other' company, had actual fun being together. You can blame anyone you want for what has happened to us, but we've done all we can together and it didn't necessarily take another person or persons to force a change."

"I'm leaving for California. Think this all over before you make any further decisions. Maybe you should get some therapy. Let me know what you decide when I get back."

"I'll think it over," getting in last word as I left for the kitchen and then upstairs to get dressed, but my mind and my heart were almost leaping to be released from this enduring pressure. And I ran errands and pretty much kept cool and quiet for several days.

One of the errands was finding an apartment, and I did find one that I could afford right away, answering an ad from an agency that wanted the former tenant's name to be unknown. It was only one block from my house—one bedroom, second story apartment with a living and dining room, bath and kitchen in respectable building with a side view of the lake. But it was dirty and the carpet had nasty stains. I later discovered that a federal elected official used this apartment when he stayed in Lakeshore Bay with his dog that did pretty much what it wanted to do. I signed a year's lease right away. It would be only one block from Jenny and one block from work. My timing was right on. It was a good sign. Meanwhile I'll sleep around or stay in my room until I can move in.

Jan's attorney on September 13, 1977

"Dear Mr. Carnigian:

"Your wife has conferred with me in respect to the problems in the marriage and her desire for a separation or divorce. I suggested to her that, in view of the circumstances and the possible harmful effects of their publication upon you and your wife, your children and others, a conference to discuss the situation might be worthwhile.

"She informed me that you had consulted an attorney some time ago. With their training, experience and objectivity, lawyers are often able to suggest procedures which are helpful in cases like this, and I hope that you will attend such conferences."

"Very truly yours

<<◇>>

I'll keep out of the way after Alex gets this letter before he leaves for California. I'll be gathering up Bea and heading for Eau Claire for another Hospital Public Relations-Wisconsin (HPRW) conference. But while Alex's away, I'll go home to take care of Pepper.

On other fronts, Lakeshore Med gave me a good raise with my job responsibilities expanding with new projects to achieve.

Bea on September 18, 1977

We drove to the HPRW meeting in Eau Claire. Wednesday night's pre-conference fun ended again with most of us in or around the hot tub, drinking, talking and singing around the circle. Because Eau Claire was close to many Minnesota hospitals, our organization invited the Minnesota hospital PR group. But that's no excuse for being as close as one of those guys was when he put his hand on my crotch while I was in the hot tub. That's when Jan and I retired to our room—and I told her why. I didn't want to make a fuss with that guy in front of the others. It was 1:30 anyway and I was really beat. After our workshops, we had our banquet with award plaques for hospital PR achievements. We picked up three and one-half awards: one for Jan's patient information booklet and another for the "memo" series sent to corporation members and community leaders. The half award with two plaques went to the Nordstrom agency's expensive publication to explain Lakeshore Med's building project. It also countered our struggles with the city and with our neighbors. It was filled with our pictures, research and writing.

Jan's greatest award came for her work during Lakeshore Med strike. She compiled a comprehensive, 250-page report called "A Year of Union Militancy Challenges a Century of Caring." The judges' written comment from for Jan's prestigious award were:

"Congratulations to Ms. Carnigian for the positive moves in the PR department that will result from the handling of the strike situation. Excellent writing job under tremendous strain. The idea for a daily communication very well carried out. Components well used to keep hospital management and personnel well informed. Excellent media coverage, as well as union tactics. Employee moral obviously kept up by PR efforts."

We really had a swell evening pulling off all those awards for such a small department.

Jan was concerned that Alex didn't try to contact her after all this time. Maybe he wasn't back from California. "God," she said, "maybe Pepper's been alone since he left." Jan called Adele. She told Jan that yes, Pepper was alone, hungry and that she fed her. "I'm sorry to ask you, Adele, but will you keep on doing that until you know that Alex is there, at least until I bring Jenny home on September 25? I don't know where Alex is, but you can reach me at this number, at work or at my room if you need to talk with me." Jan thanked her, hung up and cried.

Jan on September 20, 1977

When Alex finally returned home, he found my attorney's letter and called me in the evening at Bea's. I agreed to talk with him on Monday if a third party was with us. He must have called Tony then and we met in Tony's office at church. It turned out to be the same old, same old. That's when I started editing and retyping my divorce notes that I sent to Alex. Maybe that would stick in his brain so we don't have to go over all the pain again and again.

Dear Alex,

Roots of separation go back a long way—many years—lost opportunities for coming together when the coming together was valid and possible

You tell me that I 'shit on you' when I do the things that has meaning to me. If that is so, then I must leave you and stop your suffering. I do not want to 'shit' on anyone, and I will not give up nor diminish what is important to me.

My priorities in the past have been to balance my needs after fulfilling yours and our children. They are outgrowing the primary needs from me but you are increasing them and their hold on me. I cannot and will not have your needs depress me any longer.

I will seek light and growth and creativity and joy; your shadow and your stare no longer have power over me.

After over thirty years in your possession, I am giving myself a gift of freedom. I want a legal separation until time can help resolve our material possessions when we can make decisions based on positive gains in understanding and acceptance. I do not want to take away or destroy any home or property rights from anyone. I will continue to work and support myself. If time passes and you want to make a settlement based on kindness and fairness, then maybe we can work something out together for the benefit of all, especially the children.

Through all these years, sex has been our only intimacy, our only means of communication, and in recent months, over a year, you have communicated, through sex, your dislike and disgust of me. I cannot tolerate it any longer.

At every other level other, we have been at odds. I must live fully and participate in life fully and in joy without your stifling restrictions. I have books and poems to create, visions to fulfill and goals to reach. I cannot any longer use up my energies in your negative pull of duty and responsibility. I have been responsible for too many years at the cost of something very dear to me. It's time now for others to understand and to let go of me so that I can fulfill my dreams for my life—try to anyway.

I actually wanted to complete the responsibility of being at home until Jenny became eighteen. But I cannot continue there for two more years. Matt will be settled in his race to achieve. He's away from home and doesn't require my daily tasks in his name. And Jenny would eventually dislike the idea that I hung around the house suffering and making you suffer just to keep pretending for two more years.

You can be a happier person if find someone who will give you the love that you need. Many fine women would be happy caring for you and give you the love you deserve. I feel more like a mother to you than a real wife. And you're at a suitable stage now where you've learned and you've grown beyond the smothering person you've been to me, paternalistic. You can and will make someone a very fine husband and/or lover—but it's too late for us after all these years.

You've been a wonderful father, Alex, and I respect you for that. But you've missed being a husband to me and you've missed, most of all, being a friend. I have loved you in many ways—now, only as the father of my children.

I have played a role for you and for the children. Today I will become an authentic person all the time.

Vietnam, civil rights and the assassinations of the Kennedys and Martin Luther King, Jr., the police riots during the Democratic convention in Chicago, 1968, commitment to church and Montessori, my sense of humor, my work—all that was important to me, all turned to anger and loneliness and were merely tolerated by you. During the McGovern campaign, for example, all you worried about was what was for supper—then your empty words or no words at all.

I feel so free when you are not near me. Free from fear and intimidation and judgment, free to be what I am—a human being filled with joy and concern and talent and love and creativity and the desire to succeed in something greater than what is now.

I'm drinking too much to kill the frustration of each empty evening. I am not free to create what is important to me—you do not accept that as valid. You never have. Domestic chores, redecorating for companionship or nothing at all. Your judgment dries up my positive skills and leaves me scrawling angry verses on torn paper scraps to be hidden in secret places.

I've left you before. I've run away. I remember screaming at you to let me go folk dancing, that you're keeping me a prisoner. But I've always come back because I've wanted to be responsible to the children and to my role as a wife as much as I could be. Now I must be responsible to my life as a resourceful human being, a woman with potential to grow.

When your anger diminishes, we can talk and see that this is the best for all of us.

1 will stay in my room until I can get an apartment with a kitchen and room to entertain and to spread out my work.

I have said for years that you love me only for what you want me to be, not for what I am, and I have kept that "am" in another part of my life to keep my marriage together. I cannot do that any longer.

The priority of time is weighing on me. I do not have time to lose. I do not have time to waste. Last year at this 45th birthday, I thought I'd go crazy with time passing by. Last year at my birthday party, I knew I'd not have another at my home again—with you staring and angry and hateful.

<<<◇>>>

Before Alex could get to Matt and before Jenny got home, I mailed a long letter to Matt. I wondered how he felt being so far away from home when his family is breaking up. I could identify with this because my mother finally succumbed to being permanently institutionalized after she was found by sheriffs and taken away again to Winnebago—after I left home to begin my junior year of college.

Jan on September 26, 1977

Yesterday at 5 p.m., I picked Jenny up at school after her two-week bus trip with her classmates ended. It's also her 16th birthday, a day that should be one of the most delightful times in a girl's life.

Jenny hasn't had the greatest birthdays in her life. We seemed to be traveling in September so many times and she'd end up with a cake and candles sitting with Matt and her cousin and her aunt at our kitchen table.

But this year was her 16th birthday—and the birth of her mother's new life.

On the way home, I drove her to my new address to show her where I would now be living. "I won't be coming home with you, Jenny. This will be my apartment—only one block away from you. It's time now to face the reality about continuing my marriage to your father."

She looked up at the second story window, then stared at the lake from the passenger seat of my little Toyota.

"I don't love him anymore in the ways that a woman should love a man. I respect him in many ways, but that's not enough."

"You've been fighting for a long time, even if you think we couldn't tell."

"For years I've told your father that he loved me only for what he wanted me to be, not for what I really was. I'm closer to what I really am and with the years that I have left, I must try to reach my goals. That hurts your dad and makes him angry. What is important to me, beyond you and Matt and our home, are my job, my interests in so many different things, my friends, my independence and my goal to be a successful writer. These are either ignored by your dad or make him feel hurt and powerless. Giving them up would make me feel frustrated and powerless. I can't continue living with these angry feelings, and I can't endure his hostility or the emptiness I face when I obey his expectations of my role as his wife."

"What do other mothers do if they're unhappy?"

"Many women seem to get through the day without lot of feelings of being put down or suppressed. I suppose I have "everything a woman would want," yet I have more goals, motives and incentives than most women, and I am ready to stretch out and grow without continually carrying the load of negative feelings. There are some mothers who must think they are alone in their unhappiness and stay at home, get depressed, perhaps drink a lot. Sometimes I think my sanity is threatened—and that's so awfully scary for me."

"It's scary for me too."

"Of course it is. Often mothers stay with their husbands because they can't afford to leave or because they'll be condemned for leaving their children. I know that your father will be good to you and I will be close to you always."

She looked at me briefly and turned away. "Don't I have any choice in the matter?"

"Jenny, I planned to stay with you until you became 18. But your father made ultimatums to me that I wouldn't accept, and I left the house on Wednesday."

"But you seem so happy most of the time, so positive."

"When I was your age, I said I wanted to be an actress, an impossible goal, and I guess I've turned out to be an actress all of the time. We've done a lot of good things together in our marriage; the best has been parenting you and Matt. Hopefully you will try to understand that each of us is an individual person and has individual ways of being and living. But I've been "Alex's girl" or "Alex's wife" for over thirty years. It's been a long struggle for me."

"What about Matt? I knew this separation was coming, Mom, and I think Matt does too."

"Matt's away now. That's what he wants. And you'd eventually hate it that I hung around the house like a robot pretending to be happy with your father. I can actually be a better mother to you if I am happier doing what I was meant to do, and your dad can be a better father if he stops suffering long enough to find someone who will give him the love that he deserves."

We cried together for a while before I could say. "Alex and I must stop being hurt by each other, even though the hurting isn't done on purpose. We each have different expectations about our lives; and now that you and Matt are getting older, these differences have been impossible to tolerate.

"Jenny, your dad's pride is badly wounded. He doesn't want to let me go. It seems like a relatively sudden event to him because he thought I would never leave him; but to me this has been an evolutionary process over a long time. About four years ago when I talked with Adele about my concerns, my boredom, my limitations and frustrations about marriage, she said to me, 'Jan. There's a war in Vietnam, Nixon is messing up the government and inflation is ruining the economy. If you and Alex get a divorce, we'll have nothing left to believe in.' I can't carry that load anymore."

"You carry a heavy load around the hospital and at church and with all your women friends and their troubles."

"Maybe that's a key reason why I can't take you with me. Your father would never let me take you with me. I know you don't want to leave your home, and there'd be legal fights and there could be stuff in the newspapers. That's why we must separate quietly and without a contest. The attorneys suggest beginning divorce proceedings as soon as possible. Alex's attorney will notify mine that because his wife no longer loves him and does not want to live with him, he wants a divorce. No-fault divorces have just been passed in Wisconsin, but it takes four months to get the new bill into practice."

"That seems so fast, Mom. After all these years."

"It's not going to be easy for any of us. I am confident and strong, fearful and trembling all at the same time. I fear losing the love of those who may hate me for being myself. I need you to love me and I hope you will understand. In many ways, you will now be free from the tension you experience from our conflicts."

Jenny and I sat and stared for a long time.

"I found this for you, dear, at an art fair. I thought of you when I saw it and tucked it away to give it to you today."

Jenny opened her birthday package, a handcrafted earthenware angel that looked like an authentic young woman holding stars in a bag on one arm and offering a star with her other hand. It was getting dark as Jenny read her little card saying that I loved her.

"How do I get a hold of you when I need you?"

"I have a phone in my room, but I will be there only a couple weeks more because I've rented this apartment. Believe it or not, it seems to have just become available for me. I'll still get a view of the lake and I'll be close for you and Pepper to come to see me as often as you like. I'll get a phone there when I move in around mid-October. And I'm always available if you call or visit me at work. And I'd like to spend some time at Old Mill Inn if it's all right with you. Good food, there, right?"

"I guess I'll spend more time with that family, Mom, than with ours."

"Jenny, I love you desperately, and the fear of hurting you has always been the most important thing in my life choices. I don't want to hurt anyone, but especially you. Many of my decisions have been made to create a home for you and Matt like I never had, a stable and secure place to grow. But now it's time for me to stop living in a world set up for others and begin a new life for myself. You will always be, as Matt is too, primary people in my life; and you are so important, always, in how and what and where I live that life. I am excited about your potential and I hope you'll have the same feelings about me."

I started up the ignition on the car and drove her around the block to home and to her waiting father.

Jenny on September 26, 1977

What's going to happen to me now that Mom is leaving Dad? What will I tell my friends? Why did she have to do this to me—to us! It's all her friends' fault—and her working, too. Why can't she stay home like Ellie's mother and take care of us.

What will I do in our big house all alone when Dad travels for business and my brother's gone off to college? Hell. That was one tough trip taking him to school in South Dakota. The two of them argued all the way home. I guess that was the last straw. I guess I've known for a long time that this would happen. It's been so tense and frightening when they get going at each other.

And she tells me this on my 16th birthday. Great! What a present? She said Dad gave her an ultimatum that she couldn't accept and is moving out. I'm glad I don't have to move out with her. Why doesn't she make him move out and we can stay at home together. She can't afford to keep house, I suppose, but maybe Dad would fight her for it and we'd still have all the anger and tension.

Better I stay here with Dad. He's so unhappy. Why does she make life so miserable for us? Why does she have to leave!

I guess we'll be all right. I'll have my dad to myself and I'll be my own person. She says she'll be close and available—if I want her, that is.

Jan on September 29, 1977

Dear Matt,

As each day passes, each of us is getting closer to better understanding and accepting of what's real.

When I called Jenny on Monday night, the house was noisy.

Ellie and she had made supper and Var and Sona were there. All seemed well at home for her and her voice was friendly and strong.

I don't get much news in detail about you when I ask you dad how you are. It's still too early in our separation for your father and me to get together without hurt feelings.

I also hope to continue contributing some funds to your college and/or your personal expenses (and for Jenny's too.)

The new hospital's *synergy* is hot off the press and I mailed it to you. I hope you like it. It's being received with great enthusiasm in the hospital and in the community. We're tooling up for the winter issue.

I hope you're getting enough out of your classes. How does the level of achievement compare to your classes at Oshkosh? Are there other highly motivated students in your classes? Have you found some good friends? Are the instructors human beings?

I love you, Matt,

Mom

P.S. Did you get the first check I sent you?

Jan on September 30, 1977

I'm bouncing around sleeping in my room when it seemed ill-advised being with Bea at her apartment. Anxiety at work carries into the evening. Flare-ups ignite on one wrong word. Stress kindles fires of anger that burn us out. Alcohol doesn't help anything; the tension is enough to drive a person to drink.

Our psychologist friend Rachael Sandler wrote that her feelings on receiving my note were mixed: "Sadness at an ending of good people and relief that I hope you will stop hurting each other. You write that you're OK but I know that you always say that no matter what's going on. How are you really? Are you asking for what you need? I care. I'm a friend, and I'm available. Call. We can get together—here, there, or halfway between. Please let me hear from you again."

<<<>>>

My attorney is a kind and thoughtful gentleman who wrote me

this advice before I was to appear before the Family Court Commissioner who just happens to have been my father's attorney and good friend.

"The Commissioner will probably make some inquiry respecting the nature of the marital problem and may urge further counseling. I see no need for you to mention to him all of the facts that you disclosed to me. All that he needs to know is that you no longer feel physical love toward your husband and that you desire that the marriage end. If he suggests counseling, you can tell him that that has already been tried."

Jan on October 15, 1977

Moving Day! One block away from Jenny! I had one day to get stuff out of my house and blend my bunk bed, tiny refrigerator and office equipment from the room I rented since February 1976. Bea's daughter, Jill, was a lifesaver by getting her father's truck for the day, and so were my long-time dear friends: Betty plus Marie and Sandy—and Bea, of course. They cleaned up the new apartment and moved a few personal pieces out of my home, my former home: my homemade yellow desk, the complete garden furniture set of white wrought iron with blue, green and white floral cushions and some books. I didn't want to leave a big hole in the house by taking more. My leaving would be a large hole in itself.

Jenny was not allowed to help me move, according to her father's orders, and they went off together somewhere in the interim.
Built-in cupboards in the dining area became my studio where I used my office files to hold up a flush door for my large desk and worktable. I bought a few lamps and bookcases to match those in Bea's apartment, a blue bean bag chair, a floor lamp and a room-sized blue and green shag rug for the living room to cover the stains left from the previous tenant's dog.
I joined the bunk bed and mattresses together to make king-sized bed, which filled most of my bedroom. Black tiger stripes on

white sheets covered the entire wall at the head of the bed. My bed linens with black zebra stripes completed the bedroom ambiance.

To reflect my new idea of kitchen work, I selected a Mickey Mouse motif for the curtains and dishes.

I encouraged Bea to set up her art studio in the north light of my writing studio, and she soon brought in her paints, easel and canvas frames from the basement storage area of her apartment complex on the west side of town.

We planned to spend every night together at her place or mine until my divorce is resolved—and after.

Jan on November 2, 1977

Dear Matt,

I was so very happy to hear that you made the team status to be able to drive home to compete at Oshkosh in a few weeks. Jenny and Ellie stopped by last night with Pepper to tell me the good news. I hope you have a few minutes to see my apartment and to talk with me during your short stay.

When I went to Thoreau High's open house with Jenny, I talked a bit with your respected teacher Jerry Kerr about your lack of fulfillment there. He went to Duluth State College and knew how you felt, but he said that your incentive and motivation would make the best of a small college scene. He asked me how my book was coming. I was embarrassed that I didn't have much to report on that. I said I was too busy living it than writing it.

Sona and your Aunt Var are very angry with me. Anna Spence had a talk with Var and Anna described them as "hate incarnate." I think your dad may feel relief in being free from the tension that our separate temperaments created.

November is always an intense month for me—at least it's more intense than other months. This year I'm looking for a positive time of solving problems and making progress rather than coping with frustrations.

Love,   Mom

Bea on November 5, 1977

The two of us slept late Sunday but after brunch, Jan posed nude on a soft blue blanket on the studio table while I took colored slides for overnight processing. But I couldn't wait to start and began sketching while she posed from the side her body with her arms around her knees. The focal point would be the intimate white space in the center of her legs, arms and breasts. I decided to leave off her head and completed that project in oil in a few hours. It's one of the best paintings I've ever done. I'm truly pleased with the results. I love painting the nooks and crannies of her body. I'll use her other color slides for future portraits.

When we told Marge about my painting, she wanted a nude done of her. Sure. Why not? A day later she and Beth Danson came over after work for a drink. They no more than stepped in the apartment, Jan took their coats and showed Beth Danson how nicely the apartment looked with everything set up and in place, and when those two walked into the studio, Marge had already stripped and was naked, sitting on the table on the orange, green and yellow crocheted shawl that her mother had given to Jan. The surprise on Jan and Beth's faces was obvious when they walked into the studio. A stripped-to-the-pink Marge leap-frogged upon the table and I started taking slides to use for the best choice of poses. It wasn't easy because Marge is short—and her feelings will be damaged if her image doesn't come out looking like a goddess.

Of course, Jan hung hers with prideful glee in her new living room. The first large canvas showed her graceful back and dimples in her butt. The second was a side view, a profile showing her soft belly curving to meet her breasts. The third was full frontal, again with no head, but with a lovely triangle of pubic hair. More paintings arc on the way. I'm on a roll.

Word buzzed about that I'm painting nudes in Jan's studio apartment. I did another of our friends, and all the nudes were without heads. Who needs a head, anyway? But that is the last one for friends. I had enough ideas to finish the several that I wanted to do of Jan and then some of myself from slides she took of me.

After working hours at the hospital, we filled our evenings as if we lived on the Left Bank in Paris, free to be artists and writers, free to be ourselves, rather than living on the western edge of Lake Michigan in conservative Midwest America.

Jan on November 15, 1977

In Sunday's want ads on November 6, I started looking for a house that Bea and I could afford to buy. My attorney and I were beginning financial negotiations with Alex, and I wanted to buy us a little home to be together and save rent money from two apartments. The sun streamed in through the window on the small-print classified ads and blessed me as I scrutinized the pages and I felt warm and happy.

On Wednesday, November 9, a knock on the door after supper didn't startle us because Jenny and our friends would come by—yet recently a close male friend of ours—and everyone else, including Alex, a friend who had previous encounters with Bea and three others of my friends, knocked on the door and Bea let him in. I was sitting in my blue beanbag chair with my feet up on its matching hassock. She returned next to me in my garden lounge chair with our floor lamp casting its light around us and the stacks of books and magazines that we were reading. Soft music was playing. In lieu of a real fire, we lit huge candles within the brick façade of the fake fireplace.

We wondered what business or announcements he wanted to make, coming into our space and standing over us with his coat still on. "You two look so warm and loving. I only want to get in there with you, in between the both of you. Get right down in the middle of all that love."

"No thanks Pete." Bea said. "We don't need any man to get in between us."

"No thanks," I responded.

"Are you sure?" Pete asked as if he were offering us the opportunity of a lifetime.

"Yes. We're sure?"

"Well then, I wish you both the best. And I'll get out of your way."

"OK with me. Good-bye," each of us responded. "Shut the door on your way out."

Yesterday Bea and I pulled off an impromptu birthday party for me in my new apartment, our Bohemian style-painter's studio with nudes of me without heads hanging on the walls. Earlier this week, Adele came by to see the apartment and when she saw the nudes, she shuddered and exclaimed, "You've hung them!" The word about their existence had gotten around. "I insist you cover them up. Put a drape on them!"

But I discounted her prudish nature. "Adele, you should be more broad-minded. My mother had a gracefully beautiful nude statue in our house for years, until some of my Lutheran school friends painted fingernail polish on various parts."

"Well! Doesn't that tell you something about people? Take down or cover up those paintings."

"I hope my friends are more broad-minded and intelligent than those dirty kids were."

"The word is 'Broad Minded.'"

"Adele! My mother even included the statue in the living room with us in our photo Christmas card the year my dad was in the Seabees. You know her. You remember her."

"Yes. I remember her. And how will people remember you?"

Well, on a couple hours' notice and after we filled my once-garden table with booze and snacks in the sunny, windowed alcove that overlooked the lake, we celebrated my forty-sixth birthday party with thirty friends from work, including the Dixons and others who showed up at the door. Surprise! Did they want to see me? Yes! But also the nudes. Yes! It is true. The nudes on the wall and I am walking around, entertaining, being the hostess again, but also the guest of honor—in person and in nudes on the wall.

I'm overwhelmed at the number of guests and the warm response everyone gave me for my first birthday as a single woman.

We went out for a Friday night dinner and shopped at Worthman's where we separated, shopping for our different priorities. I shopped across the crowded store in the pharmacy department when someone came up behind to see what I was holding. Completely absorbed with my discovery, Bea startled me when she found me checking out vibrators "to soothe muscle aches and pains." I smiled at her and said we need more toys for each of our apartments. Of course, we had to go home and try it out.

Bea on November 25, 1977

I've been having fun for four weeks finishing five nudes from classical ones to comic, plus work and all. My latest creation is a single boob, a pink sugarplum candy mountain against a deep blue sky. We laughed and fantasized about adding troop of Boy Scouts marching in line up to the top and planting their flag at the top before marching down again.

The nasty early snowstorms keep us shoveling our cars out of the drifts and snowplow mounds as we try to live after work together at her apartment or mine.

We did manage to get through by Thanksgiving spending time with each set of our children. But Jan came with me when I took my family out to eat. She cooked for her two and ate with them without me before they went their own ways.

Her back is hurting again. It's bad. And she's so touchy that we both get ticked off at each other—at home and at work. She berates me, resents me. I try to reason but it's no use. It's good that we have separate apartments.

The truth is, I don't know how we can make it work unless she demands less. I can't be everything she wants and she cannot be in control all the time.

Jan on December 6, 1977

I received from my attorney a copy of Tom Kerry and Alex's proposal as a final settlement. Tom is a UU, but he's a shark too. I agreed to most of the terms including no alimony and Alex having custody of Jenny and the mutual funds to help both children with their education. My cash settlement of $30,000 was quite skimpy, about $1,000 a year for services rendered since we were high school seniors together in 1949. That was the amount for half of the estimated house value.

I also wanted to clear up Door County and didn't want Alex to have to sell it in order to settle. That would prevent my children from getting the land. And I needed to visit the property myself. I proposed to my attorney that in consideration for giving up all property rights on the Door County land, I would have visitation privileges and shelter for one week each summer and two weekends, one in the fall and one in the spring with visitation continuing until the property is awarded to the children equally.

Sanders said my offer was quite magnanimous, but he was wary about Alex selling the property. I told him Alex never would; it meant too much to him.

In addition, I asked for some personal possessions left behind when I moved and listed them: Matt's and Jenny's plants, personal books, my Dickens prints, my two grandmothers' sugar bowls, the painting of a seated woman, my white teapot, my yearbooks, theater Playbills and my long-playing and 78 RPM record collections, my red Venetian goblets with Jenny getting all my German China and crystal, my Toyota and a couple savings accounts totaling $4,000.

<<<>>>

In Lakeshore Med's employee newsletter, distributed every

payday with good humor and snappy stories, Bea promoted the 1978 Lakeshore Med Las Vegas weekend from February 24 to 27. "For only $179.95," she wrote, "you get round trip TWA air fare, all you can drink on board, hotel room at the Stardust, breakfast and dinner, $18 in nickels, $24 lucky bucks, $18 in drink tickets, plane-to-room baggage service, transportation to and from hotels, taxes and tips are all included."

Wow! How can you top that!

Jan on December 20, 1977

Somehow our passion, love and respect for each other balance our struggles to establish an equal partnership between us. We are both so vulnerable. I will not submit to any inequality like I felt in my marriage, and though Bea had the upper hand in dealing with her husband and children, her boldness covers a thin-skin and she is insecure and defensive when I want to make suggestions and work as a team. I have to be very careful when we are together at home and at work not to say anything where she can misinterpret my intent or meaning.

Regrettably, at work, I'm the one who gets called in, walking past Marge's desk, to see Randy in his office, to find out if there is anything submitted for his approval that he doesn't like, and I have to humble myself to his power tainted by what he did to Bea in August. His behavior and superior attitude disgust me. He never talks to her and he must know that I know what he did and that, so far, maybe Bea told Marge, but I don't think so. I have not told anyone about it—so far. I don't want us to get fired. What once was a friendly and productive working relationship with him has become a serious struggle. Now I have to second guess exactly what administration wants, produce error-free publications, advance the best image of the hospital and its employees, respond to a hostile healthcare newspaper reporter's phone calls and hope that I'll be quoted accurately, and be the best that I, that we, can be to prove the worthiness of the two of us divorced women and lesbian lovers.

Fortunately, we have friends who sustain us, invite us to their homes and stop in to see us often at one apartment or another. Marge and her sons and mother will come for Christmas, my Jenny and Matt's girlfriend who is Jenny's girlfriend too, stop by. Bea's kids and their friends come to her apartment too, especially now that her boys are home for Christmas furloughs.

Bea and I picked out my first Christmas tree for my new life and I bought thick white garlands, strings of mixed colored lights and Mickey and Minnie Mouse and other Disney ornaments for it. It stood proudly in my living room, and when I stood in the exact correct corner of the room, I could experience the rainbow colors of my shining tree lights reflect off of my alcove window glass as the moon illuminated the wintry night, reflecting its silvery rays off the millions of undulating Lake Michigan ripples.

Dixons invited hospital administrators, head nurses and middle managers to their home for a lavish Christmas celebration. Bea's and my invitation said the party was from 5 to 7 p.m. and we were in awe of the tables laden with gorgeous plates of gourmet food. The full bar almost bowed with the weight of choices of punch, eggnog, wines, liquor and mixes. Our hospital had victory to celebrate with the groundbreaking and hopes for less conflict in the future. We sipped and nibbled our way around the rooms and chatted and laughed with our colleagues.

I wondered how the bounty of food and drink would be consumed by the time we were to leave. Then I realized when most nurses and managers started to put on their coats to leave. I asked Marge if she was ready to go, but she said no, not yet. Nick and Diana's friends (and many of my old friends) were starting to come in the door for a second party. Randy started playing the piano in one of the other rooms.

"Time for us to leave, Bea." We finished the tasty morsels on our plates and tossed down what was left of the potent cocktails we made for ourselves, collected our coats, thanked the host and hostess, walked the half block to my apartment, and got out of the way for their friends of higher status—like Alex.

Yesterday though, I had to get back to my apartment to get out of the way for Bea's kids coming for supper, and I had a date with Matt and Jenny to come over to see me before Matt left for South Dakota. He was going to drive the old VW camper van with a broken heater across hundreds of miles of drifting Midwestern plains. I'm really worried about that, but he doesn't seem to think it will be a problem.

Matt, Jenny and I have another problem to face. It's the first time that we will have a chance to talk without others around so I made them supper and served some holiday cookies in the living room near the Christmas tree. They sat on the garden sofa under two of my nude paintings on the wall behind them. I sat on the carpet across a coffee table at their feet to begin to tell them, somehow, why I've left home. What would I tell them? How would they respond? Where would I begin in my plea for their understanding? Who could I name to share the responsibility, yet take full responsibility for what I have done—to them, to their father, for me? How can I be so selfish?

"I need to explain why I'm here in this apartment and am leaving—am getting a divorce from your father."

Both pairs of eyes stared down at me. What had their dad told them? Perhaps they already know, but surely not the whole story. How could I even begin to tell them the whole story? They needed me to explain my decision. I took a deep breath to try to stop the tears already gathering. Don't cry now. Hold back the fearful joy of finally living the life I want and suppress being responsible for inflicting pain on my children—and, yes, my husband. Are these conflicting emotions my form of schizophrenia? Another deep breath and I straightened my back, my aching back, as I sat cross-legged before them.

Looking at my two beautifully maturing children I started. "I have not been happy for a long time."

"We know that, Mom," said Matt. Jenny shook her head yes. Her eyes were filling up too. Luckily, I had a box of tissue close by and we both grabbed for one to pinch at the tear ducts and stop a flood.

"Jenny, I tried to wait until you were 18."

"I know. You told me."

"Matt. I'm sorry I had to leave when you were so far away from us and you had to think of all this from such a long distance."

"I'm OK, Mom. That's OK."

(I didn't think of it as we spoke, but I do now as I write. How devastated I felt every time my mother left or was taken away, especially the last time when I was a student in Madison. How could I do that same thing to my son? My daughter is only a block away. It is bad enough to leave her, but Matt is in South Dakota, for Heaven's sake.)

I said again, "I have not been happy for a long time—but that's not exactly true because most of the time I am happy, but not when I am with your father. I'm happy when I'm work, most of the time, and I'm happy when I am with my friends, most of the time. And I'm happy when I am with you all of the time. You are truly great people and I am so proud of you and how you are becoming such wonderful young adults. And I love you so much."

That did it. The dam broke. Even Matt's eyes welled up, but Jenny's and mine overflowed.

"Actually, love is the crux of the situation. I had a deep affection for your father and married him for practical reasons because he is a good man and I knew he would be the best person for me to be with and an excellent father for my children when we were ready to have a family. But since I restarted my career, he holds me down and he keeps me back from what I need to try to be. The more I succeed, the more he seethes. But I've given him other reasons to be angry with me. And that is love again, but a different love that I found with another person, a soul mate that I love very much for a long time, someone who is so important to me."

I wondered as I paused to take a long, strengthening breath

again. Did they know who this person is? Is a list of men's names running through their minds? It would be a shock, I supposed, either way. Their mother has left them and their father for another man, someone they may not even know. Or even worse from society's point of view, could they even think their mother would leave them for another woman—someone they knew, someone close to them who, with me, has been deceiving them in their presence since April 1, 1974.

"I didn't ever think it to be this way," I whispered, "but it did happen anyway." Speaking bolder, "I suppose I really did want it to happen. Yes. Or we wouldn't be here like this."

"Mom. Tell us," Matt insisted. "What's going on! Skip the past. Where are we now?"

"OK." And I pulled myself together to say out loud, "I love Bea Lindberg."

"Bea! Yes. And I'm not surprised," said Jenny. "We could always find you with her or with her and Marge if we needed you. But I thought you were only good friends."

"Bea and I are more than good friends, Jenny. I love her and I want to live with her."

After a long pause, "Well I guess we can't explain that to anyone, Jenny," warned Matt. Both of them have friends who've been harassed by their peers because of gay or lesbian tendencies. And they've discussed gay and lesbian lifestyles in their UU sexuality classes. "We'll just go on as we have, Mom. But we understand a little better now. We still love you, of course, and I'm not all that surprised either. You're such a strong woman and a feminist, too. I suppose it doesn't hurt being from a liberal Unitarian church. You don't have all that biblical crap to overcome."

"Actually, Matt. I'm not all that strong. And there's plenty of other crap to overcome."

"Well, it seems that you're strong. And Bea is the same," said Jenny.

"She's not that strong either."

"We'll get OK with all this. But what will I tell my friends?" she asked.

"Jenny, I have trouble even telling my friends! Only a few really know, like Marge and Anna and Tony. Maybe others have guessed. I hope no one gives any of us a hard time at work or at church."

"Yah. That's something to be concerned about. People can be really mean," said Matt. The three of us sat in silence, waiting for the next one to speak. "But now I think Jenny and I need some time to talk this over together, Mom, just the two of us. Don't say anything to Dad about this, Jenny. Let him tell us if he wants to."

"I think he already knows because he told me I can't come over here if Bea is around."

"Jenny, your dad thinks this is all Bea's fault. He doesn't understand that there are many reasons for my leaving, for changing the way I live. Our marriage has really been over for several years, even before I fell in love with Bea. Perhaps when he gets that through his head, he may be less angry. He waited long enough for me to change emotionally and love him again. He's known about Bea and me for a long time. That's why life has been so crazy at our house. And that's another reason why it will improve for all of us if I live somewhere else. I would hope that it's better for you to see your mother being in a loving relationship than being in a hostile or submissive relationship with your father. I know too that your father would not move out of the house and allow you to live with me. I would lose you in a custody battle and don't want this to become public. Besides, you'd really get messed up then. Plus, that I can't afford to keep up the payments and maintain the house. I don't make that kind of money."

After thinking that over, Matt said, "Well, I guess we all share a big secret together, but each in our own way. It's easier for me. I'm away in school. You'll have to make the best of it, Jenny. Maybe you can tell them that your parents don't love each other anymore and leave it at that."

"But a lot of parents seem to live like that and don't get a divorce."

"That's probably because the wife can't afford to make a move—or she's afraid," I said.

And Matt added, "But right now I don't know any women as a

couple like Mom and Bea. We'll just have to keep that to ourselves, Jenny."

"I guess so. And I will. Actually, Mom, I am making the best of it now. I'm happier that we know more about what's really going on."

"And so am I, Mom. We love you."

"I hope that's how it will always be. And I'll do my best to keep it that way. I've been afraid that you'd find out from someone else and I've been exhausted by keeping this secret from you. I think I'll be better and stronger now that you know the truth." Raising myself up to my knees on the floor, I reached forward with my arms to embrace the two of them and we hugged each other. A nervous cough from Jenny broke the tension with more sniffling and tissue and blowing of noses.

After they left, I sat there, numb. Was it all going to turn out all right? Who knows? It would seem that death is the ultimate end for men; losing the love on one's children is the ultimate loss for women, at least it is for me.

Bea on January 4, 1978

Jan is pushing us into getting a house or larger apartment for the both of us to live together. She hasn't been in hers more than a couple of months and is ready to find a place for the both of us. And she always said that she needed time to be on her own, to be by herself for a while. We actually looked yesterday at a larger apartment and a house to buy by combining her divorce settlement money and my nest egg from my father's estate.

It's no wonder we're bickering. I don't know now if I'm ready to make that kind of commitment.

Bea on January 20, 1978

I've been put through the mill this week. Whatever does that expression mean? I'm not corn, but I feel pretty ground down. I missed work on Monday with doctors' appointments, first to check off sinus problems and then to see a neurologist who put me on valium and told me to go home and stay there until I could get an appointment for a spinal tap which eventually caused me to stay overnight in the hospital. Jan came to my apartment every day to help me and of course stopped by frequently to my hospital room. Marge and others who work at the hospital came often to wake me up and ask how I was doing. They also asked me for the details of our Hep trip we're planning for Las Vegas in February. Can't the committee take over and let me rest!

I had x-rays and bone scans and EEGs that showed nothing. I was given an anti-depressant and Jan drove me home after I was discharged at about 8 p.m. She held me and we watched TV until we went to bed and fell asleep.

Jan had made appointments on Saturday and Sunday to see some houses for sale and drove me around, wiped-out and sleeping in the front seat between houses. I couldn't tell what I was looking at. I'm tired and edgy. What is this all about, anyway? When Jan left Alex she told me, "Bea, I can't live with you. I have to have a place of my own." Fat chance. Three months later she's pushed me out in the cold and snow to hunt for a house we would own together. She's dragging me all over town looking. But I'm on anti-depressant pills and I can't keep awake.

Don't I have anything to say about not being ready to buy a house? About living together? I don't even know if they sell houses to two women. Marilyn Lange, our real estate agent, seems to think so and she's going full blast to find us a house. Jan doesn't even have her divorce settlement money yet. What about the bank? Will they give two women a loan? Just a couple years ago Jan had trouble getting a personal charge card without getting her husband's signed approval. And where's the down payment coming from? From me, that's who. And then she'll back out and I'll be stuck living alone again in a house that I don't want.

It's absurd! I don't mind being together with somebody forever. I just don't want to feel like it's forever.

Jan on January 27, 1978

Bea and I went to the bank to see if she could apply for the down payment to buy a house with the understanding that I would pay half back when I get my divorce settlement. Yes. Her inheritance would float a mortgage on her own. But she doesn't trust me, I guess. Ironically Bea wanted to prove she could have a life of her own after her divorce. Then when I could only fill the cracks in time to make myself available to her, she was depressed and unhappy about that too.

We worked off some agitation together by taking down our Christmas tree, finally. It was so dry that I thought we'd shed needles down two flights of stairs and have to sweep all the steps. Bea grabbed the naked tree, walked through the apartment to the kitchen and out on the wooden porch that we never use and threw the tree over the railing near the dumpster. That solved that problem in a hurry.

Our arguments intensify, especially when after work when we're drinking, which is intensifying too. One evening we realized that the lady next door must have been hearing most of what we do and say. Perhaps her bedroom is next to mine. We knocked on her door recently to give her some mail that came to me by mistake. We were all smiles with this opportunity to finally meet my neighbor. She recoiled when she saw us, gave us a strange, unfriendly look, grabbed her mail and closed the door as quickly as possible.

With work and all this house business going on, there's too much, much too much now. Somehow we let our first feelings control our responses and our lives can turn surprisingly dreadful. I think Bea's afraid now to move in together, to make a financial and emotional commitment to me and officially, in the eyes of others, to live as a lesbian.

Bea on February 2, 1978

I had sent some slides of my paintings to the Wisconsin Women in the Arts and they chose a couple of nudes for a women-oriented art show in Madison. I took off in my car on my own and dropped them off, turned around and drove home.

Jan on February 5, 1978

Dear friends and relatives who may understand,

I can think of over two hundred persons who love Pepper either because of first-hand experience or because of the love that is revealed by others who love her: a Christmas card saying "cheers" when all you can see is a hairy face and forelock with a sad pair of eyes; a story in *The Bay View Times* from years long gone by about what it feels like to be an underachiever, a drop-out from obedience-training school, but, in reality, the happiest creature who outsmarts us all.

Those who love her first hand do so for many reasons, but most of all, I think it's because she was so accepting. Without rules or reasons, except for a bark or two for protocol, she accepted anyone who would be gentle and kind with only an idealistic hope that some of the time she, in return, would be accepted with kindness too by friendly, playful persons who'd respond to her.

An accepting nature—that's important between creatures.

I like to remember the time in Door County when Pepper met up with a skunk early one morning. Those two black and white creatures scrutinized each other closely, carefully and quietly. Perhaps they recognized that they could be meeting up with a kindred cousin of sorts. So, after acknowledging that fact and accepting the reality that one could be cousin to a skunk—or a dog, each turned away without fault or reprimand. The visiting skunk left

Pepper's territory and Pepper turned, unscathed, and crawled back into someone's warm sleeping bag for a nap.

And Pepper was trusting.

She would trust her vulnerable underside indefinitely for a rub, but if you stopped too soon, she'd nudge you—insatiable for more.

She would trust you to know her endurance because she'd follow you to infinity if that's where you wanted to go, even if her paws would get swollen from running next to you over sharp gravel in the unpaved country road.

She would guarantee a playful response if you felt the same after a hard day's work.

She would lead you to the outhouse at Woodridge past the woods at all hours and through all weather, trusting that you needed her for protection and company.

She would trust with the trust that meant that you'd be accepted and loved for what you are without some expectation of what you were supposed to be.

With her immediate survival needs taken care of, all that she needed or asked for was a pat on the back for encouragement or some positive reinforcement to acknowledge her worth, and it was so easy to do for her.

But Pepper died on January 25. She acquired an infection that shattered her physical support system, an infection that neither she nor the vets could conquer. She would have been ten years old in July.

Little could one have realized how her physical limitations could shatter human beings' emotional support systems for the while as we feel so deeply how much we need the accepting love that Pepper and some few other creatures on this earth dare to offer to one another.

Sincerely,
Jan

I thought I'd taken care of all the details when I left home, but I didn't think that Pepper would die. I counted on her to give Jenny support in that big house when she came home from high school. I counted on having Pepper visit me with Jenny in my apartment. I knew she loved me no matter what. I counted on her too much, I guess.

And she is gone.

Bea on February 11, 1978

We made an offer on a house today on Westwood Lane. I can't believe it! It's perfect for us. A brick and frame tri-level—well, really four levels, and two bathrooms—and a bar in the family room!

I have been so exhausted, but Jan forced me to house-hunt again with Marilyn Lange making appointments. Jan told me she drove us past this house weeks ago when I was so tired and told her I didn't like it from the outside. Of course, then she had to wake me up to glance at it. It seemed too small. But when you get inside, as we did today, it opens up into space after space. The sellers were smart too, setting an atmosphere to sell. Simmering on the stove was a pot of spiced tea and Donavan or someone as subtle was singing on the phonograph, "Our house is a very, very, very fine house."
Jan told me that she and Marilyn knew I was sold on it when I went to the back yard and hollered back to them from the end of the yard, "The tree is on our side of the fence!"
It took them almost a week before they owners accepted our offer of $47,000. We didn't even bicker. What's a thousand or two more or less? That house is meant for us. We'll close the deal at the end of March.
Meanwhile I've been getting little sleep with people stopping by all hours and a folk dance party where I really got sloshed. I didn't think I drank that much, but those pills make me vulnerable to the booze.

Jan's dream of having our house is coming closer to reality, and when we struggled to her apartment through the blowing snow again, we cuddled together under her feather quilt and made love until we got thirsty and hungry again. Then we spent this rest of the day having a business meeting about our assets and making financial plans.

We had to decide what to pack for our Las Vegas trip on Friday. She said her dream for this trip is to celebrate the purchase of our very own home and to have the two of us have fun in a new kind of adventure in Las Vegas: good food and drink, good shows, some slots, interesting people, and enjoying our Lakeshore Med employees. "Get HEP!" is our motto.

CHAPTER 7

Jan on February 24 to 27, 1978

The stewardess handed out free drink miniatures soon after the Lakeshore Medical Center HEP tour group lifted off in their Fun Jet plane to Las Vegas. "Have fun," they toasted. "Yeah! We work hard. Now let's play hard!" And they clunked their plastic glasses together.

"What a way to fly," celebrated Bea, the hospital's tour organizer, as she opened another miniature and poured it onto the ice in her glass. "What a relief. We got all our people in the air. I can relax for a while. But I'll really unwind when we get back home and they tell me they enjoyed the trip."

"You deserve to have a good time. You've done a great job, Bea."

While I looked out the window, Bea spoke quietly as she pretended to look over my shoulder and breathed closely on my cheek. "I love you, Babe."

I glanced about the area to see if anyone heard or saw us. "Yes. Me too. Yes. Just think. Soon we'll be in our own home. We'll actually be living together. And I'll be divorced from Old What's His Name." I leaned even closer, "I cherish you, Bea," I whispered, "and we're going to celebrate this weekend, but—not just yet for me," as I reclined my seat. "I want to rest up for our first Las Vegas adventure together. You get up and visit. You be Mrs. Hostess with the Mostest."

"I'll do that," while unclipping her seat belt, "especially when the drinks seem to be on the house, or on the plane—or whatever."

Among the many co-workers Bea joked with were Marge and her escort John. Marge usually hung out with us; we were a threesome, like sisters, bosom buddies, but if Marge had a man—almost any man—he came first.

After Bea moved on to converse with others, Marge remarked to John, "Those two are getting too friendly in front of people. There's more gossip about them now. I'm glad you're here with me—and I'm not with them."

I love watching the way Bea moves. Enjoying my drink, I studied Bea as I had since we admitted our secret love to ourselves and then to each other four years ago. "'A love that dare not speak its name,'" she thought, "according to homophobes. But it's magnetic tension, that's what it is—a lifelong need fulfilled. Yes!"

Bea and Donna exchanged repartee, and after Bea moved on, Donna suggested to Edith, "Bea and Jan seem too happy to be real. Have you seen how they come in to work together every day? They're close and smiling. I wonder what's up?"

"Do you think they are more than friends?"

"Heaven's sake. What can you be talking about? I heard that Bea and Marge have been known to pick up guys the Sexual Revolution, you know. And Jan's always seemed to be happily married, I guess, until now. Besides, why would they dare losing everything they have—including their children?"

Edith grew quiet as she tried to imagine what homosexuals do in bed. "Excuse me," she said, clearing her throat while reaching for a magazine to signal an end to this topic.

<<◇>>

Usually guarded with others, Bea and I had shared almost every intimate thought, including our fears and, sometimes, our confusion. I once suggested, "We need someone to talk with, to help us get clear about what we're going through," in one argument among those that were growing more frequent. "I wish there were other women to talk with."

"Never mind, Jan. We can manage on our own. And don't ask me to see a damn psychiatrist! I trust no authority figure. Are they not human? Do they not have problems of their own? Is their intelligence any better than mine? I'm suspicious of anyone who tries to tell me what's right for me."

I knew that was correct—for Bea who keeps me off balance with her unpredictable mood swings. I had thought, "It's too scary to confront her; she'll explode even more and then where will I be? I hope she realizes when she's had enough to drink now, especially at this altitude and, particularly, on this trip. I worried about Bea's continuing alcohol consumption, the effect of the altitude, and her overly zealous claims of being "responsible for the success of this tour." The stewardess straightened up the galley before landing and unloaded the leftover miniatures into Bea and other passengers' Fun Jet bags. "Must be part of the package deal," said Bea. "Those little bottles are cute but they don't last long."

Several passengers, including Bea, were plastered when they landed.

The loud banter of well-lubricated passengers above the plane's engine noise and the confined cigarette smoke seemed tolerable compared to the airport waiting room's thick yellow haze with one-armed bandit handles clanking and cylinders spinning bell fruit gums, cherries and plums. Gawking and tumbling into and through the nicotine-coated passageways to collect their baggage, the Midwesterners inhaled their first windy Nevada air just seconds before the bus exhaust. The February sun melted into the hazy dessert horizon as they climbed aboard to the Stardust Hotel.

In their room, Bea said, "Well, we made it so far," dropping her suitcase on her bed and her body beside it. "And now that we're here, why don't you get us some ice cubes like you always do, dear, and we'll have a quick one before we head out."

"We could rest up a bit. This town goes on all night and that's when the action is. Our group agreed that we'd all meet in the lobby after an hour and decide where we want to eat and what we want to do."

"Well, I'll get our own booze out of the suitcase and we'll freshen up," Bea said as she opened her bags.

"I love you, Bea. Don't go away," I kidded her as I stepped out along the second story walkway with the empty ice bucket. The dry breeze whipped through the parched desert plants. "Some wind, but it is great to be outdoors without a coat." Looking up, I studied the city's highest cocktail lounge on its slender tower above the sand-blown concrete walks, streets and lots surrounding it. "It does make you thirsty," and I filled the bucket with cubes overflowing.

Bea flashed out her make-up kit and put on a slimming black, sleeveless top and pants outfit. Her silver belt draped at hip level; her boots fit under her flared slacks.

"I have me one intelligent and beautiful woman," I thought as Bea applied her blue eye shadow. *"My Emma Peel."* Bea's long, dark brown hair framed her artistically made-up features. "I should be so beautiful, Bea. What a creative artist you are. I still have to chuckle when I think of how our Lakeshore Med friends reacted when they saw your nude paintings of me at my apartment-warming party."

"I love painting your body. And you give a great party."

"We are so bold, Bea, to celebrate our freedom and to travel together like this. Everyone knows we are a team. But do they know how much of a team we are?"

"Hell! Women travel together all the time. Look at Donna and Edith—and they don't even like each other," she said as she sipped her vodka martini. "Let's go. I'm ready," Bea announced, downing the remainder in her glass.

"OK. I can't wait to play!" I popped up, ran a comb through my hair, a lipstick across my mouth and I followed Bea tumbling out the door and down the stairwell leaning firmly against the handrail. "We'll be all right as soon as we get some food."

"Yah, OK. I know."

They found the other Lakeshore Med people and Donna and Edith, a Las Vegas regular, in the bar right off the lobby.

Most didn't know what to do or what they wanted:

"Do you want to buy show tickets here?"

"Who do you want to see?"

"Depends. Who's here and what do I want to spend to see them?"

"Some slot players said that Frank Sinatra stopped by Sammy Davis Jr.'s show last night."

"There's always Liberace."

"Ugh. That fag."

"He's got a good show."

"I like the nudie shows."

During the planning, one bar stool became available between two brawny men. Bea spotted it, staggered slightly away from the crowd and fit into the space, her wallet in her hand. "Let me buy you a drink, pretty lady," said the man in a western vest. "You're looking very pretty, very attractive."

Keeping an eye on Bea, I did my employee relations routine and kept talking with the others. Marge appeared but kept her distance. I went to look for her minutes later, hoping Bea and I could go with them, but Marge and John had disappeared.

"What will it be?" asked one of the tour group.

"Where to go first?" asked another.

"Where do you start?"

"I need to eat."

"Well, I want to gamble."

The larger group started splitting off in different directions.

After the others seemed organized, I went over to Bea and leaned over her shoulder, brushing the front of my body against Bea's back ever so gently and I whispered temptingly—warmly close to her ear, "We're going now—to get something to eat, dear."

Bea stiffened her back and turned, staring boldly at me. "I'm staying right here. Can't you see that I'm having a conversation with this gentleman? You go on with your women friends. I'm staying here until I decide where to go and what to do."

"But Bea—"

"Don't Bea me. I can do what I want to do. Now go!"

I felt a jolt like a hanged-man's trap door had opened under me. My breath wouldn't come. Pain surged through me. Rejection flushed my face to gray with shock, then to red with embarrassment. Recoiling, I backed away to gain perspective, watching Bea's back with her profile turned to the man, her lips moving in conversation with him.

"How could Bea do this to me? How could she abandon me like this? What's going on? What did I do wrong?"

"Come on, Jan," said Donna. "Go get Bea. Let's find someplace to eat on the Strip."

"Bea is not coming. May I come with you?"

"Is there anything wrong?"

"I hope not. Let's go, please," and I followed Donna and Edith while I strained for breath to fill my lungs, to feed my brain, to try to understand what had happened. My chest would not expand. Tight, aching bands restricted me as I stumbled along. Faking indifference at my wrenching separation, I inhaled shallow breaths. "I'll just follow where they lead. I'll pretend that I'm OK. I can do it." The women's small talk mixed with the desert wind and echoed my despair.

"Why does she do this to me! So sudden. Unpredictable. So painful to be thrown from joyful expectation to—misery, like living with my schizophrenic mother! Be brave, Jan. Show them you are strong and smart, that you haven't thrown away your husband, your children and your home for a crazy woman with erratic behavior. You're too intelligent to do that. Donna, I can trust; Edith, I can't. She'll tell her husband and he'll tell Nick what happened on this trip—in front of everyone, and Nick will tell Randy." I released a slight groan as they walk toward the glittering lights.

"What'd you say, Jan?"

"Oh. Nothing. I'm hungry, I guess."

"Well, here's the Strip," declared Edith, starving more for gambling. "Here we go—" and they turned the corner to face the shocking electric smear of lights.

Undulating, flashing, pulsing glare whipped around us. I felt blasted like a metal ball spun off the pinball mallet. Snap. Bang. Bong. We passed the jangling casino blasts, open doorways releasing discordant noise masked by snaking spirals of neon. My assaulted spirit recoiled.

Their passage found us in the center of the Circus Circus casino where tight ropewalkers balanced overhead. Jugglers and unicyclers performed. Fire eaters inhaled. The ringmaster cracked his whip. Enveloping the entertainment ring, slot machines jingled in low-ceilinged aisles lit only by each slot's fringed lampshades. Low-slung, shadowy light fixtures outlined roulette wheels and blackjack players who circled under their lights. Against a dark and distant background, a purple red blush illuminated the baccarat players and their ladies in glass-enclosed Victorian Barnum and Bailey rooms.

"Let's order some food over there and watch the free show," directed Donna.

"Then we can play the slots, right?" Edith responded.

After they ordered, Donna asked, "Do you think Bea will be all right, Jan? Why didn't she want to stay with us?"

"I don't know," I bravely pretended. "She's her own person. She does what she wants to do." Choking down a quickly ordered circus hot dog, I studied the performers with fake enthusiasm. "I really did need something in my stomach to soak up the booze," remembering that those former drinks were consumed in celebration. Now the food would only absorb disappointment and disillusionment. With no comfort, I swallowed again and realized we were so far from home now, a half a continent away. "What should I do? Where should I go? What's happening?"

Looking at my naïve companions, I suggested, "Tell you what, you two. I'm going to find the ladies room and then go back to our hotel. I'm exhausted and I'll feel better playing the slots closer to the Stardust. You go on and have fun without my tagging along." My stomach warned me to find a bathroom—fast. Standing up, I patted my stomach gently, furrowed my eyebrows with a pained expression for emphasis, said good-bye and raced up the ramp to the mezzanine to find the rest room.

"Where am I? Is this a dream? It's a scene from Pinocchio's Pleasure Island where bad kids get turned into jackasses." Children bearing stuffed animals roamed in circles through a kid's gaming arcade. The lights were brighter than below, illuminating the carnival barkers hawking their games and sodas and popcorn for the offspring of parents gambling below.

Going against the flow of kids and their bulky prizes, I pushed my way under the women's room sign and practically fell into a stall.

"I made it," I sighed. "I made it."

In this safe cell I released emotional restraints. "Who would care if someone heard me cry. Who would be able to hear anything but the damn pinball sounds and arcade games, the circus music and jackpot bells."

Abandoned and in anguish, I shuddered with frightened imaginings of my immediate and future loss. I stared at the graffitied back of the compartment door and thought, "Life is not a game of chance. Losers are truly lost. You win a time or two, but the prize has little value. Great poem, Jan! Lots of luck. What have you done, Jan, to your life? And what have you done to Bea? Where is she now? Risking her life. Out with some male getting laid to prove she's not a homosexual. Then everybody on this trip would know she's not a lesbian—and that she's not in love with me."

Bea grabbed her bag off the bar and walked unevenly toward the exit wearing a cowboy on each arm. A gust blew dust against her and she gripped each man close to keep her steady. *"These guys know where to go,"* she thought. She'd find out what the real Las Vegas was all about. *"To Hell with Jan. She is supposed to be with me, but she goes off to do her PR thing. She left me sit there and wait for her. I always have to get her leftover time."*

They hauled themselves into their Ford pick-up, headed away from the lights of the Strip and stopped at a crusty saloon that reminded her of a recent Gary Cooper movie. "Give us three tequilas, Sally," said one, "and we'll start with an order of chips and cheese for starters. The lady here needs some food in her."

"And let's have a round of beers for chasers," said the other. "I'm looking for Charlene. Have you seen her tonight? She must be working a double shift at the casino if she's not here. It's getting late."

Bea was still on Midwestern time when she looked at her watch. "My God. No wonder I feel swacked. I've been chasing around for sixteen hours. And I need something to eat, you guys. Don't you know how to treat a lady?"

"Sally. Bring us a bowl of your chili right now, to hold our lady steady until Charlene comes, like she said she would."

After the food and a few more rounds, Bea said, "Excuse me, guys. I have to find the ladies room."

"All right, but don't stay away too long now."

The wooden door was off the hinges and Bea had to fit it back into place to have some privacy. "What a dump." Looking into the mirror, she saw a mask of herself that she recognized after focusing her eyes carefully on the image. "What a frump! Hell! What am I doing here!" Holding on to the basin, she looked more closely. "Me with my clown makeup on. Fool! Shit, my father would be proud to see me drinking it up with those cowboys. He'd even buy us a round rather than have me be with Jan. To think I have anything to hope for, to believe in impossible possibilities—Jan and me? Who am I kidding?

"Like he rejected my brother, he and my mom. He told Cal to

take a jump in the lake. Perhaps I'm following a script. My brother committed suicide because of what he was. I remember that I saw them recover his body on TV. A reporter called me in the afternoon. I couldn't stop watching, and there he was floating face down and they were pulling at him with a boat hook.

"God, I'm shaking right now. Nightmares. How am I going to get out of this place? Laugh, Fool, laugh to keep from crying."

Heads propped on their elbows over their beers, Bea's buddies were almost aware of her return. "Well, I guess it's time to wrestle me a pretty girl and kiss me a grizzly bear," she said. "I gotta to get back to my own corral, boys. Besides, I've had enough of the hillbilly music in this joint. Time for me to hit the trail. Thanks for the hospitality but I'm heading back to the ranch."

"You take her, Sonny. I'm going to wait for Charlene," as he waved goodbye to Bea and her cowboy. Sonny boosted her into his truck and wove his way back to the Stardust parking lot. She opened the door quickly before he turned off the motor. A gust of wind ripped her door from her grasp. He reached and struggled to close it, followed her, asked for, and then demanded a good night kiss from his lady of this evening. He leaned in to pin her body against him and the truck, and Bea could feel the heavy, hard impression in his pants imprint on her body.

"You are not going to get to rape me this time, you bastard," she shouted, pushing his sodden weight away.

Stunned, he said, "I never seen you before tonight, have I?"

"And you'll never see me again," as she ran and hid among the parked cars and landscape foliage.

Our empty Stardust room sent me searching again, rejected. "I'll look for her. I will find her." I paced through the Stardust gaming rooms. From carpeted corridors, I looked into bar lounges. I glazed over the Keno players and played the nickel slots near the lobby where I could watch for Bea. I even won enough to keep on playing my $5 limit for the night until I heard my name being paged. I rushed to the reception desk and the clerk told me there was telephone call from our room.

With frightful apprehension and hope, I opened the room door. Bea lay fully clothed sideways on the bed on her back, arms tossed above her head, and the back of her head hanging by her neck over the side of the mattress. "She's dead! No! Damn! Oh, God! Oh, she's passed out. But she's safe at least. Do not disturb. Let sleeping dogs lie," I whispered as I moved her off her back and on to her side as close to the head of the bed as I could maneuver her. Feeling ill, I closed the door quietly and retreated to a deck chair near a poolside cabana that sheltered me from the wind, inhaling fresh night air to calm me as I stared at streaking clouds flowing across a moonless sky.

Bea was still sleeping when I woke from my bed, went for brunch and brought food back for her to eat when she woke up.

"God, I don't remember how I got undressed and under the covers?"

"I put you there. You could have choked to death the way you were."

"Thanks. Do you want some hair of the dog?"

"Why not. Do you want some of the food I brought you?"

"I'm not hungry. God, this is a crazy place. It makes you crazy. Hyperactive."

"I guess it can do that. Are you OK?"

Bea looked into my anxious face, "We're not going to talk about last night. I'm not ready to and I won't."

"Have you seen Marge?"

"Hell no. She's off with her man. Why would she bother with us?"

"What does a person do in this place during the day?"

"Well, let's go and see," as Bea picked up her bag jingling with the remaining few miniatures from the plane. It was cool at poolside, but we soaked up what we could of the thin sunlight. To try to keep control of the day, I avoided talking about last night's fiasco. Bea was alive and seemingly well—and proud. She actually seemed in better shape than I was. Bea was quickly bored watching the women and men come and go—honeymooners or couples celebrating anniversaries, holding hands, being close—so the two of us went into the casinos to look at the expensive gift shops and to play some slots until we returned to our room for some serious martini cocktail-time drinking, a snack and then a nap.

"What a relief," I thought, propped up in my bed, matching Bea's breathing while she slept in the bed next to mine. An image of my mother came to me as I gazed at Bea sleeping, and I remembered asylum Sundays, visiting days. *"Who's the patient? Who's the visitor? I hope neither."*

Quietly, I poured another martini. "I need some rest. I'm brittle. I've been walking on glass all day."

When I woke, Bea was gone.

When Bea returned to our room well after midnight, I dared to challenge her. "I thought we were here together—as a team, as a couple."

"So you say."

"I don't understand what's going on. Why are you making me so miserable? I'm afraid you'll get hurt or mugged or raped."

"I can handle myself. I did what I wanted when you were off with your husband. Why do I have to cater to you now? Because we're going to actually live together? You talk about being afraid. What about me? When we were each in our apartments, we spent almost every night together and we had big fights even then. At least I could walk out on you and I had a place to go."

We heard our Stardust neighbors close their door. Are they going out or coming in, I wondered, and thought, "Get some fresh air, Jan, and some fresh ice. If I have a drink, there won't be so much for her. And I need one before I hit the sack to rest my aching body for another tense day."

When I quickly returned, Bea said, "Where are the values in this place. How can people sit there squandering their money? Did you look at their faces, Jan? How wasted they look."

"Yes, Bea, I did. Many times. We're in another world. A world that doesn't care about our lives—and perhaps no one else's either. Maybe we can get some sleep and tomorrow we can enjoy some companionship."

After Bea dozed off, I took the half-filled glass from her hand and finished it and my own drink before I gave in to exhaustion. Ice cubes clinking on a glass woke Bea.

"This place makes you crazy. It's insanity here," she proclaimed, pouring herself more vodka. Turning on the bathroom light, she started getting dressed again. "You and I, we're crazy too, trying to make a life together. You're crazy to think we can. Two women. And I'm going to throw all my money away on a house to prove that I'm crazy too."

"That's not true, Bea. We'll be OK."

"You aren't even divorced yet, and I let you talk me into buying that goddamn house with you."

"Please, Bea."

"You can go back to your husband anytime, back to your family and you'll leave me alone with a house to pay for."

"You know I won't go back."

"And you talk about gambling. I'm the biggest gambler of all. No security. No kids anymore since they left me. No future." She paced in front of my bed. Stopping at the mirror, she added her make-up and jewelry. "I'm supposed to put up all the money in lieu of your divorce settlement which is still months away. How can I trust you? First you told me you had to have a life of your own. 'I vant to be alone,' you said, like Garbo, but you started looking for houses only weeks after you moved into your apartment."

"In my heart, I wanted only to live with you, Bea. I love you, Bea. Why don't you relax now! It's after three."

"I don't want to relax. Stop telling me to relax! It's like you're talking to your mother! You're always trying to get me to go to sleep. What the hell did we come here for anyway!"

"Please Bea. The neighbors."

"Damn the neighbors. You worry about neighbors?" Bea paced

and pointed her finger at me sitting on the bed. With each gesture, Bea increased her volume. "We had that fight in my apartment and you shouted, 'What do I have to do to make you realize that I love you—kill myself?' Jesus, Jan, the whole apartment complex could hear you. And I had to face up to my real neighbors. You're the crazy one, Jan! Do you really want what you think you want? I ask myself this all the time. How can I be so stupid to have fallen in love with you—You are safety and you are danger. You are life and you are death. Why did my brother choose that way to die?"

I rolled over on my stomach and pulled a pillow over my head.

"Damn you, Jan. I've taken enough from you and your perverted love." Standing in the darkened bedroom, Bea focused on the bathroom light. She threw her glass, and its contents smashed against the bathroom tile.

The sound enveloped me. "Oh, my God! Oh God!" I said into my pillow that muffled my groan. "Maybe she'll stop now—I can't stand this anymore."

"Fuck you, Jan! Fuck you!" Bea roared into my pillow.

I lay there, exposed to physical violence. Burning rage rose in waves up each of my vertebrae and exploded into a hot red burst within my brain. *"Electric shock? Could electric shock be like this?"* I moaned inside. *"Should I just give up and die of grief?"* White waves of current flashed in my brain. *"Should I surrender myself to insanity—finally?"*

Bea pulled on her boots, marched out the door and slammed it behind her. The neighbors? Oh well, people aren't supposed to sleep in Las Vegas.

"I'm glad she's gone. I need the rest. I have to get us back home." But before I could let myself give in to anguish, I went into the bathroom to pick up the hazardous glass shards in the bathroom.

Bea was still gone in the morning so I grabbed what was left of the booze and hurried to Marge's room to wake her up. "I need you, Marge. I'm afraid Bea has lost control this time. Take these bottles for yourself and maybe she will stop drinking."

"This time! You two lost control weeks ago—months and years ago. I told you she would be bad for you way back then and here you are. And keep the damn booze. She'll only go out and buy some more to drink anyway. You know that. Everybody's talking about you and Bea. Someone saw Bea getting picked up and put on a luggage cart by some security guards who found her in the parking lot. They dumped her in your room."

"She didn't say anything to me."

"Maybe she doesn't remember—or else she's too proud."

"I just need help until we get back home."

"We all used bad judgment when we hired her to work with you. And now that you're getting divorced, you're on the road to ruin. I don't want to be a part of your fall-out by being involved with you anymore. That's why I have John here to save me from being compared to you two. Besides, I want to have a good time on this trip. I won't get involved—even if I knew what to do."

Like a child scolded by my mother, I withdrew from Marge's room.

Bea returned after 8 a.m. "I just met Howard Hughes up in the tower. That's who he said he was, and he should know. He is a friendly fellow and he bought me a drink. We had a long talk, and I like him."

"Oh, that's memorable. Howard Hughes! Is he still alive?"

"Yes and he wears a heather tweed hat and has mossy teeth. He lives up there in that Stardust tower and only comes out in the middle of the night. What a crazy place this is. Wild. I'm exhausted," and Bea finally collapsed in bed.

"I can't wait for this ordeal to be over and we're safely back home," I thought. Bea was gentle and quiet after her few hours nap. *"Her chat with Howard must have been comforting. I think he's dead. But what do I know."*

"I've been so mixed-up, Jan. Having that talk with Howard

made me realize you can have everything in the world and you can still be so painfully lonely. Look at us. We have each other. At least I hope we still have each other, Jan. I know how scared you are when we have these fights. The tension around us is unbearable. And this place is Hell. I never want to come here again."

"Yes, Bea. All I want to do is get the two of us home where it's safe."

"It's not safe, Jan. Not for us, ever."

I could hardly move my body or lift the suitcases to the airport bus loading area. Bea discovered that her heavy period had started before we left our room so she could change her clothing. "Thank God I wasn't on the plane when this surprise came."

The bus was late, but all of the obedient Lakeshore Med group were on time, patiently sitting poolside in their Wisconsin winter clothes, most appropriate for the chilly but sunny mid-winter Las Vegas morning. The windstorm had blown to the east beyond Las Vegas.

Each person stared into space, avoiding eye contact.

"Jesus. We have to go back to work with these people," I thought, observing that no one seemed to care. As the hospital PR person, I didn't give them a pep talk nor survey them for their opinions of the trip. *"Let it be."*

It looked as if the photographs that Bea posted of the tour group proved the trip was not a success. If posted, those photos would not convince others to join them on their next hospital trip, if there would be any. Certainly, I wouldn't be going with them again. I vowed that if my life were to be so unpredictable, I'd avoid a plane of co-workers—and a place like Las Vegas.

Most of the plane's passengers were quiet on the way back home. Bea slept now and I was alert. I drove Donna and Edith and Bea from Milwaukee's airport. I was angry with Bea's chatter to the back seat audience with glib talk as they led her on. After dropping them off, I drove Bea to her apartment.

"Thanks for the ride."

"Yah, what a ride."

"Do you want to come up?"

"Yes, I'll help you with your luggage, but I think I'll head for my place tonight."

"I wish I could sleep longer and come in to work later tomorrow."

"OK. Sleep late. I'll cover for you, Bea. And I will never give you up. I haven't before and I won't—ever. I will not lose you. We can make a life together. We will make it work."

"I wrote you a note this morning. No. Don't read it now. Read it when you're at your place. I'm too tired."

We parted after an embrace. I cherish the soft skin of Bea's face against mine. I drove alone to my apartment, turned up the thermostat, poured myself a glass of wine and opened the note.

Dearest Jan,

I don't know what will happen. I know neither of us is happy apart from the other, but are we ready to take the step that would put us together? Commitment is here after all these months and years, but it is frightening. Must we play out our roles? We must! There is no turning back. They are written for us; in spite of the deviation we have written for ourselves. You said once, "I love show business," and we both know the show must go on.

Bea from February 24 to 27, 1978

Left for Las Vegas and The Lost Weekend. Insane place. Gambling. Robots. Wild. Crazy. Bad misunderstanding with Jan. Ended up being delivered to our room. Real bad time. Angry. Hurt. Wild. Emotional. Crazy. On Sunday, I met man with a heather hat and mossy teeth on top of Stardust Hotel. Home about 9 p.m. on Monday.

CHAPTER 8

Jan on February 28, 1978

My heart hurts. It's so hard to breathe. What will people say? What will happen next? Tight bands bind my aching chest that struggles for breath.

I went to her apartment after work but she wasn't home and this evening I tried calling her from my bedroom and no one answered. I don't know where she is. Is she in a car wreck? Has she fallen somewhere and freezing in the cold?

I needed someone to talk to and I thought of our UU friend Nora Carpenter, an alcoholic counselor. She was home when I phoned her and Nora listened and asked me the right questions. I could be honest about my love, fear and grief. She lessened my hurt somewhat, tried to calm my fears and cried a little with me. I didn't want to tie up the phone in case Bea would try to reach me. Nora said she would be available at any time of the day or night.

I don't know how much more I can take before my heart actually—physically—shatters within me.

<<◇>>

The day after we returned from Las Vegas, the busy phones kept me close to my desk. I answered a 10 a.m. call as usual, "Lakeshore Med Communications."

"I was afraid of this, Jan." It was Randy. "I knew you two would get into trouble. This is a disaster. In addition to both your behaviors on the trip, Bea told someone there that Nick is learning disabled. Is he fuming!"

"What she said was that he was brilliant, that she respected him for his intelligence and success in overcoming a learning disability."

"That's not what he heard. You better get this all straightened out now." And Randy hung up—hard.

I looked at the heavy, dead phone in my hand and could see his flushed, furious face on the other end. *"It's OK for Randy to step out of line with co-workers, but no one else had better do it,"* and his fucking fiasco with Bea flashed through my mind, an event that no one but the three of us knew about. *"I wish I could erase that from my mind—and more recent nights as well."* I put the receiver back and let my heavy eyelids drop to shut out the glare off the piles of mail and reports that were waiting to be processed while I kept answering the incoming calls. *"It's strange that no one is walking into the office. It's usually like Grand Central Station when we get back from vacation. And I need Bea."*

I gave Bea time to sleep late and rest up, but I finally called her apartment at noon. "Are you coming in? I need you. I'm worried about you. Are you all right?"

"Hell yes, but I'm not coming in today. You'll have to survive without me." And she hung up too.

I stayed away from joining our gang of friends in the cafeteria, waiting until the lunch hour crowd disappeared. I went in to pick up the last ready-made sandwich to eat at my desk. *"I need Bea,"* as I gnawed on the tasteless tuna and wilted lettuce leaf on limp white bread. *"Do I look like a fool? I feel like one."*

When I called Bea again, there was no answer. *"Oh my God! What has she done now? How can I concentrate on this other crap when my thoughts are with her—and my heart is so damaged. God help me."*

Yes, Bea was angry but she slept some, she told me, before she headed to Madison to pick up her paintings on the day the art exhibit closed. She slept in a motel that night, picked up the artwork and started for home. She made a wrong choice at a split in the Interstate, ended up in Rockford, one hundred miles away, but she finally made it back by noon the next day and finally called me.

Hoping for Bea's call and anticipating another call from Randy, my nerves twitched each time the phone rang.

"Hello, Jan," said the quiet voice that I was yearning to hear.

"Where are you? I miss you. I'm worried about you."

"I'm worried about me, too. I've had visions and I'm scared. Will you drive me to the Crisis Center at St. Paul? I asked someone there to connect me with Nora and she had some social worker make room for me on her schedule. I need to talk with you. Can you come to my apartment now? I'm waiting for you."

"I'm on my way!"

I forwarded my calls to Randy's secretary. "I can't help it, Shelly. I wouldn't ask you if I didn't have to. This is an emergency. Please answer any calls and take my messages for the rest of the afternoon. I have to leave. Thanks," and hung up before I could be turned down.

Bea, now sober, seemingly alert and strong, said, "I have an emergency appointment in an hour and a half and we can just make it if you drive me, Jan,"

I released a sigh and held her. "Thank you for getting help."

"We're seeing Nora's referral counselor." Bea had changed to a springtime-yellow pants suit that made me think of daffodils.

The Interstate was quiet, and without conversation we drove against the late afternoon traffic coming out of the Milwaukee. We made it in time. I was told to wait outside the office because I was not immediate family. *"Maybe Bea will finally go to an AA meeting or get some outpatient counseling,"* I hoped as I waited.

Emerging from the room, Bea announced, "I signed myself in."

"What!"

"Yes. I'm doing the whole thing—for twenty-eight days. I've check myself into this detox hotel. No outpatient stuff for me. I need the works," declared Bea to disbelieving me who knew how much Bea mistrusted, even hated therapy. "I'm making this commitment to be committed."

Nora left her office and found us sitting together at the admissions area. She knelt down to embrace us both, and all three of us cried with apprehension yet with comfort to have someone there who knew of our relationship.

An aide escorted us to a shiny, enamel-painted, high-ceilinged room with two metal twin beds and metal dressers and long, green and gold metallic striped draperies and matching bedspreads. It looked like a recycled Army barracks, except for the curtains. A bare radiator, connected to two floor-to-ceiling, chipped-painted pipes, ran next to a tall window facing a brick wall. "Your roommate is probably out to supper or having a smoke in the day room," said the aide. "We'll bring you some supper. Your medications should come after that."

Standing in the doorway, I watched Bea, with her back to me, pull aside the coarse draperies and look outside at nothing. *My proud Bea. This must hurt her terribly if it hurts me so much."* My eyelids blinked back burning teardrops.

"I wasn't prepared to do this, so I don't have any other clothes. I hate to bother you again, but could you get me some? I don't want to sleep in a hospital gown tonight."

"Of course," and I approached her, but Bea gave a halting gesture to stop any closeness or comfort. "Yes. Of course. I'll go and do that right now so I can come back before it gets too late." I turned to go with the image impressed in my brain—the bright, yellow-suited back of Bea turned away from me, looking at the blank brick wall beyond. "I'll hurry and get back as soon as possible."

"Drive carefully," she said with a gentle hint of love in her expression. Her thoughts were hidden under her calmness.

I could only imagine what she could be thinking. *"I've done it* now. Finally, I'm confronting my demon that numbs my fears. Yet I drink, too, to celebrate our daring adventure. To risk all. To be discovered. To be a lesbian. To be loved. And I am scared."

"I'll be careful," I said, responding with knowing eyes reflecting their secret. I turned quickly and with firm steps to hide my shaky misgivings, I followed the aide who unlocked the door to let me out of the detox ward.

"She'll be moved into a different room after she's here for short while," the aide explained, as if new patients must pass a passivity test before they get more costly and comfortable furnishings.

I gasped when I was released, stepping out of the brightly lit lobby through glass doorways into the fresh air of the red and orange sunset. "I don't have to be so brave for a while now," as I sat with my car keys in my hand, staring dumbly toward the western sky. Finally, when I felt calm enough to drive, I found the Interstate ramp that would catapult me back to Bea's apartment.

I trusted my driving skill to maneuver through high-speed traffic rushing around me. What was really driving me were thoughts of how to sign their mortgage next month, how to complete their work deadlines, how to tell people what happened, their families, their failure, their submission. "I cannot believe that the person I love is in an institution."

Entering Bea's apartment was awful when I thought of where she is. And strange to open her closet to find her suitcase and pick comfortable clothes that she'd be proud to wear. She's the one who dresses me up when I have to do so. Though I know most nooks and crannies of her body, I've never ventured to pull out dresser drawers to choose her socks, bras and panties. How close we are, yet we've never shared a basket to wash and dry our clothes together. But that will all be different soon when we buy new appliances for our home, I hope. Like married people do.

Find what she needs. Keep is simple. Come back tomorrow to straighten up the place.

One small black datebook from a pile of little books three or four years of succinct daily notes, had fallen off her night stand and landed on the bedroom floor. The year 1977 flashed off the cover of one resting down and open next to the pile. I turned on the lamp and found July, almost into August, of squeezed, difficult-to-read scribbles.

> July 28, 1977 "Home to get ready for party—All organized—Great bash—Drank 6 bottles of Champagne. Randy played piano while Tom played trumpet and I the tambourine."

> July 29, 1977 "Didn't go to work cause I was trying to forget. J. left at 2 AM and Randy became #12 spot on my Neckovic—Oh well—Good for him. I don't remember it all. Day went. J came 2Xs. Tony came in PM."

That's IT! "#12 spot on my Necovic!" She props this damn Eskimo graphic image that she bought at an art fair on her bookcase shelf near the TV. Necovic, or Sedna is a mermaid goddess with white spots on her black body and two baby seals with human heads swimming under her, reaching to her breasts for nourishment. I suppose I'm a baby seal. I hate the picture but I've tolerated it. When Bea had another man, she'd add a white dot to the scene. I don't know when she started adding up her conquests. It got easier for me to try to ignore it as time wore on, but I hate it. I'm probably the only other person to know that those white spots mean. Who knows. She'd remark that I had a man; why shouldn't she? Except that I feared for her physical and emotional well-being that has been compromised by her one-night-stands with acquaintances and a stranger or two.

Enough already! Try to forget that now! Focus! It's late. I'll come back here when she has time and a mind to write a list for me of what she wants.

<<◇>>

My trusted friend Marie rode along with me and helped me get through the drive. I said little, remembering Bea's changing moods. What did I do? How can I cope? Do I have to deal with craziness again?

As Marie and I approached that off ramp, the hospital's name loomed above the turn like a monument to sobriety with blazing neon letters reaching into the northern night—St. Paul. My mother's hospital had no bright sign to call attention to it and its patients. Of course, my thoughts were of my mother, of the miles of roadways my father and I had taken to visit with her in the asylum—hours, days and years. A thought came through from my grandmother too, who told me once, "Whistling girls and crowing hens always come to no good ends."

It was past visiting hours when I returned with a suitcase so I couldn't see Bea until tomorrow afternoon or evening, and after dropping Marie off, I returned to my empty apartment.

> I don't know how long I can bear the heartbreak hurt
> and surrender myself to fearful insanity.
> Grief overcomes joy with sudden oppression
> and slashes at the fragile feeling so longingly sought.
> The thread that holds me from the edge
> is sorely frayed and frazzled.

Jan on March 3, 1978

"Yes, Marge, St. Paul." I pulled myself up to her desk early before others came in. "Bea admitted herself as an inpatient. Please start the insurance process to cover her treatment."

Well. It's about time," said our best friend and bosom buddy, colleague and comrade in arms in all sorts of marginally acceptable standards of behavior, suddenly turning sanctimonious. "She's been on the edge waiting to fall for a long time, Jan. It's for the best, you know."

Humbled and in hushed tones, I groaned, "I never thought it

would get this drastic."

"I told you so, and she went bananas on this hospital trip of all places. I'll let Randy know right away," as Marge picked up her phone, waiting for me to leave without further conversation.

"Thanks for doing that. I don't want to get involved with him in any way, especially now. You both know where to find me if he wants any more information."

Returning to my empty office, I sat facing the wall at my typewriter—alone, numb and immobile. Bea's chair and desk behind me cast mocking condemnation about how we had gambled and lost—in Las Vegas and everywhere. We gambled on our courage to risk all to loving each other. It is an act of courage to love another, no matter how out of favor that love may be. Gambling for love, every day, is a risk. The ending is forever uncertain.

Is this the end? Sharp, burning, constant devastating pain wracked my body and my spirit. My heart wanted to burst through concrete lungs so I could force in a shallow breath. Finally, a sigh sent pounding beats from my chest, through my throat and to the pulsing places that live just below my skin.

I wanted to, but dare not crumble over on my desk. Could I crawl under it and hide? *"I'm too mature to get into a fetal position, but it would probably feel better that sitting stiff and straight. I pray that no one looks in the window, comes in or calls me on the phone. Just let me grieve my loss."* I felt my shoulders fall as I exhaled a heavy, mournful load of grief. *"We have to sign our mortgage. How will we get Bea out to do that? We will! We will get her a pass! Life will correct itself now. We will be better, but humble. Yes. Humble. We'll have to beg now, for sure. No feminists now, singing 'I Am Woman. Hear Me Roar.' My heart is broken."*

I heard a slight tap at my window and the doorknob turning. The sound registered and I turned hesitantly, seeing a man I did not know. I couldn't turn him away. He was a hospital volunteer and he saw me sitting there through the window. His red cotton jacket identified him as well as did his hospital I.D. lanyard. What could I do but let him come in.

"Hello. I'm Arnie Patterson. You don't know me but I've been around, especially volunteering on the Psych Unit." I could see that his kind eyes identified with the grief in my eyes. His craggy face showed compassion.

"Yes. Come in. Sit down here in this chair next to my typewriter." That way he's facing the door window and no one outside the office can see my face. "I'm sorry, I don't know you. I guess I don't go to the psych unit often. It's not the most PR-oriented unit, I guess, unless something goes wrong, and it hasn't so far. How can I help you?"

"How can I help *you*?" asked the male stranger.

Surprised at this reversal of roles, feeling abandoned by Marge and not being able to tell our families, I was vulnerable to accepting comfort from anyone. The palpable pain in my heart reached up to choke me, and the tears started whether I wanted them to or not. I became more concerned about guarding my secret than discovering who sent him or how he knew I needed help. On guard, I thought, *"How can I tell this stranger of the depth of my love for Bea, my woman, my lover, who checked herself into St. Paul, the hospital for alcoholics."*

My deception continued with small talk until I couldn't think of any other words to say. What the hell! He was a stranger—and kind. What could he do to hurt me anymore than I already ache? "My lover, Bea, is at St. Paul and I'm here not knowing what to do or what will happen to us."

"I can help," he said.

My emotional dam cracked at this offer. I was not alone and my lover and I would not be defeated.

Bea's withdrawal symptoms began with insomnia, night sweats, hyperactivity and fear. While immersing herself in vitamins and group therapy, chapel and meditation, exercise and craft projects, I existed alone, following procedures by rote through my days at work, avoiding others and their avoiding me. I'd enter the cafeteria and felt like a derelict with a disease. Then I'd drive each night to

St. Paul's AA meetings which I hated: the Twelve Step process, the maleness of the implied Power of God, the male pronouns, giving up yourself to the Higher Power. The priests. The chapel with its crucifix.

And I gave up alcohol, a significantly hard decision on those lonely nights when I couldn't sleep and would work to finish that impossible employee benefits book that was past its deadline.

Bea too had similar qualms about her hospital experiences but went through the motions to conform. But she refused to get her kids involved in any family therapy. "No kids! Just me!" she insisted. "Or you can ask Jan to come. That's all." Do they know of our relationship? How can they tell? Did we think we were the first and only two women to come to therapy sessions who seemed to be "more than friends?" Can they treat the patient without knowing the details? A masquerade. Another drunken lesbian. Defensive. Beaten.

I went to all AA meetings with her, enduring the agony of driving there, alone, walking in to find the meeting room, finding her and not touching her. Bea was the stronger one. I was a mess.

The first Sunday afternoon visiting hours included Tony Logan's cheerful company. But as we sat visiting, all of Bea's children entered the cafeteria lunchroom and sat with us around the table. At first happy and surprised, then Bea was shocked that they knew and she looked angrily at me.

"Josh called me to see how you were when you weren't at home or with me, and I didn't lie to him."

Everyone settled down and Tony left. Everything would be OK.

Then in walked our friend Betty bringing her new live-in girlfriend Kitty, a sturdy dyke with short blonde hair and wearing a black leather pants suit. Of course they livened up the afternoon, but Bea winched each time Kitty pulled out her Zippo to light Betty's cigarette.

When everyone left this festive Sunday afternoon gathering, Bea told me to find her father's flask and throw it in Lake Michigan with some pomp and ceremony. "Don't you want to be involved?"

I asked.

"No. Please just do it for me," and after we parted, she went into the chapel to meditate.

Jan on March 7, 1978

Dear Love,

Our closing date is set at 3 p.m. Friday at the bank! I heard from the Marilyn Lange this morning. So far, I've been too involved in much work—We Need You Here—to make too many other arrangements, but I'll be taking care of insurance, the bank, etc., according to the list you gave me.

Why don't you think about drawing a sketch of our house from the realtor's copy that you have, and I will use it as a cover for our house-warming invitations.

When I drove past Westwood Lane, I looked at our house, and it has so many bright lights on it to welcome people to its front door.

There's a warm breeze in the air this morning, a touch of spring at least, but it was nothing compared to the warm feeling I have in my heart when I think of our future life together.

I will call you tonight.

I love you.

Jan

Jan on March 8, 1978

Randy finally called me to his office and the naughty child in me stumbled slowly through the corridors to the principal's office to receive her punishment. I was even made to sit on a chair near Marge's desk outside his office until he was ready to see me. It's not the first time I've been to the principal's office, but it hasn't been often in my rebellious life.

"Jan. It's true, isn't it," Randy stated with what I thought was a sneer, "That you and Bea are buying a house together and will be moving in soon?"

"We're signing the mortgage papers tomorrow."

"Well, I'm sorry to inform you that a hospital rule says that a supervisor and a subordinate are not allowed to live in the same dwelling, so we are having to let Bea go. We could place her in another department, but her specific skills complement your department here. Actually, one or the other of you can go, but we assume that you, with your higher salary, would be the one who would want to stay on the job."

"No one has ever told me of such a rule. Besides, I'll bet at least forty combinations of couples, family members, brothers and sisters work at Lakeshore Med. Even Marge's niece and sister work here!"

"But they either do not live in the same home or apartment or are not in supervisory/subordinate positions at work like you and Bea."

"I never considered Bea Lindberg to be my subordinate—nor I her supervisor because I know we are a team—and of equal status."

"You know that's not a fact, Jan."

"I know a lot, including the employee benefits package, and there is nothing there that states that rule. I would like to read in the policy manual where that is written and dated."

"Be that as it may, Bea will be officially laid-off when she is discharged from St. Paul. She will be able to collect unemployment compensation,"

"How can you do that to someone under these circumstances?"

"I can and I am. Besides, what will Mr. Young say when he finds out about you two?"

"He's a wise and compassionate man. And I thought you were humane! At the heart of this all, on what grounds are you really making this decision?"

"You should be grateful that you both aren't let go."

That shut me up. Bea's getting a pass to get out of St. Paul tomorrow afternoon to go with me to the bank that is approving a mortgage for two gainfully employed, respectable women to buy a house. Of course, Bea's $30,000 down payment helps pave the way for that approval.

Thoughts swiftly crossed my mind: *"How can I fight this injustice and keep my job? How can we pay for our house if I fight and lost our case? Who will hire her or me if this all comes out in the open? How can I sue for job discrimination and get hired by another company? Lakeshore Med has its board members from industry all over town. After all these years of excellent work and loyalty, if Lakeshore Med doesn't want me, who would?"*

"And I suppose, Randy, that I have to be the one to tell her while I'm visiting her in the hospital."

"I could write a letter."

"And who would be there to support her when she reads that letter?"

"It could be worse, Jan. At least as it stands now, Bea will get unemployment compensation."

"That's some comfort! Have we finished this meeting?"

"You still have your job."

"Perhaps I should get a job that's less visible."

"That may not be such a bad idea."

"Maybe I could drive a bus and wear a grey uniform and a jacket with a zipper."

"Who knows, Jan. If you have any more questions, write them down, send them to me and we'll discuss them later."

When I left his office, Marge had disappeared from her desk.

How will I tell Bea?

<<<◇>>>

"What a trumped-up crock of shit that is," sputtered Bea after I whispered the details of this betrayal to her in the quiet of the chapel. I had to be the one to tell her the horrendous news, the appalling injustice. I had to be the messenger of rejection.

"First thing at work tomorrow, I'm making a list of all the women who live in the same house—lots of nurses, lots of husbands and wives, family members, siblings, lovers, whatever combination and throw it at him. I'll bet there are forty combinations of employees who work and live together."

"So what! They don't care. They only want to get rid of me, and maybe you too?"

"And we trusted Randy. I told him about us before he hired you. And that hypocrite Nick, to cheat us out of our careers."

"And Jan, who told Randy about the mess in Las Vegas? I wouldn't be surprised if our friend Marge betrayed us to cover her panicky butt. And Randy's crack about you or I not qualified to work in another department so we can confirm that so-called "policy." That's a farce! We won't let them ruin our careers, Jan. We'll sign our mortgage and we'll make new lives for ourselves. You'll have to keep the job you have until everything gets settled. You're not even divorced yet and we have to be careful not to let the bank know about me."

"And HPRW too. We need all those hospital PR people from around the state as friends and possibly as employers—at least references. But let's get our house signed for tomorrow before we take another step forward. We can do it."

"We will do it. It's more important to live together than to work together."

Ironically, five thousand Lakeshore Med advocates and area decision-makers received the spring issue of our Lakeshore Med *synergy* magazine. It was Bea's and my last issue. She wrote on complicated topics and made them simple to understand with her photos and writing. She wrote "It's Great To Be Alive" about survivors of larynx and lung cancer; "Four Physicians, Four Pharmacists May Equal Four Medication Problems" with charts to help understand the dangers of over- and cross-medications.

Her final magnum opus, however, was taking my summary of three years of Lakeshore Med struggle to get approvals and funds for the hospital's new expansion. And Bea taught us how to understand it all by making it into a board game.

Bea on March 10, 1978

I was out on a pass for a few hours. It was a good feeling. We signed the papers for our house. I put down $30,000 and we financed the $17,500 at 8 3/4 percent. The owners are out tomorrow. We get the keys and move in on March 30.

What am I going to do when I get out of here?

I'm learning new artistic skills in therapy. Big Deal! I'm making four ceramic mugs. Too bad I can't use some of my newly learned skills to solve my grim job prospects.

Jan comes every day, sometimes twice on the weekends. One evening when she was walking out the double glass doors, a wife, with help from perhaps her teenage daughter, was holding up her teetering husband who was clutching several booze bottles across his chest on his way to detox. What an image. Poor bloated fat man holding on to his bottles, slobbering like a baby, and his wife so shattered as he would be if he should fall and land on all his broken bottles. Broken lives.

Jan attends AA meetings and is involved in counseling sessions, which are not helpful because I insist that my kids not be involved and we insist that we do not let anyone know that we are lovers. The "L" word is never mentioned. It's bad enough putting up with all their psychobabble and platitudes.

Now Jan has to take time and get busy ordering curtains, cleaning and painting so that everything will be ready for me when we move. I'll get all my kids to help us move from her apartment and mine. But we'll have to bring everything in via the kitchen door because the former owners installed a lush white carpet in the living room and I don't want anyone tramping in on it.

I'll be so happy when I'm free again, yet I suppose this confinement is doing me good somehow. It's great practice for being bored. I'm so pissed at what they've done to me at Lakeshore Med. And Jan now, more than ever, has to swallow her pride and keep her job so we can make the house payments until I get another job and add my income to pay the bills.

She says people at work don't know what to say to her so she's feeling isolated, especially compared to the full-blown happy and friendly atmosphere we had before. I'm sure everyone is talking about us.

And she has to start interviewing people to replace me! Ha! That will be a tough job. Let them just try to find someone who can do everything I can do.

Jan on March 12, 1978

Of course, now, I have to write the employee newsletter again and pretend that the department is perfectly wonderful and everything is peachy keen. The March 6 letter had my story on the Las Vegas trip, all golden and glowing about missing the snow banks, winning at gambling, losing but having fun, the airline's round-trip open bar and my magnanimous quote, "We drove home from the airport Monday night through sleety snow on icy roads and we could still feel the warm sun and wind on our faces. That alone was worth the trip." Bea always said I was good at turning shit into sunshine.

I researched personnel records on that "new rule" that a supervisor and employee cannot live together, yet forty-seven couples/relationships/family members work at Lakeshore Med including Randy King who's involved with a nurse, and Nick and Diana (though she works for a clinic). An RN couple who've lived together in their own home, even a vacation cottage, and have worked the PM shift for many years asked their Nursing Director Donna Durand if it's safe for them, as employees, to go on vacation together now. What would await them when they returned? Supervisor and subordinate?

I requested to see a written policy about this rule many times, but I never saw one. I feel betrayed by administration and I sense employees treating me like I had the Black Plague. Like a fearful epidemic, truth mixed with rumors spread that Bea and I are a lesbian couple and she got fired after misbehaving on the Las Vegas trip. Like a pest house, our office is strangely quiet as if quarantined.

When I enter the cafeteria, I sense people stepping away from me as if they would catch something from me. What is the value of what I have accomplished for six and a half years; and what of Bea's work for one and a half years:

The employee relations project, newsletters, photography, creative posters, exciting promotional materials.

I have had to cope with masculine power too long. Too long it wants to enter me; too long it wants to control me—too long! And I'm collapsing from the weight of bearing it too long. If anger burns me out, does my creative spirit yield to peaceful submission like electric shock treatments? What a choice to have to make if that is true.

I haven't written a poem for so long. Perhaps because I've experienced life so crushing that my words get lost behind what's real and hard to bear. Lyrical, tender words will return again, I know, to help heal those wounds that I exposed in my dangerous search for love and resolution. Outlines and lists of writing goals and projects that first hung crisp and fresh on my storyboard said, "Yes! Go ahead! It's worthy! Do it!" But time has turned those white pages of story outlines and lists change into dusty beige as those goals and dreams fade from neglect.

I fear I will die of grief. It's worse than my remembered loss of my mother to her madness. How can I be going to an institution again to see the woman in my life! How can I bear this again? I've paid my dues before I owed them many times over. Who cares? Self-pity appeals to no one.

I am afraid. I've left my children to be with Bea and this is the result.

I'm scared too that St. Paul will find out that we are lovers—as if they couldn't tell. We double speak of our relationship. They insist on getting kids involved. "Keep my kids out of this," Bea insists. Just me. Without her children there she felt abandoned. The proposed family therapy session was a farce. We didn't want anyone to know or to discuss being lesbians in their conference room where we were outnumbered by male and female staff who had all the power to evaluate us and seemed to be ganging up on us. We knew they would judge us. Who are they to do so!

One strong cultural taboo is leaving your children. The final taboos are being a lesbian that comes just before pederasty and cannibalism.

I was walking alone through the cafeteria gauntlet at work when I felt hands touching each of my shoulders. Skittish like a wounded animal, I turned and found Laura Williams guiding me to sit at her table with Pam Holmen. After this touch, my shoulders did not strain nor feel the need to hold me up. I could let my bones do that. I could relax for a while. A kind person had touched me and let me know that I still had friends.

Homophobic Marge may just as well have disappeared, unless I caught her in her office; but my avoiding Randy kept me away from that department. One night at a church house party at Dixon's, Marge said to me, "No more good time Bea, I guess." And when I asked our hostess for a soda rather than my customary martini, wine or Bloody Mary, a tense and anxious Diana stated loudly, "You're only doing that for Bea, aren't you. Surely you'll drink again."

All conversation stopped while I stammered out an uncertain answer with everyone listening.

Bea on March 19, 1978

Great field trips here! After a Saturday night AA meeting, we boarded a bus to visit the County detox ward. Oh Boy! Cold and scary. That experience shook me up. Talk about a motivator to stay sober. Yuck! Good thing Arnie Patterson is trying to get me into a professional AA group that meets in Lakeshore when I get sprung out of here.

Jan's cleaning, painting and hanging draperies at our new home when she's not at work or here visiting me. I actually was given an eight-hour pass and the kids borrowed their father's truck to help us move my bookcases and books to our home.

I'm working on getting out of here faster than the required twenty-eight-day stay. The social worker threatened me by saying I'd have no insurance coverage if I left early—as if a day or two would make a difference.

Last time Jan and I sat in the chapel, I told her that I wanted us to have a house-warming and April 1 anniversary party, which would be the next day after we moved into the house. I also asked her to ask Tony to give us and the house a blessing with our friends present. Wouldn't that be a great new beginning for us! Nothing like having a party right away! But I don't want my kids to come and Alex won't let Jenny be there. He's forbidden Jenny from visiting our home.

Jan on March 24, 1978

What's your own risk? Check the Social Readjustment Rating Scale" that is based on Holmes, T.H. and Hahe, R.H. The Social Readjustment Rating scale. *Journal of Psychosomatic Research* and printed in the current issue of *Pulse Magazine*.

"If you scored below 150 points, you are on pretty safe ground—about a one in three chance of serious health change in the next two years. Remember, you already have a ten percent chance of winding up in the hospital sometime during the year. If you scored between 150 and 300 points, your chance of risk is about 50-50. The odds on Russian roulette are better than that. If you scored over 300 points, be sure your health insurance is paid up—your chances are almost 90 percent."

From March 1976 to today, my score is 1020! Bea's is 868! Highest life event changes for me, and many of the same for her, started at major risks: divorce, marital separation, death of a close family member, personal injury or illness, change in health of family member, sex difficulties between two people; change in financial state, change in number of arguments with spouse, and a mortgage over $10,000.

Other changes involved responsibility at work, offspring leaving home trouble with in-laws, outstanding personal achievement, revision of personal habits, trouble with boss, vacation, Christmas, changes in work hours or conditions, residence, recreation, social activities, sleeping habits and family get-togethers.

Bea has already been through the divorce stuff, but scored high on being fired at work. Fortunately, she'll get unemployment compensation and health insurance coverage that's allotted to her. How do you get that when you're told you no longer have your job?

Bea on March 31, 1978

We've moved in. We're here! Joel, Jim, Jill and friends helped move in Wednesday from my apartment and Jan's; but Jan hadn't realized the significance of signing a lease. It was for a year, but by finding another divorced woman needing an apartment at work, she was released from her rental agreement.

My Easter Sunday pass from St. Paul gave us the chance to paint out the orange walls in kitchen. Then on Wednesday, I demanded an early release from St. Paul and escaped to our home without an official discharge. We gave the kitchen a second coat of white paint. Hell, I'm sober. Two more days isn't going to change anything. All they want is to collect a couple more days of insurance payments.

When the kids finished lifting the last loads, we worked at settling in. We had our stove delivered, my Josh installed a vent fan and we cleaned my apartment. I treated myself to a haircut and worked hard to prepare for our housewarming party for tomorrow,

Jan on March 31, 1978

On the first night in our very own home, both of us rested from exhaustion. She lay like a child with her head on my shoulder in the curve of my arm that embraced her, our bare bodies fresh from the playful shower we shared, standing in our own tub, lathering each other, wiping away the stressors of our outside lives. On our newly made bed, she wrapped her leg over mine as my arm drew her even closer to my side. Now we have all the time we want to be together in our own bed. Each night will be a sacred rite of being together. The moon's rays enveloped us, blessing us with its tender light and generous fullness. We are gently joined as one in our private world, a place of peace, a refuge.

It has been so long.
She moved her free hand and with whispering fingers, she touched my face, hair, ears and throat. I turned my face to smell and kiss her hair. Her lips caressed the sensitive skin under my arm where she lay, and the sensitive pads of her five fingers danced on my breasts so gently. It's been so long. Inhale. Exhale. How good it is. How true. How bearably arousing,
Our vulnerable selves awakening again in sensuous harmony fused into oneness with a hungry, unquenchable intensity inflamed by our courage over adversity.

Bea on April 1, 1978

We finished installing the last of the draperies when our company came on the dot at 4 p.m. The small gathering included Tony, Marge, Betty, Em, Nora, Pete and Marlene with their daughters. We'll have my kids over tomorrow.

It seemed a bit awkward at first. Our guests seemed to huddle together as if they didn't know what to do. Should they have a drink or would that encourage me to drink. Hell. We started them with their drinks of various kinds at our bar, fed them snacks and showed them our house and yard on this beautiful day.
But what really turned awkward was when I turned and saw Tony get ready for the house-blessing ceremony. He actually donned his robe and stole, lit candles and had his silver shaker to

sprinkle water around the place. I had asked for a couple of words to bless this house, but he turned it into a full-blown ritual that felt like a wedding ceremony. And he almost made our family room bar into his altar.

Again, our guests were speechless as he called Jan and me to stand together. Surprised? I could hardly concentrate on what he said. He asked our friends to stand up and he actually blessed us as a couple living in love and peace in this house. Wow! He charged those present to give us support and encouragement and asked us to repeat some words I can't remember because it turned out to be like a wedding, and we were all surprised and in awe. He even he sprinkled us with his wand as well as the four directions of our home.

I guess that's what we needed to help us begin to heal and to start the tremendous responsibilities of being a couple living with a house, paying our mortgage, getting financial security and finally, yes, finally making our dreams together come true. I guess I must really be a lesbian now. But how can that be. I've been a heterosexual all my life. I was married for twenty-one years and raised four children? My husband was dead to me so I made up for that and I've had sex with thirteen men since I became divorced. I had my Inuit Goddess Necovic, or Sedna, with her black mermaid torso needing extra white spots for all of my conquests. When I moved from my apartment, I took her picture off the bookcase and put her in a box. I am starting a new life.

Jan on April 3, 1978

My life will never be the same. Nor will I. But that's OK. We have the determination and strength to survive. We did celebrate our housewarming with singular fashion that tied together what Bea had requested, a blessing on the house, with what I needed: a blessing for us to be safe, secure and sober.

I wrote Matt many details to explain what happened to us, about Bea's job loss, especially when she admitted herself into a treatment center and put up her whole life savings for the down payment on our home while I make the payments and pay the bills.

"So, I'm alone again on my job with thousands of pounds of pressure and terrible feelings about the integrity of my hospital with Randy King, and of course, Nick Dixon. Bea's not officially laid off yet because we're both involved on the faculty of a state HPRW workshop. Then Bea is out of a job, just when she needs reinforcement and support as far as her new, sober lifestyle is beginning. I've stopped drinking too. I've lost all taste for it. And heart too.

"And I'm hanging in at Lakeshore Med because I must make this game work here in order to meet the expenses and financial promises we made so we could find peace in our lives. We're not too badly off financially, but we're emotionally battered. Yet, what can you expect when you scoff at the established traditions and society's norms, even when you don't want to confront anyone or anything anymore."

Security is an issue now that I am the breadwinner whose job is at risk if I don't play the game and keep my life as much of a secret as possible. I don't see that I can with all that has been gossiped around and about.

We have each other in our very own home, yet each of us was depressed this morning when I went to work: I, because I had to go and face them and she, because she was rejected by them. I will have to work harder to prove that we are worthy people, good persons and valued employees.

Bea on April 8, 1978

I made an appointment with Randy to have him tell me to my face exactly why I was fired. Both Marge and Jan were jumpy when they followed me into his office. Perhaps they thought I'd knock his block off or kick him in the groin. I could get even by telling everyone how he fucked me last August at my apartment. Talk about a supervisor over a subordinate! But all that would make Jan's job more tense, and she's has enough to worry about now.

I was dressed in my slimming pantsuit and looked great as I stared at him. I suppose he expected a row too. Good! In a few words of my official exit interview, he told me what my situation is, I asked one or two questions about compensation details, signed some papers, and stood up and walked out.

That was that.

I'm reading the want ads and writing resumes and Jan has to interview many people who want my job as her assistant. She says it's a painful process; no one can replace me. I went to the unemployment office on Monday and bumped into another Unitarian from Lakeshore Med's clinics who had been let go. Jan has to watch out or she'll join our ranks. Maybe Marge too. I suppose the only Unitarian who's safe is Nick Dixon.

I've been attending a couple of AA meetings with Arnie Patterson who said he'd find me a group of professionals. So far, these are not good matches for me. I see them merely substituting the alcohol itself with the addiction. Let's get on with it and forget about all the alcoholic trappings and crap like that. Each Wednesday morning, I have gone to St. Paul for private counseling. The first time I went, I couldn't talk. I just sat and cried for the whole session and the counselor let me cry it out. I was a wreck.

> Dredging up muck and mud and silt,
> riling clear water again and again.
> Dig to the bottom, probe the depths of memory
> until the water of life is murky and dark, undrinkable.
> It is needed sometimes, to deepen channels, make new waterways.
> It is needed sometimes to induce the water to flow in new directions.
> When the dredging is done, time settles out the matter.
> Clarity returns, freshness, sparkle.
> The water of life can be savored again, quenching old thirsts.

Jan on April 10, 1978

Dear Rachael,

Bea's off to her first AA meeting tonight that hopefully will be set in a more positive environment than most other meetings have been. As Nora Carpenter said, "It's bad therapy for women whose alcoholism is primarily based on depression to have that typical AA guilt trip laid on them."

This group is made up of individual professional people who meet in a home rather than the church bit. If this doesn't work, Bea may skip the AA meeting route altogether to concentrate on individual therapy at St. Paul or somewhere else.

Nora is great help for both of us.

You are too. I realize that you did not send me a bill for the listening and helping time you gave to me during the initial crisis time.

Bea is reacting to this absolutely negative job situation better than I am. I'm furious, astounded and in grief over the treatment we've been dealt at work. It's been cruel and inhumane. Better timing and giving Bea some chance to return to work with an agreement to find another job elsewhere would be such a better way. But not to be shunned and treated as a leper.

Randy is calling it a lay-off so Bea can qualify for unemployment compensation. This is the first time an ex-employee can apply for compensation without a fight from Personnel, according to another department head who's been here for twenty-five years. It smacks of salving their guilt. Meanwhile, though I can't afford to lose my job. I am The Breadwinner for the first time in my life.

In many ways, this power they have over me is the worst part of the situation. It's a threatening drama that has been badly mishandled. I once thought they were sensitive and humane. In many ways I've exchanged a marriage to a benevolent dictator to a job for a ruthless dictatorship.

Bea's started looking for work in several directions. Resumes are out with a striking photo of her at a desk with dramatic press type saying "Introducing Bea Lindberg. May I call your office to arrange an interview at your convenience? (Enclosed is my résumé & a postcard for your reply.)" The resumes went to several college and healthcare employment contacts, but she's planning projects at home while waiting for the resolution of this temporary setback.

One morning she set out for the lumberyard and when I returned from work, she had built herself a complete carpenter's workbench for the tools she's inherited from her father.

Jenny seems to be coming over to see me more. She picked out a new puppy, a black lab, no less, and she seems happier than I've seen her for many months.

At a divorce court counseling session, Alex had said he would forbid Jenny's visiting me in my home. I said that if he wanted to alienate her, he should continue with that stand. He doesn't think it would do so and said he definitely would forbid her. That's something the two of them have to work out, because as far as I'm concerned, she can come and see me anytime she wants to.

He also referred to "my recent problems," saying that "the compassionate side of me is sorry, but the angry side of me is glad." I asked him if he felt better having said that and he answered with a yes. I didn't get caught up in any argument or hostility. He's a bitter and angry man.

Good news. I even received a long, newsy letter from my son! I think he's going to work out west this summer at a gold mine and in forestry.

Our house is wonderfully peaceful and comfortable. Though we've had to purchase some appliances, all of our furniture has fit beautifully into various rooms. We'll have you over soon and then we can talk more.

I know you are there, Rachael, and thank you for that and for being you.

Jan

<<<>>>

Meanwhile Bea continues to collect unemployment insurance,

looks for jobs and releases her stress by painting and pounding about on her worktable. One day I came home from work and found a pool table in the basement that she bought, had delivered (and it barely fit being carried down the stairs and under the heating vents) and she put all the parts together by herself using a rather light-weight pulley that she hung off a rope from a basement I-beam. She said that later she'd make us a large, white double headboard for our bedroom that has a slanting cupboard storage so we can prop our pillows against the panel and store our many travel books and maps within it. The custom unit will also include cabinets and shelves on each side.

Jan on May 9, 1978

Dear Matt,

I'll be getting some help at work on Monday. Fifty people applied for the job that Bea lost. Marge interviewed ten and I interviewed six. We narrowed it down to two and then Randy interviewed and we made a unanimous choice of a woman by the name of Carolyn Schafer. I didn't tell anyone, but I knew that she took Bea and Marge's course, "Employing Your Total Self" at church. And she really did employ her total self. She divorced her husband, then graduated from college like several others from Bea and Marge's class. Carolyn has been supporting her six grown or almost grown children by working with Pete and Em Kuiper making wire retainers for kids with braces. I remembered meeting her once at a church Supper Club a long time ago.

I have been in quite a fog dealing with my grief through all of this. I wonder if Carolyn knows what she's getting into. I hope she is a brave soul who can do some of the work that Bea has done.

I'm deeply angry and upset and need to resolve these negative feelings. I can't accept that Lakeshore Med could do these cruel and unjust acts to Bea and me.

It is significant that Bea was given an uncontested unemployment insurance compensation; a first for Lakeshore Med, according to some sources that reveals the guilt of this unjust layoff. She's sent out several resumes, but it takes a long time to get answers and interviews. Meanwhile, my attitude about my job isn't good and I dislike having these negative feelings,

Everything else is good. The house is warm and wonderful with a lovely backyard with three five-foot evergreen trees. In a small garden that Bea dug for me with a garden fork and spade, I'm planting flowers and vegetables, and we're going to add a birch tree among the evergreens. I love to hug a birch tree.

And I have some poems and freelance work out in the mail.

Love,

Mom

Bea on May 12, 1978

I'm still going to the unemployment office each Monday to pick up my check and report on my job search. I go to outpatient counseling at St. Paul, to AA meetings, read *What Color Is Your Parachute*, wait for responses to my resumes and personally network at Midwest Women's Bureau, UW services, and various school personnel offices in Lakeshore and Sheboygan—I even applied at parochial schools.

Another helpful connection is through the Wisconsin Women in the Arts show in Madison before I went nuts and checked myself into St. Paul. Someone from the feminist bookstore, Room of One's Own, saw my painting and asked me if I would hang my work there in June. Of course, I accepted and am finishing up on some of those that I started in February when we were hippy bohemians painting nudes in Jan's apartment studio.

Jan recalled with a chill that she had wanted to go to Room of One's Own once when she was in Madison with Alex and the kids. To her it was a quest; to Alex it was a threat. It seemed that all he wanted to do was get out before he was emasculated while Jan explored rows of empowering subjects. She felt his discomfort and left without buying anything for them or herself.

Except for that news from Room of One's Own, the empty days can get quite depressing when Jan goes to work. She tried to cheer me up by "christening" the white living room carpeting. We lit candles all around the room and made love like two pure virgins in a sexual ritual on a soft, white cloud. We were blissfully happy that no one dropped by unexpectedly during our lovely liturgy.

<<<◇>>>

My counselor at St. Paul wanted me to do a timeline of my life and it's quite compelling. Good thing I have these little black and brown date books with terse comments and asterisks to help me remember hours and days of episodes and affairs hidden behind clues in case my kids or someone else would find the books. Someday someone will, I know, but then I'll be dead.

I guess I inherited that habit from my mother. I still have all her little notebooks, but they were mostly boring like mine in the old days when all I had to write about was how many loads of laundry I did, the kids' Scouting events and what I cooked for supper. My life certainly became exciting when I started sending out my novels and magazine articles in the late 60s and early 70s and got involved with Jan and after I divorced Jake. My life certainly is more adventurous than my mother's—and most other women, too. In fact, I better think about getting bigger notebooks.

After showing my counselor my timeline on Wednesday, our session went quite well and I felt pretty good. Of course, including Jan in it forced me to own up to my situation. But there's plenty of other info in it to keep him busy analyzing me.

Our therapist friend still keeps in touch. Rachael came over for supper and to see the house—and probably to check me out. I'm being a good girl and staying away from booze. I worked too hard to get sober and I'm not going to let that crap get to me again.

Jan's birthday note to me quoted Whitman, "I am larger, better than I thought. I did not know I held so much goodness." Inside she wrote, "Please say this for me every day and every time you look into a mirror. Say, 'I am a fantastic person!' and 'Jan loves me!' Happy Birthday! Me."

Bea on June 1, 1978

Good old Charlie called on Memorial Day and I invited him over. I don't know what he expected but all he got from me was a drink of iced tea and a quick chat before we sent him out of our space and on his way. Goodbye Charlie. Maybe he went back to Marge's.

I'm getting ready to spring my nudes onto Room of One's Own Bookstore walls with an opening on June 3. I've had business cards printed, created new paintings with parts of women's bodies, had them framed, and of course, prepared our headless nudes and other close-up and/or whimsical women's breasts for the show.

My photocopied flyer reads, "The Altogether—Paintings by Bea Lindberg at A Room of One's Own. Opening June 3 through June 30. Sponsored by Wisconsin Women in the Arts."

Then I added this explanation: "When I tired of painting lighthouses and seascapes and decided to try my hand at nudes, I was amazed at friends' reactions to the paintings. I thought we had come a long way, Baby, from my mother's milk. She couldn't pronounce the word 'breast' in more than a guarded whisper, but in many cases I was wrong. I found women so uncomfortable with their own bodies that they reacted with embarrassment to the idea of the paintings. This convinced me all the more that something needed to be said about the naked female form, and said by a woman about women. 'The Altogether' exhibit is a beginning."

For the illustration, I had Jan take my photo as if I were nude, but I held one of my frontal breast paintings with one arm and hand over the top of the breast and the other hand and shadows on my stomach. This photo had my real head and shoulders on the top and my bare legs extended below the painting's frame. I think it's going to attract attention. Jan had to use a new photo-processing guy to replace me, and Jan told me that he joked, "I don't know what that photo is all about—and I don't want to know either."

CHAPTER 9

Jan on June 3, 1978

We were up at 6 a.m. to load the car for Madison and we pulled in front of Room of One's Own feminist bookstore at 9:45 to unload. I took photos to capture Bea's personally historic one-woman show as Bea hung her nine nudes that encircled the room above the bookcases. When she finished, we sat in the lounge chairs and she proudly surveyed her paintings above the hundreds of liberating books, their covers facing out to us from the bookcases.

After I showed her some of my college sites, we went back to Room of One's Own to sense customer reactions, but they seemed quite blasé. The clerk told us the nudes really warmed up the place.

We went to a late lunch at Lysistrata, a classy, new women-owned restaurant and bar, and ordered a gourmet salad and a bottle of alcohol-free champagne to toast our accomplishments. With our conversation inspired by this feminist atmosphere, I asked Bea what she would want to do if she had a dream to fulfill.

"I've always wanted to own a bookstore."

"What a perfect idea. With all the books that you have read, and with your intelligence, your owning a bookstore would also make a dream of mine come true because I have wanted to do that too. We could work together to make it happen—you have the brains and I have the place. Together we can make this happen. My dad's storefront is a mess, full of lifeless artificial flowers that are collecting dust. He sits in the back and waits for business to walk in the side door while the storefront sign and window displays fade with neglect. His dream of pulling something off the shelf to make something saleable went bad after buyers bought boatloads of artificial flowers from Hong Kong and every drugstore and supermarket sold artificial flowers."

"Could it be possible? Would your dad let us use that space? It's close enough to the end of Downtown, only a half-a-block out of the way, and on a major street. And there's enough parking on the street. We could fix it up if he would let us."

"And I'm sure that the rent would be right—like free!"

"I wouldn't want it only to be a feminist bookstore. I don't think that would get enough customers. We'd have to call it a general purpose bookstore with a special interest for women. That way I could have some best sellers and even some boating books. I'd love to sell boating books to those people in the new marinas around the river."

"I remember hearing Studs Terkel on Chicago's fine arts radio station interview Colleen Dewhurst. She was playing the lead in Bertolt Brecht's anti-war play, *Mother Courage and Her Children*, and I was truly impressed about Dewhurst, the Brecht play, and of course, the tragedy of war. We're mothers, Bea, and we're courageous. We could think about calling our bookstore something with Mother Courage in it. I'll find the play and we'll read it aloud to each other to see if it fits us."

Bea took a napkin and started drawing. "We could have a female figurehead, like those on a schooner, and use a hawser line around her and our name. That image could serve as a life-line to rescue women." She created a full-breasted woman's profile with a daring look in her eyes and an oval circle of rope to enclose our name.

It seemed as if everything fell into place on that day. Our brainstorming flowed. No. It flooded us with excitement and its potential to take our resources and create a partnership and a service that would help others and us as well.

Jan on June 8. 1978

My new assistant, Carolyn Schafer is determined to do whatever it takes to get the job done and do it well. I think she senses that she's filling a grievous loss for me, and her compassion helps my healing. She's very astute as to what and who has power here. I've been quiet about it, hoping she would make independent evaluations without my prejudices. Her friendly warmth and cheerfulness add so much to improve the atmosphere. That helps bring employees and volunteers back looking for us to help them. She's dependable.

My guardian angel has sent her to me.

Bea on June 20, 1978

Jan's Carolyn seems to be working out. The three of us went together to an open house for a local printer of Lakeshore Med's publications but Jan and I felt a cold shoulder from the once very friendly wife and co-partner in the business, so we ate and ran. Jan told me, "It's hard to maintain the same spark and flashes of creativity that both of us gave to our Lakeshore Med publications," and she added, "My new helper is like a candle flame compared to the rocket that you were when you were there."

I'm still going to St. Paul each Wednesday morning. What a waste of money. But Lakeshore Med is paying for it. I guess I have to go in order to follow protocol and get my unemployment compensation of just less than $100 a month. I did stop going to those AA meetings a while ago. You shouldn't have to be addicted to an addiction program.

One of my paintings was accepted for a juried art show in Milwaukee next month, and we'll be driving back to Madison to pick up my nudes. Meanwhile I'm painting, carving, writing, and

Jan and I will be going to take a pottery class together. That should help with her stress.

We finally took Marge's nude painting to her house for her birthday present. I was afraid she wouldn't like it because I painted her back rather than her front. Her proportions are not flattering for a frontal view. But she got a bonus because her nude painting also included her head, the back of it at least. And she said she liked it.

I think I've had it with my nude period for a while.

Jan and I had fun collecting my paintings from Room of One's Own because we could also do research on their store and others in Madison. Too bad we can't be closer to a college or university, but we will make a success of what we have.

It is so exciting to see so many new titles on women's issues that were hardly acknowledged before—and from women authors and scholars. There are a few women-owned presses too. I picked up info on what they publish.

I wonder how many women's bookstores there are in our country, in the world? Not many, I'll bet.

Jan on July 9, 1978

Bea and I signed up for a pottery class and on her first try at the potter's wheel she threw a perfect bowl. Not wanting to deal with any more stress, chose to play with the clay by making slab pots and sculpture. I made the right choice because Bea's been having a heck of a time throwing another pot without it getting lopsided time and time again.

Yesterday I took my dad to lunch and we discussed the bookstore proposal. I showed him where we would put all his stuff in the basement so he wouldn't feel too displaced. He was happy. All systems are a go. He's happy he'll have something new to keep him interested.

He's never said anything about our relationship. I knew he liked Bea. Nor about my getting a divorce though I am sure it hurts him. He loves Alex like a son. Over the years, I have learned from him to be sympathetic with others and not pass judgment on their decisions.

He revealed to me that what he really miss is being touched. He has no one to touch him except Chico.

He also showed me Chico's coffin that he had someone make out of heavy-duty aluminum. He made rectangular pillows with some foam rubber that he found among his supplies, covered the rubber with red plastic sheeting secured with masking tape and made a soft lining for the box. He wanted me to know about it in case he "went" before Chico did.

When I drove him home, he showed me where he has dug a hole for the box in case the dog dies in winter. The hole is covered up with a wooden lid with grass growing over it.

When I told Bea about the great news of the bookstore, I skipped the details of Chico's funeral plans until later.

Bea on August 2, 1978

When Jan and I read *Mother Courage and Her Children* aloud to each other, we identified our compassion with Mother Courage's strength and cunning to survive under soul-searing experiences. The name was a natural for our new lives together.

We met a lawyer and signed the partnership papers for Mother Courage Enterprises that includes a bookstore, art gallery, freelance creative artistic and copy writing services! Jan will stay at Lakeshore Med for a stable income, as far as we can count on Lakeshore Med, and I'll manage the bookstore full time. With only two bookstores in Lakeshore, not counting the religious and porno ones, I'm sure to be busy.

Things really got rolling after the 4th of July. Before that Jan and I spent leisurely weekends in bed—reading the papers, talking, and stuff. But most weekend evenings we'd go to a play or movie or have family and friends stop by.

I'm done with job interviews. My latest one was at an insurance company in Milwaukee, which was OK, but then I had to tell them all about me and I feel bad about that.

So, I really got busy making plans and seeing Barney about using his building. That all seemed to be going OK while I bide my time. Jan's money is tied up until her divorce and I really can't proceed until I know about our cash flow. Then on July 18, she was told her court date would be August 24. She will have the money by October 7 and it looks like we go with our plans.

Jan and I consolidated all her dad's stuff on the street level to move around the block to get to the lowest floor of his building. It's dusty, dirty work moving years of artificial flower inventory stacked in boxes. She says some of the tools that are piled on tables have been in the same place for years. He'll keep his office and sign-writing room and a separate front door of a hall lined with more than a dozen 12-foot long boxes of colored paper rolls used primarily by professional photographers.

When I'm home, I'm pouring over book lists from distributors. I have so much to learn, too. What a thrill to shop for hundreds of titles to create our bookstore. Jan wanted to get in on the purchasing, but I kept her out of it because she'll only slow me down if we stop to discuss what titles she doesn't agree to have in the store.

We took a crowbar to pull the old shelves from the walls and piled it all on top of Barney's Nash station wagon. It looked like the Grinch's sleigh in Dr. Seuss' *How the Grinch Stole Christmas.* When we made sharp turns in the middle of Main Street, we begged the Powers That Be that the tottering stack on top of the car and junk hanging out the car windows would not topple over into the busy street as I drove slowly around the intersections with Jan jogging behind to catch any debris. Gaunt and dirty, wearing tattered shirts and jeans, we looked worse than the Joads from *The Grapes of Wrath* making their way from the dust bowls of Oklahoma to reach the Promised Land of California.

Then we got a look at what labor lie ahead to clean, spackle, paint and renovate to make a proper space for our dream to become a reality. The empty room with an open display divider is pretty small, but we'll fill it with large and lively ideas. The entire south side has a low platform and full-wall windows joining our space with the sunny city beyond.

Now I've got twenty-two letters with our Mother Courage logo stationery, ready to go to suppliers for quotes and information, letters of credit, etc., plus a list to do at the bank for business checks, credit accounts. Then I'll head to the lumber yard to buy new shelving that I will build and peg board that we will install above the bookcases so we have a gallery for art exhibits. Soon I'll be off for gallons of battleship blue paint for the walls and ceilings. We're going to have everything nautical, of course.

Barney's faded and flaked old metal sign came down from standing on its wooden grid over the storefront since World War II ended and he bought the building with G.I. loan. He made a change once by adding "Artificial Flowers" on the sign. We had to clear some basement space for the sign to lie flat on sawhorses because it was going to get a fresh new life too.

We bought ship's figureheads made of weather-resistant material and chose Jane Elizabeth to stand in front of our red and gold sign to add a third dimension when it was put back in its place. She's a bold figure breasting the wind in her 19th Century blue dress flowing, her hand resting on her forward-reaching knee.

I started framing the four x eight pegboard panels that we then screwed eight feet up onto the twelve-foot walls after painting. Were they ever heavy! And Jan and I didn't count on having to drill screws into the solid brick or concrete east wall. But we hung fourteen of those damn pegboards reaching our heads while standing on shaky wooden, widow-makin' ladders.

When I was at home in the evenings "resting," I was pouring into the blackness of our BookFinder microfiche files on the dining room table and placing orders from our chief distributor.

Jan is addressing her name-change cards inscribed: "Jan Anthony Carnigian wishes to announce that she will be returning to her birth-given name Jan Delores Anthony for all legal and social purposes."

Jan on August 24, 1978

Gentlemanly Conrad Sanders was waiting when I left the building to be driven to the Court House. Alex and his attorney were there when we walked in the room.

As the plaintiff, Alex took the stand and swore that we had done everything possible to save the marriage and that the plaintiff is entitled to a judgment of divorce. The plaintiff is a fit and proper person to have the care, custody and control of the minor child. Both parties shall be responsible for her support, but no monetary amount shall be established for the defendant.

And that as a full, final and complete division of the estate of the parties and in lieu of all alimony, the property shall be divided as follows:

And so on and so on with my pitiful little list of grandmothers' sugar bowls, a white teapot, etc., going to me.

Another item is that "Real estate in Door County, Wisconsin; the defendant shall execute a quit claim deed conveying her interest in said property to the plaintiff," etc., "that the defendant shall have the right to use the real estate upon reasonable advance notice for one week," etc.

I am to receive "cash in the amount of $30,000.00 payable not later than 45 days."

When Sanders asked me weeks ago what should happen if Alex decided to sell Door County, I said that he would never do that because he loves the land so much and will want his children to have it.

Alex was off guard when the judge read, "That the defendant's maiden name shall be restored to her, to wit: Jan Delores Anthony."

What caught me off guard was Alex's attorney speedy flight toward me, pushing a pen at me with his claw to have me sign away my Door County land without even so much as giving me a chance to breathe.

<<<>>>

That was it. It was over. Easy. Painless. Enlightened treatment. No fault. No one to blame. No fight for child custody. No nasty scandal. No sexual deviant. No headlines. Who knows why that couple broke up? What a shame. Such nice people.

Sanders took my arm and led me from the courtroom and I walked past the elevators to the west windows and started to cry as he stood by me patiently. I didn't want to look at anyone nor did I want anyone to see me. When I felt that Alex was out of the way and out of the Court House, I put back my brave face and let Conrad drive me back to Lakeshore Med.

"Please let me off at the parking ramp. I don't want to walk in there yet."

With comforting words, he said, "I hope that you are pleased that the problems in this case were resolved to the mutual satisfaction of you and Mr. Carnigian and that there was a minimum of unpleasantness experienced by you." I thanked him and he wished me the very best in the years ahead. While walking to my little brown Toyota, I wondered how many cases he's had like mine. Not many, I'll bet, and I grew stronger each step.

Later, I returned to the office and thanked Carolyn for holding down the fort. "I had to go home and cry for a while."

"You deserve to cry for a while, Jan."

I called Jenny at home when I felt her father would be gone and I asked her how she was. "I asked Dad how it went," she said. "And all he said that everything would continue to be the same except for your mother's last name."

Jan on August 28, 1978

I found out that my new colleague Carolyn has a lover who is well known in his field and ten years her senior. Roger lives in

Washington, D.C., but he travels about as a consultant and gives lectures. I encourage her to meet him as often as possible. To do that, we looked for work she could do away from the office to build up comp time to use when her lover's around. That's when my banner idea came to me. A heraldic banner will be created for each department with its individual department logo and Carolyn would bring them into reality at home while she dreams of meeting her lover when he flies to be with her.

She went off on her first vacation with him, and her 80-some-year-old mother warned her not to get pregnant. Six children are enough. "Don't worry, Mother. I'm prepared," she almost laughed, "and so is he."

Bea on August 28, 1978

Wisconsin Women in the Arts
Lowell Hall, University of Wisconsin Extension
Madison, WI, 53706

Dear Friends,

Jan and I have something to shout about. We are opening a new bookstore in Lakeshore Bay in October. As you can see by our logo, we are calling it Mother Courage Bookstore and Art Gallery at 214 2nd Street, Lakeshore Bay, WI, 42424. There are several layers of symbolism in our logo. A woman is emerging from an egg; she is "breasting" out of bondage (an oval rope); she is breaking the way wherever the ship goes. And it's time real women are allowed to sail the ship.

We would like to announce our opening in an ad in the program for the Milwaukee conference. Could you send us rates and deadlines for such an ad?

We hope to become a women's center of vibrant creative energy and an influence in the women's movement in the Lakeshore Bay area like A Room of One's Own in Madison and Sistermoon in Milwaukee have done for their areas. We're also members of a microfiche service for fast order response to the general trade.

Please check to see if you have our new addresses on your records. We are now both living at 2026 Westwood Lane, Lakeshore Bay, WI 42424.

And Jan has reclaimed her birth name from Carnigian to Anthony.

Please send the quote to this address.

Thank you very much.

Bea on September 3, 1978

I picked up lumber and light blue stain for our entire bookshelf wall that goes all the way to the ceiling. I ordered a library ladder to go with it. I've always wanted a room full of books with a library ladder.

I've scrubbed the front of the store and built and stained a counter for our cash register. We've acquired marine maps of Lake Michigan that we've decoupaged on to the shelf surfaces. Jan is taking advantage of the sunny weather by painting the front of the store a fire engine red that also will be the background color of the sign with golden yellow bold letters of Mother Courage and the lower line smaller, saying Bookstore and Art Gallery. Jane Elizabeth, our impressive figurehead, will look stunning standing proudly next to our name in her primrose blue dress.

Now I am calculating how I'm going to make Mother Courage's bookshelves fit around a damn, dust-encrusted radiator that Jan will clean and paint the same color as the shelves. We also salvaged a long, tired storage chest with four wide drawers to use as an island in the bookstore space. Its countertop will be perfect for displays, especially when we paint it the same color of the walls and decoupage Lake Michigan charts on its top. We'll fill the other two walls with wire bookracks for paperbacks. That should add lots of color to the room—glorious book cover colors.

Jan on September 23, 1978

Last week I had to take out a loan to pay for our book order because Alex has not yet settled our divorce account. He has the money or he can get it easily by hurrying up the process of refinancing the house from our credit union. The loan officer was very understanding to me when I signed my loan and negotiated my interest payment. He said these things happen.

I also paid my attorney's bill of $600.

Months ago, when Bea lost her job and was dependent on my salary, I gave her my check and let her manage all of our money. It was only fair because she put in all that money to buy our house, at least until I could get my settlement from Alex. Some couples, I know, keep separate accounts. I surely did in the later years of my marriage and felt I needed escape money in case I had to leave my husband. I don't fear that with Bea, but it was actually scary to have both of our names at the same address printed on our checks. I did keep a little separate checking account in case I had to pay professional membership fees or write an occasional personal check. Now it seemed natural that she takes care of all of our resources. Besides, I have enough to worry about.

Then on September 17, I got a raise from Lakeshore Med from $1,150 to $1,500 or $7.22 an hour. Of course, the hourly rate doesn't matter because I don't get overtime and am strictly on salary. And I deserve every penny of it. But they cut my hours down to thirty-five a week and informed me that my divorce put me on a single status so the government would withhold more taxes than before. I get a salary increase and end up with less money than I got before. As if I have been a clock-watcher and left on the minute for all of these years. I've worked hours and hours over without overtime pay and now they cut my hours. Carolyn will have to fill in that time, that is if I leave work by the clock.

Speaking of hours, if Bea and I knew the total hours, days and weeks of drudgery we would have to put out before we remade this drab old storefront into a sparking and colorful reality, we probably would never have started. But no. I guess that wouldn't be us. We'd finish what we said we'd do even if it did us in. Subconsciously, we could think of doing only one step at a time and when that was done, we tackled the next. Our funds were low, but if we ran out of physical stamina, our motivation energized us for the next task.

For example, I never thought we'd take on the job of refinishing the wooden floor on the back side of the divider, but when we completed staining and sawing and building the bookcase to cover one whole wall, and saw how attractive that beat-up old chest of drawers looked with its fresh coat of paint and its snappy maps pasted and lacquered to the top, we looked at the dingy floor and knew that we had to rent a sander and just get that job done.

We now both weigh about 140 pounds or less, losing weight without booze calories plus plenty of stress and hard work. When I got the floor sander, the rental staff put it in the trunk of the car, but when I got to the store, I was the one who had to lift it out of the car and push or drag it into the building. Fortunately, I didn't put too many gouges in the floor surface after I got the hang of it. Good thing I started in the rear of the room. Bea got down on her knees a lot when finishing the three coats of shiny new varnish on the floor several days later and we were proud of what we accomplished. The topper was installing Bea's beautiful new walnut library ladder to the top edge of the ceiling-high, blue-stained bookshelves.

I drove Bea to the airport to fly to Denver for the American Booksellers Association Booksellers conference for first-time booksellers. Two women from Chicago were there too as owners of the Women and Children First Bookstore. Jan called me most nights with the news of what she'd learned, but it usually was late when I got home and I was exhausted from Lakeshore Med work and going to our shop to clean up the trash on rickety shelves carelessly built over the stairs to the middle landing. The middle landing still had stuff piled up from World War II that needed to be cleared away. Then I painted the ancient wooden slat walls down those steps toward the 1930s toilet and sink with only cold water.

Never in my life did I think that I would be on my hands and knees trying to clean and paint that ramshackle toilet room with an antique wooden toilet seat that was always in the upright position for decades. The thin, plank walls gave some privacy if no one else was on the landing that hung from the beams of the floor above with a bracing timber or two from the cellar below. But I did it in case a customer had to go to the bathroom. Over the years, I knew I'd have to do this job after inheriting the property, but I never guessed I'd be able to do it while fulfilling a dream of owning a bookstore and an art gallery to promote women artists in this area.

My goal was to have all this shit completed by the time Bea returned from Denver. And I missed her so much and wanted a beer to quench my thirst, but keeping on task kept me on track.

My dad is relieved and happy that he can maintain his business and that someone, especially me, is spending time at his place and holding the building together. And the price is right for us. He's not charging us any rent. He even got out his old wooden extension ladder and tarred the roof. He was astounded at this improved status of the landing and toilet almost as much as he was with the front of the building and the store that had been neglected by everyone except spiders and cobwebs.

Bea on September 30, 1978

We'll open the store tomorrow for a trial week on the mechanics of the store, the cash register, etc., and we'll have our Grand Opening on Sunday, October 8 for the Old Main Street Association Oktoberfest celebration.

The main order of books finally came in on September 25 and totaled twenty-one cases. It was better than Christmas. After Jan came here from work, she choked back the tears when she saw the boxes stacked in the middle of the store. Jenny appeared too and Barney came out of his back offices and we started opening each box to check the order and cherish each book and its smell of ink when you page through its contents.

Madge Leighman, our first artist, was surprised when I showed her our high art gallery, but with good spirits, she climbed Barney's shaky ladders to hang her work high above the bookshelves and the room divider.

We've paid for Mother Courage pins and pens, t-shirts, bookmarks and flyers galore. But we still haven't had our metal bookshelves delivered. Jan's found some wooden crates that we've piled up attractively for many of our paperbacks.

YIPES! We're opening tomorrow!

CHAPTER 10

Bea on October 6, 1978

Many friends came to our preview opening. We looked so smart and attractive and so did the store. Jan isn't comfortable with the cash register, yet she's not intimidated by our new Bookbinder microfiche machine that sits in the window with books, our marine gifts and striking figureheads, especially the one with the nude torso.

Barney expressed some concern about the bare-breasted figureheads and also about the powerful life-size cardboard Wonder Woman super-hero figure propped up in the back corner with her bosoms wrapped in red and gold and the rest in blue with sparkling stars. What would he have done if she were three-dimensional? We listened to him but didn't make a change.

Jan on October 6, 1978

To Randy King; copies to Clark Young, Nick Dixon
The 1978 Communications Review of the Hospital Public Relations of Wisconsin differed from the past by elevating the award standards. Only one award of Communications Excellence and only

one, or at most two, Certificate of Merit were presented in each of 12 categories. No awards nor certificates were granted in some categories.

Top honors were awarded to Lakeshore Med Communications for the 1977 annual report, "Lakeshore Medical Center Is in the Black," the insert with the calendar in the winter issue of *synergy*. I received a creatively designed engraved plaque for this honor.

The Communications department also received three Certificates of Merit: one to Bea Lindberg and me for the Lakeshore Med News publication; a second to me for non-patient information: the memo on "Hospital Costs Confound You;" and a third to me for a special area, Comprehensive Public Relations Project, describing the Lakeshore Medical Center Costs informational campaign from September 1977 to June 1978.

For the second year in a row, no other hospital in the state received this many awards, and this year's competition with its even more challenging standards is truly a record year for Lakeshore Medical Center.

Thank you all for helping me acquire the detailed information required to explain these complex issues and for advising me about the most appropriate ways to present them.

Bea on October 9, 1978

Mother Courage had her big Grand Opening yesterday and lots of excitement! Barney found banners to hang from the store to a U.S. flag on a flagpole in a hole he had finagled when the new sidewalk was paved several years before. Now he finally can use it for a flag to call attention to our store and to the gorgeous red and gold sign he made with our Jane Elizabeth figurehead standing tall above our red front door and gleaming windows.

The excitement level rose as noon arrived and people started coming in. Jill came to help too. Jenny went down Main Street and handed out Mother Courage pins so people would know to come our way around the corner. Never were there more people in this building. The happy noise of supportive customers was music. They're positively enthusiastic about having a new bookstore, and one that is woman-oriented appeals to people. We sold $296 worth of books and got thousands of dollars in goodwill for the store.

After our grand, grand opening, Jan, Jill and Josh helped us take down the outside banners and I joined Barney and his bottle of brandy that he extracted from his office desk drawer. It was the first alcohol I've had in seven months. But who's counting. We went out for supper together and I celebrated again with some wine.

Today's paper had Oktoberfest pictures of clowns, bratwurst grillers, and Anna Spence and Jenny folk dancing with others in the street.

Bea on October 10, 1978

I'm rich again! Jan finally received her settlement money from Alex on Tuesday. Yeah! What a relief! Happy Days!

People come in and out of the store. I'm chatting with customers and reading in between. I love to look across from my elevated counter chair next to the cash register and gaze proudly the impressive nautical and general interest books we have, including coffee table editions like *Chapman's Piloting* and the large-formatted, clever book on gnomes. We also have many parenting titles on pregnancy and non-sexist child-raising, women's health as in *Woman's Body, an owner's manual,* and, showing no favoritism, *Man's Body* and *Child's Body*. Jan loves biographies and my favorite is adventure fiction plus varied non-fiction paperback and hardcover books. Erica Jong's *Fear of Flying* keeps selling in paperback even though some customers say they have to hide it when they take it home to read.

We're fortunate to start our business with new best-selling titles to offer our customers: Marilyn French's *The Women's Room* shows how wives of the 50s became women of the 70s. Ha! How true. And Nancy Friday's *My Mother Myself* defines why we want so much to have different choices from what our mothers had that we neglect to honor their strengths in our search for independence.

Rita Mae Brown's paperback of *Rubyfruit Jungle* is now readily available for all readers and is really popular. Daughters Press, a small feminist press with limited distribution, originally published it but Bantam picked it up and it's a new best seller with a decidedly lesbian heroine. Brown's new hard cover title, *Six of One,* will be featured in our November *Courier* newsletter that Jan's beginning to write.

I found many influential books to sell: Bea Ehrenreich and Deirdre English's *Witches, Midwives and Nurses and Complaints and Disorders* and *The Sexual Politics of Sickness;* Betty Dodson's *Liberating Masturbation, a meditation on self love;* Mary Daly's *Beyond God the Father* from our own UU Beacon Press; and of course, Virginia Woolf's books and Simone DeBeauvoir's *The Second Sex,* Adrienne Rich's poems in *The Dream of a Common Language* and her non-fiction work, *Of Women Born.*

Jan sobbed with joy last Saturday afternoon when she sat at the store reading Ntosake Shange's play *for colored girls who have considered suicide when the rainbow is enuf* that ended, "I found God within myself, and I loved her. I loved Her fiercely!"

In most books that I devour, I found bibliographies that gave me more resources like *The Malleus Maleficarum (The Hammer of Witches)* that gave authority to begin the burning of women as witches in the beginning of the Dark Ages of Europe.

In addition to all these heavy political and feminist subjects, we offer books with a sense of humor on these issues when we can find them. Erma Bombeck's book, *If Life is a Bowl of Cherries—What Am I Doing in the Pits?* is an example.

And I ordered children's books with girls and women as heroes.

When Jan comes in after her Lakeshore Med stint, she loves to find books for customers and tells the feminists she knows about the new women's records that we're selling: Alix Dobkin, Margie Adams,

Meg Christian, Cris Williamson, Malvina Reynolds, Holly Near and Kay Gardner, all founders of the women's music industry.

A Milwaukee woman came in and gave us a selection of demos. We ordered a few and hung the covers on the wall. I put a stack of albums on the machine and let it play, but I have to be careful that Barney doesn't hear some of the words, especially in Alix Dobkin's *Lavender Jane Loves Women* album. Kay Gardner's *Mooncircles* is truly remarkable, but the last song, "Wise Woman" always gives me a jolt when she sings, "Wise Woman, WHAT (with emphasis) do you know of life." I turn them off and then when Jan comes in she asks me how are we going to sell the records if people can't hear them, and she puts them on again while I go crazy.

Jan almost died of rapture when she heard Margie Adam's "Best Friend (The Unicorn Song) and "Sweet Friend of Mine." Cris Williamson's *Changer and the Changed* album hits lesbian consciousness that celebrates and stimulates our lives, especially in "Song of the Soul" and "Waterfall."

These courageous authors, scholars and independent musicians risk all to rewrite women's history and invent and sing women's lyrics and music. Together and with others are creating a revolution, and I know that we're a part of that same revolution for women's rights—and human rights too.

Jan on October 19, 1978

We're celebrating the best that we can be. Being sober helps a lot. Without alcohol, our new body chemistry makes our touch erotically intense again. Adversity and injustice that we have lived through fuels our proud determination to comfort and heal each other's wounds back to wholeness.

Our bodies bless each of us in sensual, sacred rites in our own hallowed home, in our own divine bed, to worship with the moonlight blessing our bareness, we embrace a sacred organ,—our supple skin that contains us from scalp to toes. Bundles of tissue sensors surrender and accept the fondling from knowing fingers, stroking of soothing hands, bonding with willful arms and legs enfolding and supporting while sensitive lips and savoring tongues maneuver to strategic destinations. Moist ringlets of hair, like electric energy, slide to tingle our noses, faces, breasts, the hills and valley crevices. Mother Earth. So primal. So immediate. Basic. Wanting. Laughing. Playing with our vibrating toys. Intense. Trusting our lover, we let go to joy and satisfaction, to oceanic orgiastic tidal waves, to exalted exhaustion, then breathing and sleeping as one.

Coming together or taking turns makes no difference. Receiving pleasure and giving it are the greatest gifts.

When cool sunshine wakes us, hugging, fuzzy fun begins again. Eyes can focus sharply in the light, seeing clearly the downy fluff of cheeks and arms, velvety stomach and silky thighs. Noses inhale fresh morning shower sprays flowing, lavender cool, soapy fragrances as we anoint each other with warm water blessings. Returning for a morning ritual, we Goddess pilgrims travel gently again on the smooth and supple paths of nerves that stimulate the connective links and slowly travel to the surging mons, the goal to reach ultimate intimacy again.

Sweat, salt, frankincense and musk. Sweet iris, engorged blood red rose, makes blood rise in mine.

We share more than our sexual senses. We speak with kindness most of the time except maybe when our deadlines and people-problems put us on edge. We are each other's physical, emotional, intellectual and spiritual sanctuary. Sometimes we try to protect the other from emotional letdowns that we've experienced. Our lives are complicated with maturing children, ex-husbands, relatives, insecurities and judgmental adversaries of our less-than-closeted lifestyle.

Our financial security is always a worry with the bookstore and our customers, my co-workers and my work at Lakeshore Medical Center.

Though our increasing sexual coupling and experimentation is delightful, what's important to our survival is how we react and perform with others each day. Bea and I love each other, and this love that so strong affects our lives and sets us apart. We know who supports us, but most often, we don't know who is intolerant and perhaps even hostile.

For one small example, our neighbors across the street set out some cobblestone-type pavement blocks for the city to take away during its annual clean-up week. I was sure the heavy, rugged bricks were granite and could someday enhance my garden; so, I backed our car up to their curbing, opened the trunk lid and started loading the heavy bricks. The weight in the car caused me to drive a couple times back and forth across the street to load and unload.

The neighbors' little boy, probably four years old, came around to watch and started talking to me. In a while he asked, "Who do you sleep with?"

Stunned by his boldness, surprised by the content of the topic and defensive by my vulnerability, especially with this little kid, I packed in a few more bricks while I was thinking of an answer, and I turned his question back on him. "Do you have something you like to sleep with? A bear? A favorite blanket? My son slept with his ragged old rabbit when he was your age."

I lifted the bricks quickly after that, hoping his puzzled and thoughtful expression indicated that he'd be distracted long enough for me to make a cool escape from further interrogation. The boy shrugged and turned away and I imagined him in his house, overhearing once perhaps, his parents saying, "I wonder if those two women sleep together."

A simple question as "Who do you sleep with?" caused a deeply stressful, fearful emotion and adrenaline response. We are moving along on uncharted paths like early American pioneers who didn't know what was in the forest and the mountains ahead of them. The woods that we travel through to find a place to rest has different plants and species that made us invaders, trespassers in the land of privilege and conformity, in the environment of family: mother, father and children, convention, straightness.

We are strangers here, two women in their mid-forties alone together making new trails. Watching. Wary. Perhaps in time, we strange newcomers will foster a more understanding neighborhood. How do we know that it is not welcoming? Our anxiety makes us guarded. We'll mind our own business and work hard to be good neighbors. We won't make much noise and we'll keep the yard neat. Perhaps when they get to know us, the question "Who do you sleep with?" will not be so intimidating.

Many think that being lesbian is only what we do in bed, a sexual activity rather than a gender preference. Ironically, neither Bea nor I, but perhaps I should speak only for myself, have not been sexually attracted to any other woman since we fell in love. Yet I do have loving feelings for the wellbeing of other women, and our families are our priority. If our togetherness sets us apart from society, so be it.

In contrast to what others may think about us, we celebrate the affirming experiences we share as a couple and as Mother Courage partners when we plunge more deeply into the surging waves of feminism with its powerful women dedicated to improving women's lives and preserving our environment.

Wisconsin Women in the Arts (WWIA) met at the YWCA in Milwaukee in October and we attended with great pride. We bought a full-page ad in the program book and represented ourselves to WWIA women across the state as Mother Courage Bookstore and Art Gallery.

On Friday night we went to see and hear Alice Neel speak about her fifty years of art. Good thing the old downtown building had an elevator to the fifth floor because Miss Neel at 78 would not have made it up the stairs. Probably we couldn't either. She was so frail; she must have led a hard life. But her strong mind and heart spoke boldly about her work with candid simplicity as she sat in a comfortable chair on the platform close to us. Her slides and lecture demonstrated her strength as an artist. Her early paintings portrayed gaunt "victims," she said: the poor, the unknown, a dying man ravaged by tuberculosis, many images of people's bodies as frail as hers is now.

She lived in Spanish Harlem during The Depression and survived by being sponsored by the WPA, the Works Progress Administration Art Project created in 1935 by President Franklin Roosevelt. She's finally receiving recognition. Now she paints her children and grandchildren, but someone had the foresight to have her paint *Time Magazine's* cover portrait of Kate Millet. She promised us that she's continuing her work, and she inspired us with her talent, tenacity and wit, as well as her feminism.

On the drive home we stopped at the seedy old Sugar Stop women's bar. It's been many months since our first anxious visit, and this time we walked fearlessly past the motorcycles lining the entrance and without the customary booze. Except for one bouncy tune, "I'm Hooked on the Feeling—Oga Chukka," Bea slipped her hips around and toward me, dancing together slowly and intimately, Bea whispered in my ear that this all was fantastic, but it was time to go home and make love.

On Saturday Bea staffed the bookstore so Betty Willing and I could experience Adrienne Rich, her poems and her comments at WWIA. While we waited for her, our poet friend Betty reminded me that she introduced us to the works of two of her favorite poets, Sylvia Plath and especially Anne Sexton with her bitter humor. I had read their books when I was still married, including Plath's autobiographical novel, *The Bell Jar*. The book was too close to reality for me with my mother institutionalized off and on since I've been ten years old, but Plath's book ended with some hope, in contrast to my mother's thirty-five years of being discharged and readmitted to private and state mental institutions. Plath was able to put her emotional experiences and treatment into words and have her book published so others would begin to understand her life, as did Anne Sexton who dared to write about women's experiences in her poems, including menstruation, masturbation, abortion and adultery.

"Both of these geniuses committed suicide," Betty reminded me. "Each suffered from mental illness, each had husbands and children. What more can a woman want?" she joked. "Plath put her head in an oven and died in the early 60s at age 30. Sexton, whose poetry is right up my alley, suffered from depression and did herself in with carbon monoxide about four years ago at the age of 46. These women are our generation, Jan. You have to watch out writing about being unhappy about life and lost expectations and just grin and bear it."

"OK, Betty. You better watch out about yourself as well."

I introduced Betty to our new Milwaukee friend Sue Samira, and she introduced us to her partner, Mary Vella. It seemed as if they were meant for each other with the same dark hair, round, smiling faces and short stature. Sue was exhilarated by her assignment to escort Adrienne Rich from and to the airport and to introduce her to the WWIA gathering. Sue's writings were quoted by Rich in *Of Woman Born*.

"When I met her at the airport, I actually asked Adrienne Rich if I could say in my introduction that she is a lesbian, and I was overwhelmed when she said it would be all right!" I could see Sue's self-esteem in having her own lifestyle affirmed, and her short stature seemed to grow inches taller while Mary chuckled at her partner's sense of accomplishment.

The printed program identified the much-honored poet, scholar, teacher and author only as a feminist, even though she left her husband and has lived with the feminist author Michelle Cliff for two years. Rich had birthed three boys in five years—and now she identifies herself as a lesbian. We had most of her poetry books at Mother Courage but of all her books, I chose to devour her new paperback, *Of Woman Born*. I could identify my own life with her life as a mother and wife. I underlined sentences in almost every paragraph of her scholarly yet personal prose, and I also felt affirmed and empowered.

I took photos as Rich stood back from the podium set on the floor level so she could lean against the front of the stage. She explained that made her more comfortable because of her arthritic pain. She looked tired and drawn. She's only 49, only two years older than I, and in such pain I could almost feel it when she moved.

The audience, sitting in creaky wooden chairs in the old and musty, gravy brown auditorium, hardly made a sound when Rich spoke so quietly or read from her new poems in *The Dream of a Common Language* that was published in April. We had it in our store. I brought my copy with me.

Just as Simone de Beauvoir's book, *The Second Sex,* touched me in the late 1960s, I found Rich's words living in me now. I truly connected with her when she read from "Transcendental Etude (for Michelle Cliff)" that

"Birth stripped our birthright from us,
tore us from a woman, from women,
from ourselves, so early on
...This is what she was to me, and this
is how I can love myself—
as only a woman can love me."

So moved by her, I struggled to assimilate more of her words. Her body, in the black sweater and slacks, disappeared against the dark background, but her tender hands shone white as she used her elbows and arms to support her weight upon the stage behind her. As I stared into her face with her dark eyes and cropped black hair, a spiritual white aura seemed to radiate around her head. Occasionally I looked about me and saw women crying. At times I listened so intently that I was absorbed into oneness, the shared space, the common life of uncommon women.

Putting my mind back to being the journalist, I took notes so I could write a story for a future Mother Courage newsletter. I also jotted more notes when I related my experience to Bea that night.

While Bea went to the WWIA on Sunday, I worked at my typewriter while staffing the store.

"Women need to find their power within"

"We need words, images, music which can tell our truths," said Adrienne Rich in Milwaukee at the fall conference of Wisconsin Women in the Arts.

"Women need words which do not simply reflect or imitate men's subjective fear, envy and hatred of women but which empower women to become the 'active chooser' of the culture we want."

The author of *Of Woman Born: Motherhood as Experience and Institution, Dream of a Common Language*, and more books of poetry was the one who in 1974 accepted her National Book Award in New York by reading a statement by her and two other women nominees promising to support, rather than compete against each other, "in the name of all women whose voices have gone and still go unheard in a patriarchal world."

Speaking to Wisconsin women artists and writers, she said, "This is not the first time in recorded history that the possibility has existed of grasping and ordering a women's culture."

She quoted from a generation ago when Virginia Wolff wrote, "As a woman I have no country; as a woman I want no country; as a woman my country is the whole world." A woman is not a man; her experience is not the same. Her traditions are different; her values both in art and life are her own.

Rich said that this "grasping and ordering a women's culture" is for all women, not just a chosen few.

She explained, "Living as we do in a dominant culture that degrades both our female bodies and our female minds, our creativity and our power, we need to become highly conscious and aware of what we are taking in—absorbing through the senses."

She read from *Motherroot Journal*, a feminist newsmagazine that stressed that women need to know their own minds, to have their own ideas to establish psychological independence from men. "New words and images can do this," she emphasized.

Rich called for support of women's journals and presses through subscriptions and for support of other women-oriented activities to "create our own networks, hear women's music and poetry, see women's art defining women's bodies, create space of our own for discussion and exhibition."

When this is established, "Then we can say 'No' to the culture of male subjectivity and dominance which silents and faults women and pretends to be universal, and say 'Yes' to our collective selves, to the profusion and flowering of female energy, skills and thought which means the spirit of the individual woman."

Women should be aware, she said, of the present power "who makes the decisions as to what shall be visible, who shall be visible, the way in which even the few women are chosen of ability, and, by the selection of their work have their meanings wiped out." She described the "so-called little mags controlled by men" saying that the statement is particularly true that "times change but the avant-garde remains the same."

So, women have been grasping for new power of the press and can move through support of women's cultural channels of communications. Women need "power to be, power to make, power to create; not the stale repetition of the archetype of male power systems, but a power which we invent in which we find in ourselves, and which we now have begun to affirm in each other."

She read poems from her *The Dream of a Common Language* poems to illustrate her concept.

From "Paula Becker to Clara Westhoff," she imagines what Paula would have said to Clara even though Paula died in a hemorrhage after childbirth murmuring "What a pity!"

"…I'm looking everywhere in nature
for new forms, old forms in new places,
the planes of an antique mouth, let's say, among the leaves.
I know and do not know
what I am searching for

…Which of us, Clara, hasn't had to take that leap
out beyond our being women
to save our work? or to save ourselves
Marriage is lonelier than solitude…"

And from "Transcendental Etude" she writes

"…But there come times—perhaps this is one of them—
when we have to take ourselves more seriously or die;
when we have to pull back from the incantations,
rhythms we've moved to thoughtlessly,
and disenthrall ourselves, bestow
ourselves to silence, or a deeper listening, cleansed
of oratory, formulas, choruses, laments, static
crowding the wires. We cut the wires,
find ourselves in free-fall, as if
our true home were the unidimensional
solitudes, the rift
in the Great Nebula.…"

    I staffed the store on Sunday afternoon of the next day so Bea could attend the final WWIA sessions. She limped into our home grumbling and angry when she returned from Milwaukee and the last of the WWIA meetings. Could she have been in a car accident, I thought at first. Maybe she was mugged?
    What she had done was to leave momentarily from the "Where Do We Go From Here" session and go to the women's room. When she opened the door to walk out of the stall, she forgot that the white tile floor of the cubicles was a step higher than the rest of the room, and she crashed down, grabbing for a wire-mesh waste container and landed with it in hand in a clamorous spread-eagle on the ceramic floor. She stood quickly before anyone came running in to see her, regained her composure somewhat while brushing herself off and realize she had twisted her ankle. It was good, she said, she didn't hit her head on one of the basins or she'd have ended up in a Milwaukee ER.

"And I'm even sober. It hurts more when you fall when you're sober."

Bea on November 14, 1978

Jan loved the ring I made for her and I loved making it. When we came home from the bookstore, I made supper and we actually had a glass of wine when Marge came over to wish Jan a happy birthday.

Another gift for her was Jenny's asking her to be the parent involved in her Emerson High School's "Rites of Passage" committee which challenges the seniors to analyze their lives, set goals, make decisions and meet with student colleagues, selected teachers and a parent on a regular basis to check that the student is on the right track for the future. Jan would have been so distressed if Jenny had chosen her dad rather than her.

Matt called and said he'd be home soon from his college in the Black Hills of South Dakota to run cross country at Oshkosh's national race, and he told her he will transfer to Madison for the next semester to be "in a more cultural environment." Having Matt closer to home is another present for her.

We decided to save our dessert of apple pie and ice cream for later and eventually we ate it in bed—and then we gifted each other. WOW!

I wrote my first poem in a long time.

> I am rich beyond measure.
> Your soft body is my pillow—
> Lush cushion of delight—
> Luxury that cannot be bought.
> It's my bonus that comes with love
> For the time when the tide of our passion ebbs
> And you draw a circle around us
> With our love enclosed—
> Our softness mutually comforting.

Mother Courage is doing OK, but that's about it. Customers come by to chat and sometimes they even buy something. Often friends and family stop in and since we joined the Milwaukee Feminist Writers group, some Milwaukee lesbians visit our store.

We're making new friends in Lakeshore Bay, too. One Saturday afternoon we saw a clutch of casually dressed women walking across the street. Then they crossed State Street, tumbled through our door and seemed very happy to see us. Jan remembers two of them from Lakeshore Med, Sarah and Corky whose friends were Marian and Jane. They stayed a long while and we had lots of fun showing them our books and records. We hit it off right away and now they come in often, at least Sarah and Marian do.

I sense women living as couples when they come in, but many are very closeted, except for some of the younger ones and those who come from Milwaukee. Some obviously straight women seem shy about coming in. Do they think we will seduce them?

It's hard to believe a story I heard about a woman who sat in her car for half an hour to get up enough courage to walk into our store. She wanted to read our books, she wanted to support us, but what was she afraid of? That she'd be seen in a feminist bookstore? That she'd actually talk to a lesbian? Or, as Alix Dobkin sings, "They're gonna squeeze ya and tease ya…the leaping lesbians."

Being here is either busy and stimulating or dull.

When it's quiet, I read books. Lots of books. Jan's always busy when she comes in after work or on weekends. She empties the wastebaskets and sweeps the floors, etc. She writes drafts for our *Courier* newsletter and bugs me about writing reviews, which I eventually do. I wrote an entire page on current books about sexual blackmail at home and work starting with the first new and widely read book on incest, *Kiss Daddy Goodnight*. Its author, Louise Armstrong, had placed an ad to find others who had known incest. She was worried that she was the only one who had experienced incest until hundreds of letters poured in from women abused by fathers, stepfathers and older siblings. Using hers and sixteen other women's testimonies, as well as that of experts, Armstrong exploded the many myths surrounding this dreadful, ages-old, well-kept incest secret.

She concluded that the issue of sexual abuse is an issue of the gross abuse of power. The answer is prevention; incest can only happen in secret. This book breaks the silence.

Another book too close to home is *Sexual Shakedown, the Sexual Harassment of Women on the Job* by Lin Farley. The story that emerges is one of sexual blackmail, job insecurity, economic powerlessness, and fear—fear of social stigma and of job loss. She documents cases and demonstrates that beyond the issue of equal pay for equal work, the real goals are equal job security and the right to be free from demands of a trade-off with sex for employment.

I wonder if somebody passes our newsletter on to a certain administrator and if his mind flashes back to all the Lakeshore Med women he's laid—including me.

Jan on November 20, 1978

An HPRW conference sent me to Madison and, incidentally, also to my first strip bar. Almost always open to new experiences, another woman and I and four of our male colleagues were led by one of our lustier PR comrades who was anxious to get into the smoke-filled lounge to watch the show. So, I've seen naked women before, so what. This one dances, too—without being raunchy. I kept quiet about my feminist perspectives, reflecting about what women have done to make a living, to survive throughout history. I wondered if I make as much money as they did. I added to our friendly group banter, enjoyed watching the acts and the others' reactions, my drink, and someone else picked up the tab. I couldn't help but wonder about my Wisconsin hospital male companions. "How yah gonna keep them down on the farm…"

After that conference, I met Matt at his campus co-op on the poor side of State Street opposite from where I stayed in Elizabeth Waters Hall in the 50s with its conservative women's dorm rules. His co-op was one of the ancient frame houses filled with students and hangers-on who seemed quite harmless to a mother's eye. I couldn't believe his "room" that was a closet where he slept on a padded board resting on coat-hooks and shoulder-high shelf supports. His desk, chair and books fit just below. He had to keep the door open to sit at his desk and probably to get air enough to breathe while he sleeps.

In retrospect, I slept in a closet at age five when my mother took in borders and needed my bedroom, but I, at least, had a window. And as a married woman when I "ran away from home" for three months, supposedly to write my novel. I kept that room until I really ran away from home and got my divorce. So, who am I to question Matt's Spartan but innovative living arrangements?

He's tough. While waiting for him to join me, I remembered Matt's adventure with a young adult married couple and their friend, a bachelor who's a white-water rafting guide. They paddled two canoes on Lake Michigan's northern horizons starting in the east from Ludington, Michigan, north and west to his family waiting for him early in September 1975, at Gill's Rock in Door County.

His Aunt Var, Cousin Sona, Sister Jenny, Alex and I waited for several hours at Gill's Rock before we spotted two floating specks on the horizon growing larger as they approached us after six weeks of endurance and adventures on Lake Michigan waters, islands and shorelines. After cheering them in, we loaded their gear onto and into the station wagon and Var's car and drove them back to Greenridge stocked with food for some real home cooking on our two-burner Coleman camp stove.

Matt with a beard now, had grown tall and strong. They devoured everything set in front of them. Stories of their accomplishments and travails made us laugh and cry. Being the Steer Expedition cook, Matt vowed he would never again complain about how his meals were prepared or about the weather. The three older adults respected their young friend's stamina and competence, even if his cooking was sometime raw or overcooked.

"But you never came to the campfire when I hollered for you that our food was ready," he defended himself as he looked at me with new appreciation for my years of keeping him well nourished.

Months later, our Unitarian Universalist "Adventures of the Mind" poster for Matt's talk read, "Matt is your guide to his 1975 "Blazing Paddles Trip" or "How to travel 400 miles at three miles an hour" or "The Steer's Expedition explores Lake Michigan islands" or " How to live for eight weeks on cereal, rice and beans."

The blurb floated above the illustration from *Paddle to the Sea* of a carved object, a Native American man in a miniature canoe on rolling waves. Bea adapted the illustration by adding another person to the first canoe and a second duo and canoe to the poster artwork that Bea and I reproduced to publicize Matt's program.

Matt's lecture and slide show projected his adventures, including being hungry because he was the cook in fair and foul weather and they used up so much energy paddling from island to island. They were, in turn, bitten by bugs, burned and tanned by the sun and plagued by seagulls that never stopped squawking.

(He didn't tell anyone that night how tired and lonely he was. We heard that from his girlfriend, or how much we all missed him. Even Jenny talked about how strange it was being an only child in the family.)

He did talk of watching the reflected lights of the U.S. Apollo and Soviet Soyuz spaceships link in the clear July night sky overhead without light pollution. He enlightened the audience on environmental issues and entertained many adults and youth at our church.

I'm proud of what he accomplished and surprised that Alex and I not only let him go on such a harrowing journey, but also that I seldom worried about him. He must have suffered more that summer than the average 16-year-old American boy. Obviously, that prepared him for other major character-building experiences.

On this night, Matt drove my Toyota back to Lakeshore Bay. He liked the brown Rust-oleum spray paint I used to hide the gray duct tape covering the rusty holes in the once proud auto body.

While he was driving, I could get a good look at him after all these months that quickly turned into a couple years of not being alone with him. Heart to heart, adult to adult, we exchanged potential conflicts with candor and understanding, and I told him my true feelings as well as a long, hidden secret that may have been a beginning element of the end of his parents' marriage.

Where do I start? Asking about him, of course: his degree in geography and filling a foreign language requirement by learning Indonesian, which he loved. Because of smaller Indonesian language classes, he made good friends with well-traveled, interesting people. He was happy and that made me happy too.

When we reached the highway for the long ride home, it was time for me to unload about my job, Mother Courage, his father and my secret.

As he's matured in college, Matt's stopped being frustrated and angry with me about needing to be a professional person, although he's told me that I worked too hard and that I was away from home more than he wanted me to be.

"Remember, Matt, the time you slid on the ice off 6th Street pier trying to save a stranded duck stuck on the frozen concrete? You landed in the ice chunks into Lake Michigan and made it back to shore with your heavy, wet snowsuit and boots. You must have been about twelve then.

"Yah. That was pretty dumb of me." After some contemplative silence, "I could have never made it back."

I shifted my position to help emphasize the point I wanted to make. "I had a day off from work and I drove the station wagon to the back door to unload groceries when you came around the fence dripping wet and freezing. Yes, you could have drowned. And do you know the first thing that crossed my mind after that initial shock? "It's a good thing, Jan, that you weren't at work!" I was doing what a mother and a homemaker does when you almost died—even if I wasn't exactly at home because I was shopping for groceries. If I had been at work, I would have carried such guilt for the rest of my life because I wasn't home to save you. That's what society lays on a working woman, especially one who doesn't really need to work to financially support her family."

"I guess I see what you mean."

"Yet your father and I went to Greece for three weeks and we never called home once to see how you were. Perhaps we naively assumed that because we were U.S. citizens, we could be traced down at any cheap hotel at any island we were on. But I felt no guilt about that until these last few years when you've been the one traveling and I didn't know where you were."

The car flashed by mile markers and familiar intersections when we stopped talking but kept thinking, absorbing what we shared.

"I guess I was the lucky one to be free of having to take care of Dad when you left," Matt said. "It was hard for me being so far away in South Dakota when you left. Being homesick was bad enough. I kept in touch though, and I know that he and Jenny did all right together."

"I chose an excellent father for my children," I responded, "a balanced man, the traditional male image of masculinity as a hard-driving worker. But he became a silent, closed-off person. We had a wonderful life together until I became the mother of his children and he became the Armenian patriarch and American husband, a victim of society's expectations for males. He has high morals for himself—dogmatic even—for his wife—orthodox, proud of us and what we should be—in his expectations. Yet he's liberal and tolerant of others, except me. I wanted to folkdance, play and be spontaneous, but he was always working and when I played at parties, I would feel his eyes staring at me and I knew I would be punished for laughing too loud or for holding on to someone's arm or hugging someone, for not being at his side where the introvert in him needed me. I guess that's now called 'passive/aggressive.' And I hate to say this—but he was boring."

I had to laugh at myself. "Matt, excuse the expression, but you ain't never seen me when I've pulled out the stops and played."

"Oh yes, Mom. I've seen you at folk dancing when you get funky with that "Amos Moses" number in the center of all the teenagers dancing with you. You forgot that. And remember when I was with my girlfriend and came late to the annual Brass Quartette and Sauna Bathing Party—"

My mind went in instant replay.

"You and your sauna buddies were throwing snowballs at each other outside the bay window and you never missed a beat to bend over and grab snow to throw at someone— even after your towel fell off."

"What a shock to see you there, Matt. I don't know where Jenny was. Probably downstairs with the other girls taking a turn in the sauna. I was having so much fun and I looked up into the window and saw you staring down at me just as your father would have done had he been there. Oh well. Remember that we were in the midst of the so-called Sexual Revolution and Open Marriage trends. I must also admit that I did have a puff or two of marijuana once when it was being passed around. That Tom, one of Marge's friends who had cancer, offered it.

"It seemed like our gang," I teased, "became the closest thing to being Hippies inside of the East and West Coasts, minus the hard drugs. But remember, Matt, I have never been with anyone else except your father and Bea. And that's the truth," I said, mocking Lily Tomlin's lisp when she's on *Laugh In*."

"Well, Mom. I guess I've got you beat on that count." After a long pause, "I guess if Dad wanted you to fish and cook bagels and make wine with him, he should have done what you wanted him to do when you wanted him to do it."

"And he began all that bagel and wine making stuff when I wanted to get out of the kitchen and get on with my goals. He was jealous when I was happy with other people and jealous when I was a successful newspaper reporter and PR person. He was sullen and quiet, seething inside with anger if I didn't do what he wanted me to do—and I tell you this so you don't act the same in your relationships. A good man, like the good woman, is empathetic and strong, outgoing yet connected. She or he is responsible to self, to loved ones and to society, and he or she understands how all these responsibilities must work together. Wow, Matt! Where did that speech come from? If I didn't have such a bad memory, I would guess that I read that somewhere. That's a mouthful for you to swallow when you're maneuvering through this traffic."

"What you just said is a tall order, Mom, but you have to remember that I'm from two types of people and that I have a lot of you in me too."

"Oh, thank you, Matt." I touched his arm. "Those are words of advice that I didn't follow myself. I wasn't true to myself when I was with your father because I wanted to keep peace between us, and then I betrayed his trust that I would forever be his—exclusively."

"I guess he'll get over it."

"I don't know. Your grandfather remarked once that Armenians hold a grudge for a long time—and you realize you're a lot of my dad, too—calm and non-judgmental. My dad had a hard life. He knows about people living with the decisions they've made. Remember that joke he told you last year about the squirrel who first had his tail run over by a train and went back to find out why; then he had his head run over by a second train? 'Don't lose your head over a piece of tail,' was his punch line. I don't often hear him tell jokes. He told that one for you to hear.

"Your grandfather loves your dad too, like his own son, and I know that this change in my life hurts my dad too. But now I get to see him every day when I go the bookstore and am closer to him that I've been since I became Alex's wife twenty-five years ago. He likes Bea. He suggested that she take over the sign business, but she'll have none of that, she said."

"How is Bea?" he asked, shifting in his seat after the long time in the same driving position.

"We're doing all right together, really great actually, living in our own home and building up our business that makes us so proud. But there's one problem. Her behavior is changing since she started drinking again at Marge's house. And I'm drinking too, but it doesn't change my personality as much, or at least I don't think so. Maybe it does. But she can certainly change her moods in a flash and for hardly any reason. Then we quarrel. I know I could step back, but I did that with your father, and I promised myself I wouldn't do that again."

"I know," said Matt, turning on to our interstate for home. "I hardly ever heard you and Dad fight, but Jenny and I knew something was wrong."

"I promised myself I'd never let anyone treat me less than an equal again. And I can argue expertly for women's equality if I need too."

"I hope you don't need to argue with Bea much."

"The damn booze fuels the flames. And the lack of customers and Bea's boredom at the store, our worries about money, and more, get to her—and me. This wasn't what I'd planned our lives to be. I counted on both of us having a steady paycheck to count on. And the tension at my work gets me so stressed that I feel that I need a drink when I get home."

"But you're always so cheerful in your letters and you seem to be doing so well with all your awards and accomplishments."

"But it doesn't impress my bosses, just like your dad's reactions when I'd do good at my work. Nick and Randy can get nasty when I stick my neck out as a feminist and promoter of the bookstore.

"Don't ever get too personal with your boss or with someone who could end up being your boss. Randy uses people now. He's a self-centered hustler, a handsome bachelor, you know, like Hurd Hatfield in *The Portrait of Dorian Gray*. You'd have to watch Ted Turner's Classic Movie Channel to see that one. If you did, you'd never forget it. I saw it at the movies in when I was a teen and remember it well."

"How'd Randy get that way?"

"He's Nick Dixon's hit man, and Nick has sided with Alex and is probably homophobic and too unprincipled to stand up for me or any woman, or man either, who dares to disagree with him. To me, these guys both are quintessential male chauvinist pigs. How about that! I feel so much better saying that out loud."

"I can tell, Mom, and in many ways, I agree with you. I never did spend too much time with the Dixon family 'cause of the way Nick talked to his kids and his wife—and I was just a kid and knew that."

"I suppose he could be getting heat about me from his board members and trustees because of my new life, if they even know about it, but I've never felt anything but affirmation, even respect from Mr. Young and the gentlemen on either the Board of Trustees. I believe they really like me. And our old dear friend Marge is pretty much keeping away from us. I'm sure she's afraid she'll be fired too if they imagine she's still our close friend, and she panders herself to men—and don't be surprised if you see her hanging around your dad too, even though at one time he hated her for being my dearest friend and a bad influence on me by being a happy divorcee."

"I won't be surprised to see her with him after all these years. It's easy for Dad to be more comfortable with someone he knows. And maybe he's learned how to talk more with Marge and Pete and that whole crowd that's taking care of him."

"Actually, I'm happy they're taking care of him because I didn't want to hurt you or Jenny or anyone when I left home. I didn't want to hurt Bea either if I didn't leave home to be with her. No matter which way I went, I hurt someone—or hurt me. Who knows what could have happened or what still will happen?"

As Matt turned east to head for home he said, "No one knows, Mom, but you said you had something to tell me from the past."

"Yes. We're running out of time and I better get to this painful secret that happened when you were too young to realize what was going on. When you were four years old, your dad and l lost a baby boy born too early at seven and a half months—like the Kennedy baby boy was lost, and the best doctors in the country treated that infant and they still lost him."

"I lost a baby brother and I never have known about it? Does Jenny know?"

"Yes, actually, I told her when we were in Door County and the topic came up when Ellie said her mother had to stay in bed because she had a high-risk pregnancy. The three of us talked in the barn. It seemed like an appropriate time to finally tell Jenny, and she didn't say much. She's good one about mulling things over in her mind before she makes a decision.

"It hurts me still to talk of it, or even remember it, but I picked myself up and continued on with what I had to do at the time. And now here you are, twenty years old, and I still cry when I think of this loss. That's why I didn't want your feelings to be hurt. I wanted to protect you—and Jenny too, but I knew all along that someday I would have to tell you. And that's one issue that started the rift between your father and me. We never talked about it together. We never shared our grief and he was angry with me because I was in the hospital when they buried the infant at his father's gravesite. And he's been angry about this all this time and finally said so when we were in marriage therapy a couple years back. He said how angry he was about the loss of his son, and that I left him with all the arrangements, standing without me at the brief graveside ceremony. But I was in the hospital. He told the counselors and also me, because I was in the room, that he imagines the boy when he's off fishing—his little son with him."

Matt pulled over to the high school parking lot because we were getting close to home and we still had more to say, but he kept the car running so we'd be warm.

"And we never talked about it, Matt. I did ask him then how he felt, but he just clammed up and turned away, started more classes toward his Master's degree, worked more hours and left me to take care of you both while he was working out all of his computer challenges and traveling for work.

"When I came home from the hospital, a few relatives came to our home but that was so unreal. Some brought flowers that I had to tend to until I could throw them out. It was almost like a routine visit because no one really knew what to say, except that they were sorry. I missed all the minister's words, which could have been comforting, I suppose. I would have preferred reading my own words. And I missed the graveside ceremony with Alex and my dad and Var. Sona was taking care of you two. I never even saw the baby and we never gave him a name—we just had "Infant Carnigian" in the death notices. I don't know if your dad agreed with me, but I wanted to protect us of having to grieve for him each time I heard or read that name.

"When I think about him, Matt, it's not about fishing and all the stuff you and your dad do together. I visualize how disabled he could have been had he lived. Is that selfish? I suppose so. But not only could we have lived with the fear of losing him at any stage of his young and vulnerable life, he could have been mentally defective with physical problems that would have either enriched or crippled all of our lives."

After some minutes of contemplating the power that fate holds over us, Matt put the car in gear and we headed straight east.

"I did share my thoughts about it though. I wrote down what I felt and sent copies to Naz and three friends then. But they didn't know what to say. Var and Sona and my dad didn't know what to say or do either.

"It's appropriate now for you to know. I would have told you before this, but it was never the right time or place to be together and talk about it."

"I'll be thinking about all this, Mom. And always remember that I love you."

He pulled the Toyota into the back yard of our, no, his house. We sat in the car looking across the long, narrow space still covered with ice and snow. He kept the motor running and the headlights shining toward the house, knowing that even if he wanted to, he couldn't invite me in. Nor would I want to go, especially with my heart so sad from the past that I shared with him.

We each took deep breaths as we stepped out of the car to exchange seats so I could drive home. He gave me a gentle yet all-enfolding hug in the chill wind that blew between the houses from Lake Michigan. It felt so good to be held in the strong, masculine arms of my very own adult son. Then he pulled his backpack out of my car and I backed out of the old driveway and parked near the Lake to watch the lake rise and fall, endlessly, calmly, hypnotically, for me to recover a bit before I went to our home to be with Bea.

Jan on November 25, 1978

Thanksgiving yesterday began our first holiday season together in our home. That doesn't count a quiet Halloween after we closed the store. Thursday started off beautifully together with a loving morning ritual of thankfulness, and then we went to Marge's for dinner. She was kind enough to invite my dad who came with his Chico. Ron, who is Marge's favorite fella of all, was there. So was Alice, another lost soul from work and, of course, Marge's mom and her boys. It was a lovely family event and Bea and I drank a token glass of wine for the Thanksgiving toast.

After our meal, we went to the basement den where I played pool with the boys while the others sat around the coffee table stacked with various liquors. Months ago, when Bea checked herself in to the alcohol rehab hospital, Marge had said, "No more good time Bea." Now I kept my eye on them more than on the eight ball and was getting steamed when I felt Marge pushing booze on Bea. After each drink, Bea felt more confident that she could handle it.

Our lives are so beautiful without booze. What is our fucking old friend trying to prove!

The next evening, we had my dad and Matt and Jenny over to our house for another Thanksgiving supper and I offered Dad his favorite Manhattans. Bea had some too, and then me—and the booze leaked back into our lives and began seeping into a flow with time and stress.

Bea arranged to have her kids over for our first supper together last week. I was busy trying to make everything all proper with her mother's chinaware, crystal and silverware on the table, and she cooked what she knew they'd like to eat. It was awkward at first but conversation picked up and everyone seemed to get comfortable. I tried to stay in the background as much as possible. All in all, it was a successful evening that freed them up to be available for their father and friends for the holiday itself.

CHAPTER 11

Bea on December 2, 1978

It's a good thing I assembled our new little Toro snow blower because now we have one driveway and three sidewalks to shovel—one at home and two at the store. And today we start our Christmas hours at the store so we're here weekdays until 8 p.m., Saturdays all day and Sunday afternoons. I get to go home to make us some supper while Jan minds the store until I bring supper back for us to eat. Jan will work on our Christmas newsletter to promote our gift books.

Last night we had to clear the snow in the dark when we arrived home. A depression spilled over me into a flood of emotions. Jan took care of me as usual, but she's getting harassed at work by Randy's assigning tasks she never had to do before, like typing out weekly reports, as if she has to justify her existence there. He also wants Carolyn to turn in monthly reports on our department expenses. And those reports take away hours from doing what needs to be accomplished, so their projects' goals are not being met in a timely fashion, including the next issue of Lakeshore Med's *synergy* magazine with its centerfold calendar and annual report that has to be in the mail by mid-December. She finally finished her latest magnum opus that she's been moaning and struggling over for months, the detailed employee benefits books in a customized

Lakeshore Med folder. Each book has a coordinated, cool, contemporary design and she used employee photos that she took with such loving care. The benefits details almost drove her crazy though, and it's a relief for her to have it distributed and appreciated, at least by the employees.

Carolyn is doing well while learning about the politics of the place. Jan said Carolyn's very brave to take on this job and be supportive of her, but maybe she doesn't know all that's going on with Jan and Randy and perhaps even Nick. But Carolyn can't be that naive. And she has many friends from our church who must have told her our story. Yet she observes everything in their small office and can see how Jan is devastated when she's called to Randy's office to face his relentless, petty grievances. Jan tries not to let others know what she's going through and she tries to protect Carolyn. She's a small woman but a dynamo who is determined to make it—and she doesn't hurt anyone else in the process. "Carolyn is Goddess-sent," Jan says over and over.

Saturday's business was better even when we closed the store at 5 p.m. to drive to Milwaukee for dinner at a Greek restaurant and drank a well-earned glass of roditus with our moussaka. We danced at the Sugar Stop with its haphazard holiday décor and especially casual when the only women in our traditional Christmas tradition are the Virgin Mary and Mrs. Santa. We didn't stay too long because we have to open the store again tomorrow at noon.

I drove home because Jan was too tired. I'm tired too and we still have until the day before Christmas Eve to keep the store open for such long hours.

Jan on December 26, 1978

I made it through Christmas with long hours at the bookstore. I smile now remembering with wonder about a recent trip to Jenny's Thoreau High for her Rite of Passage meeting. I was standing in the school office to check its location when suddenly through the door came Jenny and one of her girlfriends, arm and arm, laughing and singing "Rudolph, the Red Nosed Reindeer" and each was wearing bell-ringing decorated "reindeer horns" clamped on their heads. Happy see her happy, I followed her to her Rite of Passage meeting with four friends including their good-natured woman teacher.

Bea on February 11, 1979

With gale force winds blowing blizzardly snow over factories in the valley to the west of us, even snow crystals blow through the smallest gaps where the front window panes meet the metal connection at the corner. What a struggle to keep the sidewalks clear, but now I have to move the displays around so nothing gets wet and damaged from Mother Nature's forces. You almost need to be a pole-vaulter to get over the snow piled on the curbing. I don't expect any customers today.

I was surprised when a young man jumped out of his van and plowed past Jan trying to shovel the sidewalk late in the day. "That's what we need—dedicated customers," she shouted to him over the freezing wind. He came into the store looking for birth announcements, but that we didn't have. He looked diligently through the store and decided to buy one of our Mother Courage t-shirts. The woman in his life had just given birth to a baby daughter and he judged that our Mother Courage t-shirt was quite appropriate.

After he left I answered a phone call asking for the book *Great Stud Farms of America*—in hardcover, of course.

January's artist Nancy Peters had a solo show opening reception on Sunday, resulting in a gallery full of friendly people who appreciated Nancy's life drawings while savoring wine and cheese. Five drawings were purchased. A husband escorting his wife to the door through the crowd said—with a smile, "I have to get my wife out of here. She's getting liberated just reading the titles."

With very few daily customers, I've been keeping busy drawing a picture of Susan B. Anthony to illustrate our next newsletter and our special February 15 birthday sale in her honor with cake and coffee. All our hardcovers are on sale at forty percent off. I probably should not have bought so many hardcover titles. Live and learn.

From one of our women's almanacs, I found a concise description of Susan B: "A women of indomitable will, spirit and ability, she and her lifelong associate, Elizabeth Cady Stanton, organized petitions, conventions, canvasses and lectures to press for the cause of the vote. Although not a beautiful woman, she was not the ugly, bitter, old maid that masculine ridicule made her out to be. In the 1870s, a St. Louis newspaper conceded, 'She wields today tenfold more influence than all the beautiful and brilliant female lecturers that ever flaunted upon the platform…'"

I like drawing Susan B. Anthony and will offer copies to our customers who come to our party for her. I'll draw more famous women. We'll call them "Women of Courage" and use them to illustrate future newsletters and maybe I'll even make some greeting cards out of them.

We ran out of advertising money months ago. Jan's working hard getting free publicity for the bookstore by researching, writing and submitting commentaries to the newspaper. I hope they print it with my sketch of Susan B. to illustrate Jan's words.

Jan's commentary in *The Bay View Times* on February 15, 1979
"Susan B. Anthony led first wave for women's rights"

(Editor's note: Jan Anthony is director of communications at Lakeshore Medical Center and partner in Mother Courage Bookstore.)

Susan B. Anthony was a woman born on this day, Feb. 15, in 1820 and she had no right to vote. She died in 1906 and still had not gained the "right" but she did vote in the election of 1872 and risked a jail sentence to do so.

On Nov. 1, 1872, she read an editorial in her local Rochester, N.Y. newspaper urging all to register to vote. The editorial said, "If you were not permitted to vote, you would fight for the right, undergo all privations for it, face death for it."

The editorial writer discounted, in light of the time, that "all" could have meant women too. He also discounted that a few women like Susan B. Anthony would have the courage not only to take the editorial at its word but also, with single-minded directness, take the newly adopted 14th Amendment at its word, too. "All persons born or naturalized in the United States, and subject to the jurisdiction thereof, are citizens of the United States and the State wherein they reside…"

The 14th Amendment did not say that "persons" meant only males. The amendment continues, "No State shall make or enforce any laws which shall abridge the privileges or immunities of citizens of the United States, nor shall any State deprive any person of life, liberty or property without due process of law, or deny to any person within its jurisdiction the equal protection of the laws."

The 14th Amendment did not specify the "privileges or immunities of citizens." The truth was that it has been designed to protect the civil rights—especially the voting rights—of recently freed male slaves.

With those editorial and constitutional edicts in mind, Susan B. felt perfectly justified in demanding that the right to vote was a privilege of citizenship that includes women as well as men.

She rounded up her women friends, vouched for their court fees if they should be arrested, dared to enter a barbershop in Rochester to register to vote, did so and did, indeed, cast a ballot with fifteen other women as they voted in the November election of 1872.

Because of this "revolutionary act" of voting, she, as the leader, was arrested along with three male poll inspectors who allowed the women to vote.

The threat of jail hung over her until June 18 when she verbally defied in court the judge who had actually written his decision before the trial started. After fining her $100, he asked if the prisoner had anything to say.

She had remained silent during the feeble court hearings, but then she stood up and in a brilliant and daring speech, she challenged the court and the powers that were depriving her of her fundamental rights as a citizen.

"I am degraded from the status of a citizen to that of a

subject…(as is) all my sex," she exclaimed in her closing statements.

She refused to pay her fine and walked out of the courtroom a free woman. If she had been stopped and sent to prison, she could have appealed her cast to the Supreme Court; to prevent this, the judge allowed her to walk out.

She did pay the fines of the poll inspectors and obtained presidential pardons for them all.

Unfortunately, after her lifelong dedication to gain voting rights for women, she died in 1906, fourteen years before the 19th Amendment guaranteed the women's right to vote.

One woman, Olympia Brown from Wisconsin's history, was the only pioneer suffragette and friend of Anthony who lived through the entire movement. Olympia Brown's daughter, Gwendolyn Willis, proudly wrote about her mother, "All of it she saw and part of it she was."

Unlike the suffragettes who were wives and mothers like Olympia Brown and Susan B.'s dear friend and comrade Elizabeth Cady Stanton, Ms. Anthony stayed a single woman. This made her particularly vulnerable to personal abuse. Her single status was "proof" that her crusade was simply the ranting of an embittered old maid.

Insulting newspaper articles and vicious "battle-ax" cartoons must have hurt her, but she threw herself into her work as she unified the cause of women's rights during the fifty years of the First Wave of Feminism

The new dollar coin, to be released in the spring, honors her with an image from her later years.

She edited her own newspaper: its motto was, "Men, their rights and nothing more; women, their rights and nothing less." One month before her death, she attended her last women's conference and challenged her audience with the message, "Failure is impossible."

Yet even after all these years, failure for gaining equal rights for women does seem possible. Full and equal rights will not be legally secure until the Equal Rights Amendment is assured. ERA's purpose is only to insure that whatever is given or denied men by law should also be given or denied women by law. It says, "Equality of rights under the law shall not be denied or abridged by the United States or by any State on account of sex."

Interpretations of the Constitution will then not be distorted as they were with the 14th Amendment when the First Wave of action started women's struggle for equal rights by law.

In the light of history, the Second Wave of the women's movement is dedicated to completing what courageous women like Susan B. Anthony began.

Yes, failure is impossible. The Second Wave is now.

Bea on April 1, 1979

We celebrated our anniversary yesterday with new friends. Carolyn found amiable Jennifer Findley and Sue Manning at work and brought my Jan into their lunchtime circle. Marge's been avoiding Jan, and Randy is trying to break up the communal women's circle that usually eats lunch. He's even put pressure on nursing administrators to stay away from the group were they used to connect and build a stronger team of nurse managers.

These new gals are fun and comfortable with us so we invited them and Carolyn over for a little party. Many employees gossip that Randy hired Jennifer Findley as the hospital's new patient representative because she's stunningly beautiful with long black hair and a genuine smile, but she's smart, experienced in this field and deserves the job. But she's almost isolated because she trouble shoots for the patients to solve their problems, including those caused by physicians and staff.

Sue Manning drives from Milwaukee a couple days a week to help out in the Social Services department and adds a feminist sense of humor. They come to our bookstore too, so I know them and trust them.

They, like our clinical psychologist friend Rachael Sandler, show no signs of homophobia and we need not be guarded with them. We can air our intimate feelings because they're not like many, including a few mental health professionals who still believe that gayness is a mental defect. Now my Jan trusts people more than I do, especially when I was the one let go by Lakeshore Med administrators because of our relationship. So here we are with our feminist bookstore and "out" to most who know us—probably the only lesbians most people know or talk about.

It's good my parents are dead or they would have disowned me like they disowned my brother. "Where did we go wrong?" would be my mother's guilty concern, especially with both of her children turning out gay. My proud father would hit me in the pocketbook, and both would tell me to jump in the lake like Calvin did off Oak Street Beach in Chicago and drowned in March of '71. Poor Calvin, he even spent some time as a patient in New York City's Bellevue. I heard that cops would raid gay bars and their captives would end up in jail or in a mental hospital. God, how I ramble on; but these frightening memories surface often while I sit here alone in the bookstore in the front with Jan's father napping with his tilted chair against the old radiator in his back office with his dog, Chico, on his lap.

Anyway, after a few drinks, a snack and then supper, we discovered that Sue use Tarot cards in her private practice to open lines of communication with her clients. Just like Rachael Sandler, she's a clinical member of the International Transactional Analysis Association or TA. Rachael was important when Jan and I found each other after we experienced her two intensive church-sponsored TA workshops in November 1973 and February 1974.

Sue's been using Tarot for ten years as a bridge between the intuitive sense and the rational thinking process. The concept appealed to us immediately and we encouraged her to show us how it works using a new Rider-Waite-Smith Tarot deck that we had just brought home from our bookstore.

We were all in a good mood when we gathered in a circle around Sue who chose me to be first. What she did was to have me "smutch" the deck about to give the cards my personal energy and then I was to go through the deck to pick out the card that especially appealed to me. Then she would use that one as the key card and set up a spread of cards to do my reading.

While I searched the deck to pick my card she explained, "All of us have a store of intuitive knowledge about ourselves and others that's not always available in our everyday thinking." I don't know about that, but I did pick out my favorite card—The High Priestess sitting at her throne with a moon in her crown.

Sue laughed, "Of course, you'd pick the unconquered daughter of the moon, like Isis, Artemis, Diana, Lilith. There are some who say this card in the highest and holiest of the greater Arcana set."

"And look!" Jan burst out, "There's a "B" etched in the black column and a "J" etched in the white one. That's spooky. It's for you and me, Bea!"

I should have written down what she said because I was so taken with the idea of having control over patriarchy—Yes! Yes! Through the bookstore! And my High Priestess gown flowed into the stream of consciousness with the books that I have written but haven't been published and with all the reading of feminist ideas that are inside of me. And the "B" and "J" on the Egyptian temple columns. And the pomegranates and the ancient wisdom of the Torah in my lap. I couldn't remember much more. I have hidden power and intuitive perception that will help solve old problems, too. I know that—and the other cards affirmed all that too."

When it was Jan's turn to smutched the cards, it didn't take long to find her favorite, The Fool.

"Ha! This is me! I'm the naive one in yellow tattered clothing oblivious of stepping off of a cliff into who knows what! All of my possessions are wrapped in a hobo bag and a little dog like our Luv is at my side. This is me!"

"Yes," affirmed Sue. "You're the optimist, all right, with the rising sun warming you on your journey, your challenge. I can just see you walking down the halls of Lakeshore Med, fresh and trustworthy while your Inquisitors are plotting ways to getcha. Only the dog is warning you of danger. You are the dreamer stepping off into thin air, yet you will be able and successful because you just start it and learn as you go along."

"That's Jan, all right," said Carolyn with her affirming smile.

Somewhere in Jan's card of influence was The Hierophant representing dogmatism, strict conformity to institutionalized rules and regulations, the ultimate of "What will others think? I really don't give a damn."

I saluted the reading. No future reading for us, our first, can ever be as good as this. And we opened up another jug of wine.

Jan on July 6, 1980

A four-page document on "Appeal Procedure" from Lakeshore Med's Human Relations was distributed to all supervisors on July 1. I shared mine with Carolyn and we decided that our department's informal, on the spot, problem-solving procedures were ideal. I had to laugh at the Procedure's Purpose: "It is important that your problems and complaints be handled in a fair, equitable manner consistent with hospital policy. It has always been the intent and practice of the hospital to insure that employees with problems receive a fair hearing."

Where do I turn? My boss torments me and my long-time dear friend Marge doesn't see me anymore because she's my ex-husband's traveling companion and now heads the Human Relations department.

I called the Equal Employment Opportunity Commission and a man named George Thomas put me off from making an appointment until I had accumulated more written evidence of prejudice and abuse. I finally made an appointment and went into this imposing federal building and, after a rickety elevator ride, I found his office.

Our meeting didn't take long. He pointed out that harassment because of homosexuality is not considered a grievance and he handed me a document.

"Subject: Employment Practices under Federal Civil Rights Acts, September 1979, Memorandum #75: Court Rules Homosexuals not Protected Class under 1964 Civil Rights Act. The case of De Santis, et al. v. Pacific and Telephone and Telegraph Company, et al, arose in May '79 when two guys were discharged from the Happy Times Nursery after two years of service because one wore a small gold earring to school. "

(Our Lakeshore Med's chaplain hired a handsome young red-haired assistant who wore a gold earring in one ear and he told hospital staff, including me, that it's part of a ship crew's rite of crossing the Equator twice, or something like that—and he was believed that or ignored it.)

All the other men and two women, a couple, listed in the document because of their homosexuality and harassment by co-workers and supervisors, had their charges rejected. The appeals court held for the employers.

George also gave me a two-page flow chart of the compliance process and said it would take his office 180 days to file and 300 days for the state office to decide.

When I asked him if I could file charges of sexual harassment because my immediate boss had sexual relations with my lesbian lover while she was intoxicated. He just looked at me and snorted quietly, shaking his head in disbelief.

Jan on October 13, 1980

We headed for Milwaukee's Red Roof Inn to see what the Woman-to-Woman Conference was all about. It's grown from a small session at their YWCA in 1975 to hundreds of women participating this year. We had so many choices of workshops what to attend and plus vendors with products to appeal to women or with organizations to recruit us.

Bea went to Rachael Sandler's workshop and I went to a writers' workshop and was frustrated by the shallow topics the panel of authors wrote about, especially the fancy-hatted, bejeweled woman who wrote romance novels and is quite successful, I guess. After their talks, I asked the panelists if any of them made a living by their writing. One of the freelancers said yes, and the romance novel lady said she had a husband who supported her so she didn't need to "make a living" with her writing.

Our Lakeshore Bay Network friends planned to have a drink after at the cocktail lounge, but we were to meet Rachael who insisted on meeting us. While waiting for her, we had a drink with our Network women, especially our UU friend Robin Witte, and we celebrated the strength of purpose that we shared from all of the electrifying woman energy surging through us for the entire Saturday.

I just wish we could generate more energy for Bea at Mother Courage.

Rachael found us and directed us to a quiet corner for our second round of drinks, but she had an agenda as she described a serious problem as a school psychologist, a problem that everyone in her field has, and she has an idea that requires our expertise. She wants to write a book for children to relate to so she can help them talk about being abused. There's nothing like it on the market, she said, and she wants Bea to illustrate it and me to edit, design and publicize it.

Abused children and adults do not talk about it. They keep it a secret as if it is their fault. Bea knows about that. And Rachael thinks the three of us can open up lines of communication and free the abused from the nightmares they keep inside. She'll write it; she almost has it finished.

"No. We can't do that. We don't have any money," was Bea's immediate response.

"We'll split the cost three ways."

"That's one way for you and two ways for us," Bea replied. "Mother Courage isn't making enough to barely support me let alone pay the cash I give to my daughter to sit at the store each Saturday. It's a good thing we don't have to pay rent."

"Wow!" I said with brilliant phrasing. "I work with a good printer for the hospital."

"That's what I mean," Rachael explained. "Bea can do great illustrations and you know all about PR. I have the credentials and know what to say in simple terms that a child would understand.

What a team we could be!"

"Jan! We can't afford to do this and I can't do the illustrations. How does one illustrate child sexual abuse, for Christ sake?"

Knowing she wasn't going to get anywhere with today's meeting, Rachael asked us to mull it over. We shared a few stories and left for our homes. But I knew this wouldn't be the end of this. Rachael knows how to get her way.

Jan's commentary in *The Bay View Times* on October 25, 1981
"New light cast on witch burning: Suppression of women's rights?"

(Editor's note: Jan Anthony is director of communications at Lakeshore Medical Center and partner in Mother Courage Bookstore (The article included a headshot of me and a large illustration from a book of a woman tied to a ladder and being catapulted into flames.)

They'll be "burning witches" in West Town this Halloween, according to a news story in *The Bay View Times* on October 15.

Now I'm all for Halloween celebrations: I celebrate whenever I can. But before someone sets a torch to West Town's pyre, I'd like to cast some additional light on what witch burning really means based on research from newly published perspectives on historical documents.

Unfortunately, very few witches were left behind to tell the tales of their persecution. Also, unfortunately, some of the remaining traces of witchcraft put women with a devious lot as "bewitching, enchanting and charming" in feminine ways or a wart-nosed old crone flying across the harvest moon on a broom.

Those feminine adjectives, "bewitching, enchanting and charming" were fearful words in the past which, when directed at a woman, could have meant her excruciating, painful death.

The woman could have been a healer, a pharmacist, a midwife, an independent woman who spoke her mind.

She could have appeared in a man's dream and, if in his fantasy, she extracted from him his vital fluid, that dream could actually end with her slow burning at the stake.

In 1484 a Bull of Pope Innocent VIII authorized two monks to write the *Hammer of Witches* or *Malleus Maleficarum*, one of the most infamous instruments ever fashioned for the persecution of a class, the class being women, and the instrument, this handbook defined what witches did, how they were alleged to do it, how to try them, and how to sentence them.

One might argue, though figures are hard to pin down, that this book was responsible for more than five million executions from the date of the book until the end of the 17th century.

Witchcraft was a woman's crime. The ratio of women to men executed has been estimated from 20 to 1 to 100 to 1. The men who were convicted of witchcraft were often in the family of convicted women witches or were in positions of power that conflicted with those of the established power of the church, monarch, or local dignitary.

One writer has estimated the number of executions at an average of 600 a year for certain German cities—or two a day "leaving out Sundays."

Nine hundred witches were destroyed in a single year in the Wurtzberg area and 1,000 in and around Como. At Toulouse, 400 more were put to death in a day. In the Bishopric of Trier in 1585, two villages were left with only one female inhabitant each.

Who were the witches and what were their crimes?

Three central accusations emerge repeatedly in the history of witchcraft trials throughout northern Europe.

1. Witches were accused of every conceivable sexual crime against men. Quite simply, they were accused of female sexuality.

2. They were accused of being organized; they met in secret societies. Supposedly there were occasions for non-Christian worship rites. Undoubtedly the meetings were also for trading herbal lore and exchanging news. In this male-dominated society where

women were assigned to guild-ridden and subservient roles, no wonder they met secretly among friends even if they feared death upon discovery.

Some writers speculate that those women were involved with peasant rebellions of the time.

3. Witches not only were accused of murdering and poisoning, sex crimes, and conspiracy—but also of helping and healing.

Witch-healers were often the only general medical practitioners for the peasants who had no doctors and no hospitals and who were bitterly afflicted with poverty and disease.

They were wise women and to the peasant, the witch was often the healer; to the power structure, she was a tool of the devil.

It was especially as midwives that these women offended the established church. The Hammer of Witches warned that no one did more harm to the church than midwives. Since the church enforced "The Curse of Eve" by refusing to permit any alleviation of the pain of childbirth, it was left to the witches to lessen the pain and the death rate as best they could.

This brief comment on the shocking era of history is only one vivid example of the extension of "Eve's Curse" and the persecution of those who dare to change or eradicate that myth.

The extension of this suppression affected all our lives today because our culture accepted as part of family life the precepts that women are to be subservient to men: as sexual beings, as political persons, as helpers and healers.

As we work out our today's moment in history, we have new resources that tell us more of the history of women and hour it truly was, and at this Halloween time of the year with the so-called "burning of witches," we may find ourselves wondering to what degree the suppression of women's rites has actually been the suppression of women's rights.

Jan on January 21, 1982

Last week, Carolyn and Bea went with me to our first Bill Campion's Job Forum in Milwaukee. Campion donates his time to helping people network for jobs and improve their careers. This session, "Executive Job Search," showed us how to write a superior résumé. The meeting room in the bank's basement seated an impressive number of sixty people who learned about Campion's workshop via the job hunters' grapevine. All are welcome. There's no fee.

I was the only one who wanted to return, and when the topic came to improving employee-employer relations, participants were supposed to tell your boss where you stand without blaming "him" for being inconsiderate, unresponsive, prejudice, etc.

Someone said, "If you blow up and tell him he's a boor, a chauvinist and that you're also underpaid, you're likely to lose your job—and you won't even have told him why you're angry."

Another added, "If you swallow your anger and suffer in silence, it may fester, turn inward and affect your job performance anyway.

"It may affect your health, as well," the speaker said. "It's important to express your anger, but without losing control. One way to stop letting it build until it's unmanageable, the other is to express it in 'I' messages, instead of 'you' messages, like 'I feel frustrated when—'" And Campion joked, "It works with husbands, too."

He continued, "If you store anger for too long, you're likely to become accusatory, even destructive. If you shelve it, anger can affect your health, your personality, your job performance and your marriage."

Several in the audience spoke up with question and answers, and as usual, I come to these sessions assuming that no one knows me and I may as well gain as much as I can from the experience. I raised my hand, breathed deeply and asked, "What do you do if you have so much rage that you can barely talk with the boss, let alone think of 'I' statements. Our anger at each other has been going on too long."

The speaker asked, "What has happened that there's so much built-up anger?" He should not have asked that question. He could have encouraged me to stay after the meeting to talk privately with him.

I couldn't speak. What do I say in front of this group? That I'm a lesbian? That my boss, in his position of authority, fucked my intoxicated lover? That he unjustly fired her, leaving me as the sole income-provider for our survival together. That he has been trying to make me so unhappy that I'll quit working with the people I truly care about, find a job elsewhere and start all over again? I didn't dare speak the name of where I worked. I'm its PR person and I must only present a favorable picture of my hospital. And I am a lesbian.

I stood, silently waiting for my answer to come in judicious and inspired words that would be accepted by all these strangers. Nothing came except tears. Choking and nauseous, I gathered my belongings and left the room, sobbing in my car until I could pull myself together to drive home in the night.

It's too painful. I can't go back there again.

The Bay View Times Columnist Frank Bower on February 25, 1982

In a relatively conservative west side church there recently arose a considerable clamor. For the final hymn of the day, the congregation was asked to sing the word "people" instead of "men."

Musical purists argued that the substitution had two syllables and did not even fit the tune. Others objected to the principle of the thing. And a few doubtless, smiled in triumph as they sang.

It is nothing new in American religion that, like everything else, has been gradually offering concessions to feminist pressures.

The topic is volatile. As Jan Anthony notes, "People are hostile both ways and it is difficult to express beliefs without risking anger. But I conceive of God in personal ways, not as a man, and I would like to see God referred to with neutral pronouns."

I personally queried four feminists who were split on whether sexist language should be changed in hymns or the scripture.

One said, "I'll march against rape or argue equal pay for equal work, but Hey—leave the classics alone! Changing the words in a hymn would be like painting clothes on da Vinci's nudes."

But Betty Hannamen makes this point, "Language is so vital because it influences your thinking patterns. And how you deal with religious ideals is important. The way you feel about God shapes your thinking. Therefore, we need to re-shape our language conditioning. At present, all religions are male-oriented."

Hannamen recognizes there is a reluctance among women to change. "You're caught," she comments, "because you can't stand to part from your old thinking. What you have to do is step back and look at the issues from a distance. For our children, it is crucial that we change. And for our own self-image, when a woman sees there is no way to change something, she should go her own way and start over again."

I found many normally serene persons outspoken in one direction of the other on this very sticky subject.

Please pass the hymn/her book.

Jan Anthony's *Bay View Times* Commentary on March 20, 1982

(The newspaper's bold-type headline, quoted over many other possible choices in this essay, surprised and shocked even me when I opened the Opinion Page. I like the bio info better than the headline. Oh well. So it goes. I bet I got lots of readers on this one but no one, so far, has talked to me about it—one way or the other. The paper printed my photo but omitted my Lakeshore Med position and Mother Courage Bookstore's name.)

Jan Anthony is a partner in a downtown bookstore that specializes in women-oriented books and women artists' works. She says the church could be a leader in a movement toward equalizing the status of women.

"Erase fathergod Image"

Many dedicated persons are searching for a common language that equalizes women's places in society instead of the present language system that ignores women's existence.

People need a language that tells the truth of women's intelligence, courage, endurance and power leading to equality in a male-dominated world. Words are needed that elevate women from the subordinate position reflected by the use of the generic "he" standing for all persons and in the language symbolizing all gods as masculine.

A recent Frank Bower's column headlined "Altering hymns to please feminists a sticky subject" may be a faltering step toward some awareness of this issue, but it was just a superficial beginning of a subject that needs more clarification.

What more meaningful way to begin to equalize the status of women than at a spiritual level—the base of meaning? What better way to use the enlightened leadership of thoughtful people to erase the stern, judgmental fathergod image created by primitive male mythmakers in their need to answer religious/power questions of their time and sustained by resulting anti-female traditions across all major cultures and world religions?

Think about it.

Humankind's earliest artifacts consistently showed reverence and awe of the female—her body was the source of life. She bled painless in rhythm with the moon; her body miraculously made people; she could draw from it both female and male children. Then she would provide food for her young by making milk.

Her body itself was a living symbol of the major experiences of life.

Paternity was not recognized for a long while. In primitive cultures, copulation was not usually associated with the miracle of new life. After males discovered their biological part in the process, women were forced into possession rituals like marriage to sustain the property rights of sons.

This father-right not only established an institutionalized oppression and/or dependence of women; it also created in most religions a set of rituals to supersede and subvert what women did naturally; a religious one-upmanship that has lasted for centuries.

For example, in Christianity the right of baptism subordinated the awe of birth; communion superseded loving food/breast nutrients; life after death judgments supplanted maternal love that accepts children trustingly and without exception.

This overpowering generated by male-dominated religions not only usurped women's place as a spiritual being, it devastated women's emotions and physical well-being.

Centuries of rites to "purify" women and to break down their reinforcing sisterhood networks have mutilated and murdered women.

Though outlawed by the British in 1829, millions of Indian wives of all ages were burned along on their husband's funeral pyres in the "custom" of the Indian suttee. Today Indian widows, even those in their teens, starve to death; young wives are burned to death in "kitchen accidents" or "dowry murders" if they fail to bear sons or if their parents renege on their daughter's dowry money; women die in childbirth from filthy, destructive methods of delivery.

In China, the thousand-year-long horror of foot-binding crippled millions of girls to become marriageable and sexually desirable to Chinese males. They were made physically dependent and distrustful of their mothers and sisters who were forced by their masters to repeat the torture they endured.

To purify the church from sexual impurity supposedly caused by women, the church directed the burning of an estimated nine million European women accused of witchcraft during the 15th, 16th and 17th centuries.

The leap from Eastern, Oriental, African and European history of oppression of women to today's Western concepts on the subject is easy to make when women continue to be dominated by fear of physical violence in the streets and at home or by indifference or misunderstanding by many of their medical and psychological needs.

And, rather than take the lead in elevating and educating the women who are the major supporters of religious principles, the established church powers continue to cause women harm by the denial of their true self-esteem and of their potential as full human beings.

What harm would there be to "mutilate" a few pages in hymnbooks to neatly rephrase our praise to all people. It's such a small step in the healing of the mutilation of centuries of women.

As more women every hour become more aware and highly conscious of what has been and is happening to them, changes will have to be made toward a truly universal truth and equality for all. The church could lead that movement.

"Mankind" can be humanity, human beings or people.

"Brotherhood' can be friendship, unity, kinship, community oneness, companionship.

"Faith of our fathers" could be of our forebears.

It's easy to do such a simple step to reorder a new spiritual value system for all that celebrate the godliness within us all, that enhances rather than diminishes, that unifies rather than isolates.

Hopefully in some enlightened churches in our communities, some members will be able to sing back to the angels on Christmas Eve, "Peace on earth, good will to all people!"

And it will mean so much more.

Jan on March 21, 1982

I can only imagine what went on in Nick Dixon's office.

"Randy! You've got to get rid of her! Jan's really an embarrassment to me. She's gone too far, that damn lesbian feminist witch. This is the last straw." Nick slapped the folded newspaper down on his desk. "Writing a letter to the editor *to erase the Father God Image!* For Christ sake, can't anything traditional be safe anymore without some feminist like her bitching about it? Get rid of her, Randy, but be careful that she can't find grounds to go to court for harassment or discrimination. This could be a test case for new legislation now that more women are trying to sue."

"I've already called her and she's on her way down to my office now. I don't think she'll try to take us to court because she has so much to hide, being a lesbian and all. And she's written this heresy, her commentaries to the paper, her lifestyle—her negative attitude about us. It sets a bad example for the employees, especially the women."

A surprised Nick asked, "She has a negative attitude about us?"

"You can't tell? She seems loyal to the hospital, but she's not loyal to me anymore, that I know."

"Listen Randy. Don't you hire any more Unitarians. And don't you become a Unitarian either! We have enough of them and they are nothing but trouble. They are! Jan's inflammatory commentary is about the worst example of what can happen. She took on the whole Goddamn Christian community—and men! It's a good thing she left out her hospital title and only identified herself with that damn bookstore! Jesus Christ! I feel sorry for Alex."

<<<>>>

On my way to Randy's office, I stopped to confide in Nursing Supervisor Donna Durand who manages over three hundred nurses. "I don't like feeling that I'm going to see the principal to be punished whenever Randy interrogates me alone in his office. It's demeaning. I'm a professional. He spends hours grilling me and makes me stammer and tremble. When it's over, I can't wait to get back to my desk. I refuse to cry in front of him."

"It's obvious that he wants you to be so unhappy" Donna empathized, "that you'll leave even though you have good working relations with everyone else."

"It's counterproductive. It's toxic and it's making us all sick."

"He wants you out with a vengeance, Jan. And he's getting like that with other women now too, including me. And some men, too. He's tangled with others in some nasty exchanges in meetings over the most minor details. I never imagined we'd have to endure that."

"You'd think top administration would have enough insight to accomplish so much more in a better way." I looked to see if anyone else could hear. "They're terrible. But like Bea asked me, 'What do you imagine? There's some Utopian-type place out there? Why should you trust people and be good and kind all of the time.'"

"It wasn't like this before. Is this the real world now?" shrugged Donna.

"It doesn't have to be. Thanks for listening and giving me strength." I stood, smiled half-heartedly and left her office.

"Hang in there, Kiddo," she urged.

Walking to his office, I remembered when Randy and I were friends and officemates, when we shared too many intimate details of our lives. "I'll never do that again in the workplace," I vowed to myself. "I'm a real threat to him, speculating about his sexuality while I'm being honest with him about Bea and me. It costs me not only mental agony now when he reams me out, it also costs at least $10,000 a year lost in salary compared to what my peers are getting. And almost every time I look at him I remember Bea and how he fucked her late that night when she was drunk—and he never said a word to her after, completely diminishing her—and me too.

"Shit! If I try to find other jobs, he'll find out. I'm now on the outside of decisions made around here. I'm afraid I will lose my job and become a bag lady. How will I support us?"

I entered his office where he sat with his back to window and strained to see his face in a shadow. The sunlight's glare around his head gave me double vision. Key words he's used in the past, "Stupid" and "Tacky," kept surfacing in my mind, distracting me in my rage.

"Sit down," he ordered. "I've trusted you, Jan. You let me down—again, and you went too far. You have caused great distress and damage to our hospital."

"What specific thing did I do now?"

"What did you do! You pushed us too far this time when you wrote that last commentary. For Christ sake, Jan. We live in a Christian community. You and your radical feminist opinions have put me on the block again. Nick's received calls from Board members and he's riding me hard again because of you."

"I would have thought you two hospital administrators with your liberal humanism would welcome an awareness that the church could be a leader in fostering women's equality. I wrote the commentary; the editor wrote the headline." (i.e. 'Erase Fathergod image', a call for gender-free language in traditional religions.)

"But the editor took those words from your writing."

"From several hundred words that addressed more spiritual, tolerant intentions."

"So you say, Jan. But you challenge too many traditions that others still cherish, even revere. You have to shut up with all this feminist ranting and keep a low profile—unless you are supporting this hospital."

"A low profile? You mean when you counseled me to get a less visible occupation months ago, and when I suggested being a lady bus driver, you agreed."

He turned his back; it seemed as if to collect his feelings while I imagined what he may be thinking. *"I can feel her eyes staring at the back of my head with hate for me. I should have kept my penis in my pants when I had Bea that night. I didn't think anything of it. I'd wanted her for a long time. So what. She was drunk. I thought she'd want me like other women do. I suppose I should have fought for their rights when I was told find a reason to fire Bea when they bought a home together. I should have given Jan a raise. I should have treated them as I would have wanted to be treated if I had the courage to be true to myself as they are true to themselves and to each other. This woman is defiant! Women must not defy. Well, that's enough pity-party for today."*

It took forever, sitting, waiting, watching him, holding back my anger. I could endure the silence no longer and spoke out. "I have the right as a private citizen to air my opinions."

His body lunged across his desktop. "Private citizen, you say! Jan! You work for me! Freedom of speech? Not when you step out of bounds again like you did with that burning of witches tirade on Halloween, and take up other controversial causes—and now—to challenge our community's religious beliefs. Jesus, Jan. How can you be so stupid!"

I actually stood up to leave before being dismissed. Randy stood too, to confront me—but he was surprised at being speechless while I gained the confidence in knowing, "If he fired me I would be free to tell everything about him—or take him into court."

"Don't stand up to me," he declared, trying to stare me down. I turned and walked out. I realized then when I passed that I'm taller than he is. And he may have realized that too.

Returning to my office, I recalled researching and writing on feminist issues, practicing gender-free language, reading books like Mary Daly's *Gyn/Ecology: The Metaethics of Radical Feminism*. Randy's remark about my Halloween newspaper commentary on burning witches made me ask Carolyn, "Do you know what a prick is?"

My colleague looked surprised and laughed, "Of course I do."

"But I mean the real pricks. The first pricks. Where that word actually comes from."

"Well, I can say that hasn't crossed my mind."

"Pricking was the favorite technique used by witch hunters during the Burning Times in Europe. A pricker would stick a three-inch awl into an accused witch's flesh to locate a Devil's Mark on her body. The pricker would probe for a numb spot where the pricking would, supposedly, produce no pain—a definite sign of the Devil's connection."

"Of course, Jan, and an innocent woman ends up with lots of deep holes all over her."

"But some of those prickers would use a trick where a

retractable blade gets hidden in the handle and, Ah Ha!" I stabbed the air, "The prickers find a painless spot and the victim gets tortured even more to plead her innocence and finally dies. That's how I feel when I have to deal with that prick Randy."

"Oh my dear. Why do you have to take that over and over again."

"What can I do? I have to survive. I'm dealing from fear. Do I wait for him to okay my plans or do I get it in the neck for not taking the initiative. Instead of direction, all I get from him is criticism—and harassment."

"Jan, you've always backed down to keep the peace and you're always turning the other cheek—and you don't deserve it."

"Why do I sit there so long? I'm immobilized. But today! Carolyn! You'd be proud of me! I finally stood up and walked out. All these years I've somehow avoided abusive power. When I was a kid, I'd stay away from home, hang around other families because of my family's craziness. I've used every way I could to move out from under my husband's power over me. Now I have to endure this."

"I hate to see you go through this again." Carolyn paused. "What's behind his behavior? What anxiety is he avoiding? What could it be? Insecurity?"

"Yes. Insecurity. Anyone who wears two pairs of socks has to have a lot of insecurity."

"Two pairs of socks?"

"Yes, and long underwear, too. All year long. I know that from being in the same office when he was an intern. He'd hike up his feet and lean back in his chair and I could see the gap between his pants and his shoes. See, Carolyn, I know stuff about him that could hurt him. He joked with me about relationships with women—implying that he has to have a woman almost every night" and almost whispered, "perhaps to prove that he's not gay."

Carolyn answered in a hushed voice, her hand up to her mouth, "That has to be it."

"All the stories he told me then about his relationships, using pretty young women as sex symbols to broadcast his virility—and without any sign of loving them—or respecting them. Pawns, pawns, pawns. That's what women are to that Super Stud! And now, after these six years, he must be jealous that Bea and I are building a good life together . . ." My voice grew hoarse, ". . . after he fires Bea because we live and love in the same house." I pressed my pointed finger on my desk blotter pad like a judge's gavel. "And then he has Chuck move in to his apartment! Chuck! His immediate subordinate. Talk about double standard. Flaunting Chuck, his clone. Chuck who copies Randy's body language."

I could feel my temple veins pulsed and I slumped into my chair. The phone rang and Carolyn answered it. Staring out the window, I wondered, "How much longer will these pricks keep us—and other women—down or put us in more jeopardy."

CHAPTER 12

Jan on April 1, 1983

In 1978 when we bought our home and imagined our future together, we went to a lawyer and signed partnership papers for us two as Mother Courage Enterprises: First, I was to stay at my hospital for a stable income and she'd manage the bookstore full time. And, despite being a lesbian, I would prove that I was still the best hospital PR person and a worthy human being.

For the first year or so our plan succeeded until our bookstore dream became a nightmare for Bea. Two major chain bookstores moved into Lakeshore Bay's new shopping center.

Bea hired her daughter to free us on Saturdays. Jill probably made more cash from the salary her mother gave her than her mother earned at the store, plus Jill had quiet hours there each Saturday to study for her college classes.

When Bea was a teenager, she imagined being a Christian missionary. I once heard her say, "Now I'm a feminist storefront mission where women just come to chat." Mother Courage Bookstore was intimating—unlike other bookstores. Our books could motivate women to live without compromising, and that's scary. If a woman did come in, she'd see our biographies about feminist warriors, techniques that encouraging her to assert herself and even defend herself from violence.

She may look at us and wondered how and why we screwed up our marriages—and what about our children?

Lesbians appreciated us but we had to trust our instincts to find them. Are they out, partnered, single, deeply closeted—or are they straight but look like lesbians.

My "gaydar" sends out reliable rays to reveal women-identified-women and invite them to join us in our new lesbian rap group.

"But how do you identify for sure?" Bea challenged. "And if we approach a woman and make that mistake, she may never come back and start rumor of our trying to tempt them into our lifestyle."

"Okay. Let's start with the lesbians we know and get them to join us. Like recruiting lesbians to enter our secret society."

About a dozen young professionals, nurses, teachers came to our home, including a young nun who listened but didn't talk about her life. Once she left the circle and I found her in our back yard crying. She left and didn't come back. We lasted for more than a year until a few had change jobs and moved away, but some are still good friends.

Bea on April 7, 1983

I remember being bored and worried about our survival, then we finally ran out of money, yet Jan and Rachael forced me to partner with them. Rachael gave us two pages of her handwritten words for her children's sexual abuse therapy book, *Something Happened to Me*. Accepting the inevitable, now as a partner, I became the manager and accountant and shipping clerk. I had to carry heavy boxes of books to fill our orders, some even to other countries. I tried not to get edgy when the other partners ordering me around.

Rachael's simple text was written from a child's point of view. We created the first sexual abuse book that had illustrations of real children, not teddy bears or sad stuffed rabbits or whatever—and I did the illustrations! It's my cover that gets them with a drawing of an unhappy young girl with long hair covering her drooping shoulders and holding her hands in her lap. Jan designed the book. Each page isolates a different child, but the white spaces change with the child and adult who listens and empathizes, understands and, hopefully, helps them heal.

One older woman who read it came in the store and thanked me. She'd been abused as a child, revealing that for the first time to me. She said she could talk about it now and would find a therapist.

Jan sent *Something Happened to Me* out with media releases to professional journals, appropriate newspapers and magazines. Soon the three of us celebrated this successful project that helped so many, including us as Mother Courage Press. Her marketing sense made Shakti Gawain's affirmation our reality. Jan says it almost every day, "This or something better is now manifesting for me in totally harmonious and satisfying ways for the highest good of all concerned."

Then other authors writing about sexual abuse started submitting manuscripts. Mother Courage Press expanded with the success of *Something Happened to Me.* We took on other topics and our book list grew. We started displaying those books in a booth at the American Booksellers Trade show (ABA). Our booth drew so much attention that other small presses asked to be placed next to us. Every year, Down There Press won the prized place and staffed its booth with playful people selling illustrated adult books and interesting toys.

Jan on April 28, 1984

Bea hit the mark when she wrote a comprehensive nomination of me for Accent on Women's Communications of the Year Award. Connie Firston of our UW's Wo/Men's Bureau (It used to be Women's Bureau until the Bureau got complaints about having bias towards women's issues.) called to tell me of the honor and that she was happy for me. It's the first year awards are being presented from over fifty nominations for five categories in three counties and will be presented on May 4.

Carolyn and I've been up to our ears with Lakeshore Med's Family Fitness Run promotion, scrub shirt orders and unexpected details for May 12, and we're expecting St. Agnes' to throw us a curve on our participation for their health fair. Then St. Agnes finally responded to tell me that our invitation to the fair "must have gotten lost in the mail." so we will continue to plan our Lakeshore Med presentation at St. Agnes' Health Fair.

Carolyn volunteered to join our show-stopper tradition. Her petite and vivacious self will be this year's Cabbage Patch Doll who will walk about St. Agnes to promote free popcorn to eat while watching our own hospital's TV program. She follows in the footsteps of Pam Holmen as Miss Piggy two fairs ago and me as Big Yellow Bird as last year's comic characters. The popcorn aroma that permeates St. Agnes hallways comes from the nostalgic, red-striped tall popcorn wagon that we rented and rolled into St. Agnes. Laura Williams is always the TV star and emcee and I made this year's popcorn. To control any clutter or spills, the free popcorn was given only to those who entered our showroom, sat down and watched our entertaining and educational TV programs.

With all that going on, Randy called me to his office at 3:30 on Monday and told me that my salary compensation will be cut by ten hours a week. And he knows that I won't stop working and step away from my team and my commitments. Rather than submit to his scathing recrimination of my situation, before I left this meeting, I said that in the future I will require an associate to accompany me in all future meetings with him. He was surprised, but he agreed. Perhaps he doesn't expect to meet with me again.

Of course, all this affects Carolyn too, who always waits for my return with apprehension. She said, "Oh Jan, I wonder when he'll drop the other shoe." We know that his clone Chuck, who's now the marketing director, will not pick up the myriads of details that we accomplish for each project to be successful.

Again, I was crushed until I came home to tell Bea that I was losing a fourth of my income, but during our cocktail time she immediately started coming up with solutions. We will stay positive and after supper we lit our backyard fire and savored one of our anniversary party gifts waiting for us right now, a bottle of Korbel champagne.

Bea on April 29, 1984

What a great evening! The next morning, I felt glorious because spring has begun with the warm shining sun.

We drove to our UW's computer fair, explored various computer displays and watched our professor friend Max Morrison demonstrate the Macintosh. Jan was impressed and as dazzled as I was. We didn't waste much time going to our Mac vendor. I'd done my homework earlier and knew the Mac would be pricey but, after talking and dealing, we bought the Lisa II 512K—Mac capable. My heart was pounding when I wrote the check.

Lisa arrived on Monday! Big boxes came to our home and Joe began to set up the system. I was filled with excitement and trepidation. Can I make it all work? How best will we use it? Can we afford it now? He got it going and gave me a quick course in what it could do and how. Sure thing. It's my job now to make it work for us.

I'm actually working on my *Senior Citizen* musical that's taken me two years so far and I'm excited about finishing it and start new projects. It's a lighthearted comedy about senior citizens getting warehoused into nursing homes but primarily about my father's homophobia.

Do I really have "world enough and time" to do creative things I have wanted to do for eons? It seems too good to be true, but Jan is making this possible for me now and I must take advantage of the opportunity without feeling guilty. Perhaps I can give her the same chance in the future when I have thoroughly learned and explored all the possibilities. Meanwhile whatever I do personally will expand our musical creative horizon too. I need to get rid of the feelings of selfishness, if that's the right word. It's because I know Jan would like nothing more than to be doing what I'm doing now. But that's OK. She wants me to be doing this too. We both have mixed feelings and fortunately we can talk them over together. I feel that I never had it so good!

Bea on May 3, 1984

I must admit that the night after our Lisa arrived, I woke up around 4 a.m. with a disconcerting "Good Grief, Charlie Brown" feeling, wondering if we should have bought Lisa with Jan's pay cut and uncertain future. The old fear bugaboo reared its head again and when I worked on the computer, I only compounded the errors I'd made. But my tech friends at the Mac store showed me what to do and I'm learning so much more with every hour, day and night. I even learned how to draw on MacPaint!

But today, I spent six hours as a "user" in the center of the computer world. What an exciting day to attend the "UserFest" computer event in Milwaukee. Of course, Apple stole the show with new software demos on a giant screen directed by an expert on a regular Mac. I sensed the general excitement of everyone and got re-excited myself.

Lisa and I actually interfaced with each other. Jan told me that when I fall asleep in my chair, my hands and fingers move as if I were at my desk, controlling the mouse and key board and creating new images and formats.

Jan comes home on time now and promised she'll try to stop everything at 4:30. Because of her new hours, she'll spend time with me picking up the computer skills that I've learned.

Jan on May 5, 1984

I do have to look at this new era being "for the highest good of all concerned."

The Accent on Women conference gave us a much-needed mini-vacation including valuable publicity at the presentation of being among the first five women honored in their fields. Of course, I'm still stunned by having my hours cut at work, and the award of being the best professional woman in communications is bittersweet, but so what else is new.

Bea is aglow with finding the Lisa as a creative source for her genius, and I see its options for me as endless. She's pulled out her musical comedy and is learning how to format her songs on Lisa. Bea's putting us at the cutting edge of computer word processing and design. The potential is endless.

I'm even producing my job résumés on Lisa.

Bea on May 6, 1984

My firstborn son Josh was married in April. My ex-husband also was married one week before Josh's wedding—to my old-time, dear friend Angie Murak. That was a shock and quite an emotional strain, I'll tell you. It still is, but I'm improving.

An official invitation to a "Going Away" reception for Marge in a Lakeshore Med meeting room on June 28 arrived at Jan's office, and she and Carolyn will be attending to wish her well in her move to Carson City. We have never spoken to her about marrying Alex. Ironically, if events and her groom were different, I probably would have been her matron of honor with Jan in the bridal party, or visa versa.

Marge and Alex went off to Mexico last winter and to Spain and Portugal in August. Best of old friends—and now enemies? Honestly, don't these men have any creative imagination than to choose our best friends for their wives and companions?

My son Jim is getting serious about marrying his girlfriend now that his two brothers are married, and I had to go over to meet her parents. Jake and Angie were there too. OK but—!

Jan's also meeting at our house with her Women's Network friend Beth Johnson who comes for supper from work, and the two of them dream away, making plans to start a women's newspaper in this area. I'm staying out of this completely! I know they sense my hostility and I hope that dream of theirs never happens. How will we survive if we have to live without Jan's steady income and her benefits?

Jan on May 15, 1984

We've survived the hours of preparing and managing the hospital's run/walk on Saturday plus Mother's Day on Sunday with all of our kids stopping by or calling, and our friends planning our weekend trip to the National Women's Music Festival, a celebration of feminist music at the Indiana University in Bloomington. We'll ride in Robin's husband's van all night on May 25 to arrive on the campus, stay in the dorm and return on May 29. We'll have Robin and Naomi; Martha and Fran; our two straight women Joanne and Carolyn; Bea and me; two guitars and accompanying luggage. Carolyn's been telling us about her daughter Jane's big festival there and how she knows all of the women in lesbian music and comedy. We had checked out the details from *The Lesbian Connection* in our store and we're all signed up to go.

Jan on May 30, 1984

As if it were Cinderella's carriage, Robin pulled the van into our driveway as the clock struck midnight, and we piled into it already filled with our six excited friends ready to ride all night. Joanne, who claimed the front seat, and Bea, our driver, sang show tunes all night with Fran joining in singing "The Hills Are Alive" with "The Sound of Music." Fran surprised us revealing that she played the part of Maria, guitar and all, in a Dominican sisters theater project during her journey to become a nun, which turned out to be a short trip. The others finally fell asleep until we stopped for breakfast halfway and then I drove my shift on to the campus. Carolyn's daughter was among the first to greet us at the reception area. Jane told me she was worried about what her mother would think of being in the midst of all these lesbians, but we reassured her that Carolyn is used to being with us and truly is an ally as well as our sister-friend.

We paired off to find our rooms with Joanne and Carolyn "our closeted-straight couple" sharing our "dorm duplex" with a tiny lavatory between the two rooms. Then, without any sleep, Bea and I chose to attend Margot Adler's workshop on women's rituals ("Biologically born females preferred.") Over forty workshops are offered each day in this creative lesbian/feminist culture. Bea and I also went to writing humor and lesbian fiction and crashed for a nap before supper, but some of our friends gave in to drooping eyelids and dozed off during their workshops.

Thursday evening's Mainstage concert introduced the premier production of the amazing Kay Gardner's oratorio *Ouroboro: Seasons of Life—Women's Passages* with an all-women 40-piece orchestra and 100 festival soloists, chanting speakers and choral volunteers. The oratorio is based on ancient Celtic seasons, equinoxes and festivals that match eight aspects of women's lives from conception to death. We in the audience had to be quiet for 90 minutes because it was being recorded—Yes! By an all-women's technical crew.

After this unique, spiritual and unexpected experience compared to what we expected we found Alix Dobkin jamming in the dorm lounge until 1 a.m. We heard her singing Sue Fink's song, "Here Comes the Leaping Lesbians…We're gonna tease ya and squeeze ya…." We were too punchy after our twenty-four hour whirlwind day, but I remembered the out and proud power of the first lesbian LP records when we played in the store.

A wild Friday started with Bea wearing her t-shirt with a cow on the front with the words, "The Udder Side," with the rear end of the cow on Bea's back. That made a hit with the cafeteria breakfast crowd. Bea's cow shirt won her a kiss from Z Budapest, noted for being the mother of the feminist spirituality movement, and the shirt set a lighthearted tone for our gang as we headed through crowded corridors and campus buildings to find our various workshops. Our fee included meals so our gang did not hold back on stuffing themselves at every meal. I couldn't believe how much they consumed.

Saturday's workshops introduced us to Ruth Barrett's "Feminist witchcraft in the Dianic tradition" and then I announced to our luncheon bunch that I'm going to two afternoon workshops: "Hot sex and monogamy" and "Female ejaculation." Bea quickly coerced me into joining her for singer, songwriter and pianist Margie Adam's workshop. She, Cris Williamson, Kay Gardner and Meg Christian are considered among the women who jump-started the women's music movement. She wrote "Best Friend—The Unicorn" that made me cry when I first heard the song in our bookstore because it affirmed to me that my real best friend lives inside of me.

The financially courageous lesbian record producers, Olivia Records, would give us records to promote and sell. Some were too hot—meaning too lesbian—for Lakeshore Bay so they didn't get played unless I was alone in the bookstore. One of my many favorites was Meg Christian's "Ode to a Gym Teacher" who'll "...always be a player on the ball field of my heart." Both of my gym teachers from separate schools, who happened to live together, were players on my volleyball, basketball or tennis court of *my* heart.

Saturday's Mainstage concert was serious compared to Friday's with Maxine Feldman as the emcee and high-spirited Kate Clinton finishing off that Mainstage program.

A tradition began on Friday night. A huge projection screen filled the auditorium stage space and suddenly became alive with music and pictures from *One Fine Day*, a seven-minute video that celebrates American women, past and present, and stirred the blood and raised the pride of our cheering audience. With inspiring music, it began showing pioneer women and children living in sod huts, women on horseback, World War II women building airplanes, Eleanor Roosevelt and ending with our contemporaries: Shirley Chisholm, Billy Jean King, Bella Abzug plus Geraldine Ferraro. What a cheer went up for each one with the loudest being for Ferraro, the Democratic candidate for vice president with Walter Mondale.

<<<>>>

Though the program book's first rule, printed in bold, stated: "Indiana University Bloomington is by law a chem-free place. Absolutely no alcohol or drugs are permitted on campus." Carolyn had warned us about that but Bea and I smuggled two bottles of wine into our room. We passed that among us to celebrate the end of our first night. I hid the bottles under my shirt with the corks emphasizing booming bosoms. This was the Alfred Kinsey sex studies campus and I'm sure they'd accept some lesbians breaking a rule or two. Besides, we all were tired and silly and ready for whatever came our way.

While we walked among the formidable and classically etched limestone-covered campus buildings, I remembered the *Breaking Away* bicycle-racing movie with the "cutters" local gang of potential losers, except for the one romantic and optimistic dreamer. Occasionally I'd break into a joyful impromptu and improvised "These Are a Few of My Favorite Things" from *Sound of Music* and Bea would respond to me with her "Shut your Von Trapp, Maria." Of course, that didn't stop me.

Here I am, singing in a different state: a state of polite kindness and affirming respect in this lesbian nation with its proud women's music, art, spirituality and literature in this weekend where we could find magic in being together and feeling free.

But back to Saturday's Night Stage in the historic University of Indiana's vast auditorium, Thomas Hart Benson's panoramic murals gracefully flowed with Midwestern working together in various occupations. Men, women, children of our parents' generation are revered here forever because of Franklin Roosevelt's WPA arts projects that supported artists like Hart Benson during the Depression era.

Kate Clinton's personal experiences and polished lesbian humor lifted us with laughter through the many announcements and performers. Of course, each performer had signers for the hearing impaired and they wove their graceful body language through the humor and the profound. However, profound goes only so far, and a serious drama performance where we had to behave ourselves could hold us for only a while. All that seriousness is all that Naomi needed to giggle after one of Bea's off-hand remarks in her ear.

Naomi is a big giggler and Bea isn't one to miss an opportunity for fun. We were relatively quiet in the front row of the back half of the main floor until the drama ended and thin I joined in. We irreverently laughed out loud during the next guitar group's performance featuring Ferron, Robin's favorite musician who chose to sit near the front. Naomi predicted exactly what Robin would say after they finished, and when Robin came to rave about her idol, Naomi and Bea teased her. Robin felt her opinions were brushed off and that hurt her feelings so she went back to her seat alone for the rest of the show.

Ruth headed for the dorm with Joanne, Fran and Martha, but Naomi, Carolyn, Bea and I walked a long way to the student union where we danced together and had a great time watching women couples plus dykes in black tie and tails sway and swirl in a dance contest.

We weren't going to miss a thing, but Naomi was in trouble with Robin when she got back to their dorm room. Oh well. Who doesn't get into trouble? Loving another woman doesn't change much in most relationships; maybe it's heavier hurt because of the forbidden love, I guess. Otherwise, our conflicts wouldn't be so painful.

Even on Sunday, Naomi was in emotional pain as Robin made the worst of their incident that Bea and I initiated. Those two are so new to this lesbian relationship business and have family issues, age differences and married vs. single status to get through—in addition to dealing with lesbian realities.

Martha and Fran watched over Naomi until Naomi and I went to a deliciously slippery afternoon massage workshop "for feminist warriors." Our tribe watched Naomi and me from the dorm entrance as we two came swaggering back, arm in arm, pink and playful after our deep massage experience with a classroom full of women stretched out on floor mats. Too bad Naomi's Robin and my Bea didn't share our joy of this massage.

We all went together to our women's spirituality session with Casselberry and Dupree who drummed and chanted Afro sounds, circling closely to face each of us, getting us to join in. inspiring us to respond to their affirmation, "Goddess is within me and I love her." It was a moving spiritual and physical experience with the vibrations of their drumming and all of our chanting to expand the power within us.

Once we two were too late to join our voracious gang for lunch so we sat across from two women more our age. It's always good to meet new people, and one of them looked familiar to me. Finally, it clicked and I asked the shorter one, "Weren't you pictured in the *Organic Gardening* magazine as The Worm Lady who uses worms to enhance composting?" She smiled and acknowledged that she was that same person who had devised a system using worms to recycle food waste and produce fertilizer for houseplants and gardens. Her book, *Worms Eat My Garbage*, is self-published by their own Flower Press.

Bea has stopped being surprised by my being able to recognize people as we exchanged business cards after our long conversation that started the beginning of a close friendship. Mary Appelhof and her partner, Mary Frances Fenton, knew of our Mother Courage Bookstore through their friend River, who runs Kalamazoo's feminist bookstore. When Mary Frances told me her name, I asked her if she was the person who created a Solstice Circle Garden plan based on Neolithic stone circles in a book that I study for my garden, *Saving Seeds: Metaphors of Lesbian Growth*? And she was that same, kind and gentle person. (That book also describes a creative Cunt Garden plan by women named clove and susun weed.) They invited us to stay with them in Kalamazoo if and when we travel to Michigan.

The Open Mike sessions including poets, singers and a mime troupe, piqued Bea's interest, but she resisted grabbing her guitar and adding her talents for the audience to enjoy.

<<<◇>>>

Sunday night's concert started at 7:30 with Casselberry and Dupree's drumming followed by a dramatic presentation about the survivors of the Holocaust and ended with the up-beat music and charm of Holly Near.

We were tired after that, but we managed a bit of a party in Carolyn and Joanne's room while movies and dancing and open-mikes kept going on the campus throughout the night.

On Memorial Day we got ourselves organized and checked out by 9 a.m. even though the festival was still going on. Martha's friends, Lindy and Noretta, had invited us to stop at their farm for breakfast and conversation. Bea realized Martha's friend who wrote the lesbian novel *Who Was that Masked Woman* and was actually published by the mainstream St. Martin's Press. Their home was filled with travel artifacts and I put my lips to blow on a primitive flute-type instrument until our host told me it was an African nose flute. Whoops! I then tried playing it through my nostrils.

When they toured us around their farm, I kind of lost it as we entered the barn. I remembered my barn and forty acres of Door County land that I gave up to my ex- in my divorce settlement. Bea comforted me while the others left us alone for a while.

Ruth took the first shift driving home until we stopped for lunch before hitting the Interstate. We sat in a large booth, chattering excitedly about our experiences and used the "lesbian" word out-loud and frequently. The family sitting in the booth next to us gave us dirty looks and moved to the restaurant's opposite side.

Bea drove the second shift and I did the third. Joanne claimed the front passenger seat all the way, taking notes as we sorted out and laughed about the festival events.

We merged with millions of Memorial Day travelers on the Illinois Skyway and were trapped in a three-hour traffic jam. We moved so slowly that I could have driven without touching the steering wheel. We looked down into sedans filled with families and imagined what hell they were going through.

Bea asked us what would we call ourselves if we were to become a band and play on the open mike at future women's music festivals. We laughed through the hours, thinking up names for our band and songs we would play. We could be called The Octopussys because there were eight of us. Joanne wrote them all down, including my favorite, The Tampon Strings Orchestra. Each name provoked gales of laughter the sillier they were and the more tired we became. Bea couldn't remember, she said, a laughter therapy session that lasted for so long and so hard. Even her tonsils were sore.

And that didn't end after we stopped at the only oasis in the middle of the Skyway's concrete gridlock with hot cars filled with everyone having to go to the bathroom. I pulled up to the pump and requested that Joanne ask the driver of the next car if he would please close his door so we could drive closer to the fuel tanks.

She opened her door and shouted, "Hey, Mister! Close your damn door before we knock it off!" And he did so quickly after he watched bulky Joanne and all of the rest of us bound out of the van to head for the long line of a two-toilet women's room.

Before Robin started to drive the last leg home, she said she could tell the A-types in our group; those who were drivers—she, Bea and me. She forgot to count Joanne.

CHAPTER 13

Jan on June 7, 1984

My Day of Infamy felt as disastrous for me as it did when Pearl Harbor was bombed on December 7, 1941, because I actually understood what was happening. Rather than bombs exploding, it was "the other shoe." I've been waiting for this since 1978 when it became known that I'd stepped across society's accepted moral boundary to find my true, creative, independent lesbian self.

Randy trapped me in the boardroom again. When others at the meeting were excused, he ordered me to stay. For more almost two hours I was subjected to his vitriolic listing of the angry hours he's wasted on me. I did not respond with my laundry list of injuries he inflicted on Bea and me and several other co-workers.

Though dumbfounded and broken, I didn't cry. He finally declared that my department is being eliminated. Chuck McCarthy will head the new marketing function and Carolyn will report to him. That's the final decision. No more Communications Department; no more Jan Anthony as its director.

"Rather than have you humble yourself for unemployment compensation, it's been decided to show you some compassion and allow you to stay in your office and continue to on the payroll while you may aggressively seek another position. I sure you'll agree that it's easier to find another job while you have one. And Lakeshore Med will reimburse you for any job search expenses."

Carolyn was stunned when I finally returned to our office to tell her that our department was eliminated and that she would report to Chuck. Her sisterly love and grief for me was unmistakable and her concern for herself was stubbornly defiant. "But you'll make it, Carolyn," trying to calm and motivate her simultaneously. "We both will make it," I said, trying to calm and motivate me.

Bea could tell something was wrong as soon as I entered our house by the lack of my usual gait and my "Hi, dear. I'm home!" When I reached the final step into our family room, I saw Naomi on one side of our bar and Bea on the other.

"What happened?" Bea asked anxiously.

"He dropped the other shoe. I lost my job." And I released all of the grown-up pretenses as the two of them embraced and comforted me while I finally cried in self-pity. Yes, "self-pity" as we talked it through this evening. Other people, women, lesbians have suffered worse and shown strength and courage. Martha's mother admitted her to a mental institution; friends and families rejected others. Look at what happened to Bea's brother who committed suicide. Gay bars had been raided, customers arrested and were fired from their jobs when their names appeared in the papers. What's a little blatant job discrimination among our proud and accomplished culture of feminists and lesbians.

In my venting of Randy King, I shuddered to a finish by telling Bea, "I've wasted so much disgusting energy on this bully, this Inquisitor! I want to spew out all the nasty bile he's caused me, the heartburn, and I never want to taste or feel it again! Ugh! Who does *he* ultimately report to? From what God-awful system did he evolve?"

Jan on June 16, 1984

I headed for our Lisa/Mac computer early Monday to improve my résumé and cover letters. I customized my documents into four categories: strictly business; friends from work; local and state organizations including HPRW members; and feminist allies. If my résumé's reader didn't like my individual letters printed on a dot-matrix printer, I wouldn't want to work for that dogmatic, backward-thinking person.

As I was serving supper, Laura Williams came, outraged after hearing what had happened to me. It hurt when I told my children and friends. But I'm not embarrassed about being let go. Everyone knows I deserve better treatment. Poor Carolyn must feel the same way and is left alone in the office this week while I work on my next career move. Good thing Bea is able to help me when I can't get the Lisa to do what I want it to do. Lisa is intuitive. I think she knows what I want, but it's Bea's skill and research that makes this work.

I feel distant and preoccupied. Still, I have to act optimistic so I don't drag down the people I need to help me grieve and move on.

Ironically, I was told to keep track of my job-search expenses, including mileage, so Lakeshore Med's can reimburse me. Great! What Good Samaritans! That list is on our Lisa II beginning on June 7, the day of the deed. On June 12, I mailed out twelve separate cover letters and résumés to area contacts that resulted in eight responses, three tips and an interview with the *Southport Journal*. I've also signed up and researched UW's job placement files.

I wrote Matt, "I'm not giving in to injustice, yet I must be guarded not to compromise my relations with other Lakeshore Bay firms. I'll be returning to work on Monday and I don't know how long my job will last under these circumstances. When I was subjected to my last two-hour tirade on what a negative person I am, Randy even threw your father's issues at me to score points against me. Unbelievable!

"Meanwhile, I'm getting strength and affirmation from Bea and our many friends including those at work. I'm not causing any major ruckus now because I don't want to be shut off from my salary too soon.

Bea on June 16, 1984

Jan came home from work and drove to Milwaukee for a workshop on litigation against employers. I didn't have the strength to do it and she was pissed at me. Hell, just a few days ago I ironed my dress-for-success skirt and blouse for her to wear to an interview, and now she says I'm not supporting her. Besides, I don't think she'll follow through with legal action anyway, and we can't afford it. Our two friends who did sue and struggled to win had to change their professions because no one in their field would hire them. One even lost her husband in the process. The other husband lost his libido.

I've too much input, am spread too thin and need a time with space for me. Whoosh! When she is gone, I play computer games, the piano, watch TV and take care of me for a while.

We both are depressed, but we'll get through it. The stress is fierce. She still has to go to her office, check out her files and help Carolyn. Jan endured a half-hour phone call from the prick, laced with veiled threats. Jan restated that she will bring a representative with her to all meetings and she quoted a Supreme Court ruling saying, "Any employee has the right to have mutual protection with co-workers to be present at a meeting with management which the employee has reason to believe may lead to discipline." He agreed that they would never meet each other face to face or talk over the phone. Writing everything in memos is time-consuming but possible. He said he will get back to her, but she hopes not. Jan told me when she called the unemployment office for information on compensation that the employer must establish proof to establish misconduct for termination. But actually, he's not terminating her, just her department.

Does she qualify for a pension? She started as a part time

employee. Does that count toward a ten-year requirement? She thinks not. Is that still a requirement?

Jan on June 17, 1984

A letter from my HPRW friend Linda Edwards, the job placement chair from Women in Communications, gave me some good advice.

"Sorry to hear about your leaving Lakeshore Med. I am almost glad this happened because I truly believe you'll be much happier and fulfilled with new projects and challenges elsewhere. I know you've effected a miraculous change recently, but frankly it didn't quite ring true to me. I think you'll be pleasantly surprised once you're in another position and involved in something totally different. You'll wish you'd done it long ago. Ask me. I know. A professional friend suggested I leave a job years ago, and it was the best thing that ever happened to me!

"Thought you might be interested in the Women in Communications materials I'm enclosing. Why don't you consider an ad/pr firm that has health care accounts? Are you looking out of Lakeshore Bay? I'd assume so if you mailed me a note.

"Where's all your Lakeshore Bay Chamber of Commerce work on your résumé? I 'lost' a job in Sheboygan once because they wanted someone who could join Kiwanis, Rotary, etc. They wanted someone who could hobnob with community leaders.

"I wish you the best of luck and hope you come up with some attractive offers soon. I know you'll have a lot of appeal to many employers. Once you're free and unencumbered with Lakeshore Med's business and on one of the many job interviews you're sure to have in my area, call me and we'll get together for lunch."

I wrote my response to Linda.

"Getting your letter was what I needed to recover from physical reactions to the depression I was feeling over this abusive situation. Your letter, your Women In Communications job listing and several other positive responses from my network of supportive persons in the state and in Lakeshore Bay have been truly affirming.

I took your résumé advice and made several additions and am sending thank you responses to people like you.

I agree. I see myself as a battered wife in this toxic environment who won't leave the home because of other insecurities. Yet I can still muster up my "golden glow" for my co-workers and for me.

Significant financial changes in recent months have put at least a year's salary in reserve. My car situation has improved. Our health is good, and I'm seeing this job search as one of my greatest challenges. I've never had to search for employment; it's always come to me.

You are an invaluable and intelligent, caring friend and colleague.

Bea on July 8, 1984

Jan created twenty-three customized job letters with résumés on our Lisa computer early this Sunday morning and I helped print them so we could mail them on our way to a party at Martha and Fran's cozy little cottage behind Fran's aunt's house on Walnut Street in an inner-city neighborhood with narrow streets and little frame houses that served as first homes for various waves of immigrants. Perhaps a few Italian, Armenian or German families remain in the larger homes and lots, but Afro-American families primarily occupy the smallest of homes that lean toward the concrete sidewalks. Freight trains run across the tracks on the edge of the hill just a few yards behind the neighborhood.

The weather was oppressively hot but we shopped for Martha's birthday present. Just before her party, we changed into our cowboy and Indian outfits with the fake Indian war bonnet inherited from Jan's father's float relics. We sneaked up Martha and Fran's Walnut Street driveway into the back yard and raided her party with squirt guns, shifting the party's mood from Southern plantation porch heat exhaustion to a Wild West wet water show that jostled everyone about and cooled them down.

After offering our hostess our gift of chilled white wine, we wedged among our lesbian women—and Laura Williams from Lakeshore Med! We never expected her to be here. We discovered that Laura and Pam Holmen stop after their college Master's degree sessions for drinks at Greek Feasts where Fran is the chef. When Fran isn't busy, she joins Laura and Pam for laughs and flaming saganaki, and they're close friends without being aware of our connection. Empathetic Laura, who lives in an upscale home in a classy new neighborhood, is struggling through a divorce and she told me later of her qualms about living on her own with her two daughters. Would she have to move to a tiny place like this on Walnut Street in order to survive?

We also met Martha's friend Helen Pendell, a *Milwaukee Journal* librarian and, of course, job searches came up in the conversation. As Fate or the Goddess ordained, Ellen brought *Milwaukee Journal* want ads for two positions at the Milwaukee Area Technical College (MATC). She planned to give the ads to Martha, but Martha generously offered them to Jan, saying that Jan would be more qualified for either position. Each salary range was from $22,500 to $27,300 per year.

Jan asked if it would be OK to share this with Carolyn who could apply before the July 12 deadline. The next day, Carolyn and I worked on her résumé and cover letter while Jan adapted hers on Lisa. Both mailed them in time to meet to meet MATC's deadline.

Taking advantage of Ellen's generous nature, Jan asked her if she would look for Milwaukee newspaper references on MCMC's Administrator John Jackson and send a copy to her to study.

Thank you, Goddess, Ellen Pendell, all our friends and colleagues.

CHAPTER 14

Jan on July 10, 1984

Data processing never appealed to me, especially when my husband worked in this new field for so many hours a week, sometimes over one hundred hours, while I was struggling alone with pregnancies and caring for toddlers. But when I realized what our Lisa could do, my soul and brain realized my new potential as in *The Miracle Worker* where Helen Keller kneeled at the water pump with her mentor Annie Sullivan and Helen felt the water while Annie tapped signals in Helen's hand communicating "Water." I felt the power of The Word, and having our own Macintosh magnifies that power.

Carolyn and other Lakeshore Med people are starting a weekly résumé writing session with our new computer. Bea is our leader, and I'm learning to use this awesome tool more each day. Another tool I'm building with my unofficial office time is compiling a voluminous four-inch wide, red ring binder of my publications and credentials. It's chock-full of the work my teams and I have completed. While I'm sorting through our office files, I'm organizing newsletters, memos and references for the future.

Bea on July 11, 1984

I'm bored at the store. It's difficult to keep gainfully occupied in this waiting game. Wait. Wait. Wait to see when it will be Jan's last day. Wait and see if she gets a job. Wait for the mail. Wait for Apple Mac software to come. It's screwy—heavy with apprehension about our future. Will we have to move? Can I ever get a job? That would be counterproductive if we would have to move. Bills. Bills. Bills. And no money or security in our future. We're drinking too much too. But what else is new?

Jan has to meet with Randy at 1:30 and had a psychological reaction before she left. I gave her one of my meds. I chose to space out. At bedtime, I massaged Jan's body, which was much desired—and returned.

Jan on July 12, 1984

Mondale chose Geraldine Ferraro for his running mate! Yeah! We celebrated! After a Goddess celebration. We drank wine and Bea gave me a profound rune reading that I can't remember—all under the full moon shining through our window.

Jan on July 30, 1984

I joyfully wrote to Randy that John Jackson, administrator of the Midwest Center's Medical Complex, called me today after receiving my résumé. A new position, Director of Public Relations/Hospital, is being developed for Milwaukee County. I will be meeting with him on August 15. "Plan for half a day," said Jackson. "The job will be posted and advertised on August 7."

Meanwhile Helen Pendell mailed me a Xeroxed news clipping with a torn tip of his photo remaining, showing only a large black hand. Good! If he is Black, he'll know what it's like to live in a victimized minority—like me, only my skin color doesn't identify my life.

Jan on August 14, 1984

Yesterday I covered the office for Carolyn in the morning while she interviewed at MATC. We don't administration to know that she's looking for a job. Perhaps we crossed paths while I drove to my interview that seemed like a bureaucratic inquisition, but I guess that's what's required if you compete for a posted position with a government agency. After a panel interrogated me for the two jobs, they sent me off with a pad and pencil to write a news release based on facts listed on their form. I knew I'd made a mess of it. I couldn't think without a typewriter and I edited my copy to obscurity. I was incredibly tense.

Tonight, after supper, Bea and I needed each other in a gentle and soothing way, especially after Carolyn called. She was offered one of the MATC jobs and I'm happy for her, but Shit! When Carolyn asked about me, they told her I would not be hired. I didn't make it and I wanted that job! It would be good for me to get completely out of the hospital business and return to the learning environment of an excellent technical college.

Jan on August 18, 1984

To Helen Pendell, Milwaukee Journal Company Library/Research Department

Dear Ellen,
    Thank you very much for the important information you sent me. It has been helpful in providing critical background and for giving me a greater sense of security when I meet with John Jackson on September 6. I've had two interview appointments rescheduled so that when the half-day meeting does occur, I should have myself psyched up to gain a 9.9 or a 10 and win the gold. Meanwhile, other

opportunities are surfacing, including an interview on August 20 with a prestigious PR agency with offices on the twentieth floor of the First Wisconsin Building. I did not get the position at MATC. A *Milwaukee Sentinel* woman filled it, but my co-worker did get a publications position there. That leaves Lakeshore Med without a PR department as soon as I'm finally placed somewhere that's right for me.

Again, thanks for your information and for your personal concern.

Sincerely, etc.

Jan on August 18, 1984

To Clark and Betty Young
Greetings,

I'd like to let you know that if you get a call from Milwaukee County's Department of Human Resources about my application for openings in their system, even the Milwaukee County Zoo, it's because I'm aggressively inundating the area with cover letters and résumés to find a new job.

I added your name to my references for John Jackson who wants a full time PR person in upper management at the Medical Complex when he contacted me before the County officially posted the job. I'd heard through networking that he was looking for a PR person to fill a new position, and I took the initiative to contact him. I think he liked that.

Randy King told me on June 7 that I should look for another job. I expected to have one hour and a cardboard box to move out of my office, but unexpectedly, I am still at Lakeshore Med with authorization to take time while on the job to advance my new career search. I don't feel that they're doing me any favors, however. I think they've figured out a way to eliminate me without my recourse to legal action. Meanwhile, Carolyn Schafer pulled together her résumé and portfolio and won a new position from her first interview with a great and financially rewarding position at the Milwaukee Area Technical College. She informed Personnel that her last day here is August 30.

Meanwhile, I'm getting positive responses and some interviews from my letters. I'm singing my song, "The sun will come up tomorrow," and I'm having a good time promoting myself instead of something or someone else. I'm also serving as a positive force for any unhappy Lakeshore Med people who are concerned about their job security and conditions at our hospital.

I'm including my résumé if you want to review any details from the past. It was certainly a wonderful time working for you. Then when we waged battles to gain Lakeshore Med goals, we knew that we were all on the same team.

Sincerely,

The two of us were invited to dine at Chan's Chinese Restaurant last night with our hosts, Clark and Betty Young. He was genuinely angry at what's been going on at work since he retired as Lakeshore Med's CEO. He reached into his jacket pocket and handed me his reference letter for me to hand to John Jackson at my interview. They invited us in for a drink and more conversation when we took them home.

Today in my weekly written report to Randy, I added: Carolyn's last day, as announced on her termination note, is this Thursday. Unless otherwise indicated, I will assume responsibility for the employee newsletter and her other responsibilities. I expect to be working eighty hours a pay period again with those additional duties and assignments. Will she be replaced? Will I train someone to replace her? Will my salary reflect the increased hours needed to cover office responsibilities? In my report to you on August 2, I asked for Carolyn's salary step increase. Ordinarily, it would be due on the 15th. If that is a fact, shouldn't Carolyn receive this additional amount on the remaining check and vacation reimbursement?

I never received an answer.

Carolyn's Lakeshore Med's *letter* on August 30, 1984

Editor's Note:
This is the 165th letter that I've written and it's my last. In the six years plus that I've been at Lakeshore Med, I've had the opportunity to meet and/or write about a host of employees. Their caring spirit makes Lakeshore Med a special institution.

I've been proud to celebrate the arrival of new equipment, special events with the all-out teamwork of many people from many departments and employee anniversaries and accomplishments.

But first and foremost, working with Lakeshore Med people has been a special joy. Their helpfulness, expertise, creativity, friendliness and sense of humor are treasured experiences.

I'm starting a new position at Milwaukee Area Technical College. Though it's a bigger institution, how can there possibly be warmer hearted employees than those at Lakeshore Med? I'll miss you

Carolyn's exit interview Personnel report on August 30, 1984

Carolyn shared a copy of her exit report with me.

1. *What is your reason for separation:* New position at a substantial salary increase.

2. *What is your opinion of your job with us in terms of promotional opportunities*: "I viewed my position as a dead-end position, but it's been stimulating and exciting working with Jan Anthony."

"With the help and encouragement of Jan Anthony, I have felt up to any job assignment. Through Jan's team approach to the vast number of services the department performs for other hospital areas, we each took responsibility for a variety of projects as well as sharing multiple responsibilities on special projects. It has been challenging and rewarding.

"Occasionally, as with others involved, I have felt overwhelmed when special events came back-to-back. We didn't have time to help each other as we usually did when the chips were down.

"I have often taken responsibility for projects from creation to completion. Feedback from Jan has been helpful, constructive and often the catalyst for an extra dimension in our search for excellence. I feel our department has been a positive voice for Lakeshore Med, a place where ideas from other departments have been implemented by teamwork, brainstorming and acknowledgment of the worth of others' ideas as well as our own."

On Opportunity to make use of your education or abilities, she wrote, "I have used every skill I ever learned plus some I didn't know I had, i.e. being a Cabbage Patch Doll."

On Personal recognition received, Carolyn wrote, "Acknowledgment and praise from Jan and those who shared many projects as well as state-wide HPRW awards of excellence recognition."

On Did you feel secure in your job? she wrote, "I felt secure about my job performance, but uncomfortable about financial security and recently about the hospital's future.

"Did your supervisor handle your complaints or problems satisfactorily?" Carolyn wrote, "Yes, within her power."

Regarding technical know-how and leadership ability of your department head, Jan made an enormous contribution to student interns' perceptions and development of skills. I benefited daily from her expertise.

Carolyn's answer to her opinion of Lakeshore Med in terms of salary? was "Not until the salary administration program began with grade levels and step increases did I feel I was paid fairly."

And *If you could tell the hospital president exactly how you feel about the way the hospital is run, what would you tell him?* "There is a communication vacuum that this department could not address."

Carolyn's leaving is the end of an era for Lakeshore Med and for me.

CHAPTER 15

Jan on September 1, 1984

Dear Matt,

    I haven't written much because most of my available time has been writing résumés and cover letters to flood the area and beyond—like a storm front moving its turbulence over the territory.

    I'm anxious about the possibilities at MCMC, one of the biggest and significantly important hospitals in the state that never had a genuine PR person because of budget restrictions. If I get a job there. we'll have to move, at least over the county line, or I'll rent a room to get a County address and phone listing. I can use it for bad weather and late night meetings. Apartment living or buying another home after making monthly payments on our current low mortgage rates are not appealing. But we've lived amid change and know that we'll be fine for the short- and long-range future.

    Meanwhile Bea's also sending out résumés and has a second chance with an interview as a graphic artist in a family-owned business that makes watering devices for pigs and other farm animals. Unique! And it's a growing and successful firm. She interviewed with a sailing magazine but hasn't heard from them.

    Randy hasn't met with me since June 17 and all he gets from

me are reports about my job search and weekly activities. He hasn't communicated anything about replacing Carolyn who left for a new position at Milwaukee's technical college. I know he wasn't counting on her leaving, and when I go, he's in real trouble to duplicate what we've accomplished when he and his clone have no understanding of this job's complexities, techniques, deadlines and media responses.

We're having a big potluck party for Carolyn at Laura's house on September 12 after Carolyn returns from vacation to begin her new job. We've invited all our working colleagues and chums and have completely left out all high-power and abusive power administrative types.

Jenny called yesterday saying she wanted to get career counseling at Gateway. Her St. Agnes hours got cut back again so she's going to be making some school and career moves in the right direction, I hope. I enjoy having her closer, even if she doesn't care about living in Marge's former home now that our family home has been sold. We touch base more often now that we live closer to each other. She runs over to pick produce from our beautifully abundant garden.

Jan on September 6, 1984

John Jackson's huge hand warmly enclosed my hand and his generous grin flashed white teeth across his friendly brown face as he towered over me. I hope he could feel my mutual regard at meeting the mighty man today. He's overwhelming in his custom-tailored vested suit, white shirt and subtle tie. I'm sure that he's aware of his charisma, yet he seems to want to soften his strength to put me more at ease—even though my career depends on his impression of me.

After formalities, he accepted my red portfolio, pretending to weigh it as if it were heavy for him, raising his formidable eyebrows on his broad, brown brow. I think he was impressed. He was pleased, he said, that I took the initiative to send him my résumé right when he planned to find the hospital its own PR person. He apologized for canceling earlier interviews and it seemed as if he were courting me to take the position rather than my having to prove myself good enough for it. Of course, I did try—desperately inside—to be his chosen one.

With the twenty minutes that we talked, I handed him my recently received reference letter from Clark Young.

From Clark Young on September 1, 1984

Dear Jan,

You can be certain that your record of accomplishments while Director of Communications at Lakeshore Medical Center is not only outstanding but may not be surpassed except through you. An examination of your award-winning accomplishments in special events, publications, media relations, public relations and television programming also reflects your extraordinary sensitivity and comprehension of the complex works of the hospital organization. Your knack for finding the right phrasing and pictorial depiction of the hospital world portrayed appropriately for the public, the community and all levels of government has no equal in my 44 years of hospital administration.

I wish you continued success in your well-chosen profession and I know that Lakeshore Medical Center and I are very much better for your contributions.

Very sincerely yours,
Clark I. Young
F.A.C.H.A.

"That's impressive," Jackson said and he handed me an agenda of four other administrators to meet today. "There's one more administrator coming," and he picked up the phone and called Ron Blain at his hospital across town. "Ron, I've got Jan Anthony here and I think she's going to be our new PR person after I get through all the red-tape. I need to know when you're coming. Yes. I need you soon. Yes. You can work out a compromise on the residency requirement. You will be my right-hand and Jan will be my left-hand to get this hospital competitive again. OK. Get ready to join us. Bye."

He explained that he had to interview four other applicants on Thursday to maintain County regulations as he walked over to his huge boardroom table and set my red binder standing upright. "I'll keep this here for everyone to review." And he then sat behind his desk and looked me in the eye, "Jan. Are you sure you want to come to work here for a starting salary of $28,500?" (As if he were apologizing about its small amount.)

"Yes. I am."

"And are you sure that you'll want to move to Milwaukee County within six months after starting the position?"

"Yes. I am."

"Good. Now you go and make a good impression on all these assistant administrators. I'll keep you informed of the next step."

Jan on October 24, 1984

My Lakeshore Med office is a quiet, lonely place with nothing for me to do. Since Carolyn left, I bide my time, waiting for requests for help, writing the employee newsletter. Except for the weekly meetings with Pam, Laura and our camera tech Mark, which we're to have at 9 a.m. today to plan our next TV program, my primary function is working on leaving this job. I suppose I should be grateful to my three male administrators for keeping me on salary until I find a new job, but I should be working with them, doing the professional work that would improve the hospital's mission, working as a team member like I do with the rest of the hospital staff. It's that White Male Power System that's screwing us up now. Those three guys are really into it.

My phone startled me from my musings and I answered it with charged anticipation. Yes! It was John Jackson! Yes! I have the job! Finally! His James Earl Jones voice chuckled at my professional but joyfully positive response as he apologized for the delay. Yes! I'll be there! November 5! Yes, Sir! $27,500 per year! Right! Thank you! See you then! Good-bye, Mr. Jackson. Thank you!

After jumping up and down, shivering with glee in my silent room, I called Bea with the news and we talked while it all sank into my mind. Yes! And we chatted until I said I had to meet with our TV gang now. "I love you, Bea."

"And I love you, Jan."

Our close little TV group of four reliable friends and colleagues chatted about TV scripts over our breakfast at the round table in a small conference room with one wall of glass visible to the cafeteria. If anyone paid attention to us, they would know we were the creative, witty women, Laura, Pam and Jan plus Mark who make Lakeshore Med a more humane and happy place to work. And Mark, our quiet and capable apprentice, is an appreciative young man without pretensions, a new kind of young man like our sons, because we give him opportunities to learn from us older women and to become skilled with us, together, in this new hospital audio-visual specialty.

I was still in shock after John Jackson' phone call confirmed my new job, but I contributed ideas toward our next TV project. When we finished, I shifted my position, leaned forward to my colleagues and told them, "Ahem. I answered the phone an hour ago and John Jackson told me I will be the new public relations director at the Midwest Center Medical Complex."

Both Pam and Laura lunged toward me, so happy for me as I stood to receive their boisterous hugs and cheers. What a "Yeah!" came from our room! And Mark grabbed his camera from the table to capture a photo of this glorious moment in my life.

After we quieted down, I went back to my office to write this memo:*

Date: October 24, 1984
To: Nick Dixon and Randy King
Subject: Termination of Employment

Starting November 5, 1984, I will be assuming the responsibilities of Public Relations Director at the Midwest Center Medical Complex and will be reporting to Administrator John Jackson, MCMC's chief executive officer. I received a call from John Jackson this morning. A formal letter is in the mail.

Because I have no major responsibilities to complete at Lakeshore Med, I anticipate that there will be no problem scheduling my last working day for Friday, October 26. I will complete the employee newsletter on Thursday.

I think a personal exit interview with Nick Dixon is in order because of my position and because of my thirteen-year tenure at the hospital. It could be arranged on Friday, October 26, or before I officially leave Lakeshore Med employ.

In negotiations agreed upon after Randy King informed me on June 7, 1984, that my job was being eliminated and my outplacement expenses would be reimbursed. I have already submitted expenses, which are now complete.

Sincerely, etc.

With my heart beating from excitement mixed with sadness, I started the final steps of removing myself from my beloved hospital. I wrote the final newsletter. I started it in the fall of 1971, then Bea and then Carolyn carried on until this day, my thirteen years of part- and more than full-time dedication. I knew some time ago that my years of service wouldn't qualify me for a pension because, until the six-weeks strike in 1976, my tenure was designated as "part time." I was told the requirement was to work full time for ten years to qualify for a pension. I'd worked full-time for only eight years.

I brought home a bottle of champagne and Bea presented me with a letter from John I. Jackson, Hospital Administrator on

October 23, 1984, written on Milwaukee County stationery with its prominent County logo.

Dear Ms. Anthony

I am pleased to offer you the position of Director of Public Relations at the Midwest Center Medical Complex effective November 5, 1984,

In this position you will provide leadership for the hospital public relations and marketing. This position may also include supervision of hospital information functions and other related internal and external communications systems.

Because this is a new position, and because of the hospital's unique position with Franklin Memorial Hospital, the Midwest Medical College, the Midwest Regional Medical Center and other County departments, you may be required to coordinate with a number of key persons as we develop our public relations program.

Your starting salary will be $27,500 pending review by the Civil Service Commission. I am optimistic that the salary can be increased as the program develops.

Attached is a statement of benefits. Please respond to this offer in writing as soon as possible.

Sincerely, etc.

Jan on October 26, 1984

Dear Mr. Jackson,

I am pleased and proud to have been chosen to join your staff as Director of Public Relations starting on November 5, 1984. I will be looking forward to meeting with you on Monday.

Thank you.

Jan on November 2, 1984

At one time Nick Dixon, his wife and children were family friends. He wasn't perfect, for sure, but I trusted him as a Unitarian, a neighbor, a hospitable man, the man who sought me out to work for

Lakeshore Med thirteen years ago. I considered myself a colleague until he realized that I changed my lifestyle because I am committed to my loving a woman, Bea Lindberg.

He avoids me now, passing out orders to his two henchmen who seem happy to obey him. Today I meet him eye-to-eye in my exit interview before I move into a big league metropolitan hospital with a $6000 annual salary increase.

What should I say to him? How should I behave with my parting shot? Should I vent my frustration and anger? No matter what I say or how, he will not change. But what I say may help me to heal me from the harassment he has ignored, perhaps, even encouraged.

I was dressed for success when I entered a small conference room—in clothes that I will be wearing for my upscale position starting on Monday. Nick was in his power suit as well. Were we peers now? Friends again—now that I'm leaving? I think not.

Randy wished me good luck at our final meeting. Do they know more than I about what I'm getting into? I'm sure Nick knows the complexities of my new position. But I'm used to complex dealings after the years of loyal and successful service to my hospital despite the injustices that Bea and I've endured from these sexist, abusive, homophobic males.

Ah, what greater goals we could have accomplished if they would have allowed us to work with them.

I stood tall in Bea's new black serge suit rather than my customary blazer jacket, cotton and collared shirt and slacks and comfortable wedge-soled shoes. Her soft silky white blouse with its flowing ruffled tie made me feel like a Goddess despite under-trappings of slips, pantyhose and semi-high-heeled, glossy black shoes.

"Hello. Come in, Jan. Sit here next to me at this table so we can look at your Exit Interview report together."

I was surprised that no desk separated us. I maintained my

professional poise as he read the Exit Interview report that I handed him. He read aloud the written answers and I responded when he asked for more information.

• *Reason for separation*: My supervisor told me that my PR department was being eliminated.

• *What is your opinion in the following: Training:* Little or none from my supervisors as far as direction or response, except for negative responses.

"Didn't you see Randy on a weekly basis?" he asked.

"I handed in weekly lists addressing extensive promotion and marketing plans but I seldom received any validation or approval. I met with him if something happened that he didn't like."

• *Amount of work assigned:* Supervisor is indifferent or unaware of the amount of work that is required to achieve successful projects.

"Your hours were cut back, weren't they?"

"That only affected my paycheck because I've always stayed until I've known the jobs were successfully completed."

"Yes. I know," he said. "You more than proved that during our terrible strike."

"I've put in whatever time it took to reach a successful outcome. And the strike was before there were any co-workers like Bea Lindberg and then Carolyn Schafer, both dedicated to our assignments and our hospital."

"Humm."

I interpreted that "Humm" as saying that he didn't want to talk about Bea.

• *Amount of job freedom:* Worked in isolation without supervisory direction. When I asked for help, I would end up with more work.

• *Extent to which your ideas were put to use:* Extensive results without guidance in daily operations, patient and staff relations, publications and special events.

"I would think you'd enjoy the freedom you had to be creative without someone peering over your shoulder."

"That's true," I answered. "But I paid for that freedom by waiting for the guillotine to fall on my neck should something minor go wrong."

• *Promotional opportunities:* "Zero" And I added, "In fact, Randy threatened me with demotions."

• *Your contribution to the work:* Leadership, creative problem-solving, active participation in implementing projects.

"This looks impressive," Nick emphasized.

"Yes, and it's because of the team-building we've accomplished among the staff. They gave extra time and energy to this hospital because they're loyal to its goals, not because they'll earn rewards points toward some cheap cutlery or sports equipment."

• *Use of education, skills and abilities:* 100%

• *Personal recognition received:* Yes. From outside the hospital, local and state; from inside, peers and others; nothing sincere from current administration.

"Do you think, Jan, that you may have taken too much time away from work to attend these outside activities?"

"If that is so, Nick, then some of the many planned and unpredictable matters would have been neglected. On the contrary, we took on everything that was asked of us—and more. We did it all, and I don't know how you're going to find someone who will do the same." I kept quiet for a while after that while the next comments sunk into his brain.

• *Leadership ability of your supervisor:* Negative, draining, diminishing self-worth, abusive.

• *Was work challenging and rewarding:* Yes to 99% of peers and community. No to administrative support.

• *Did you feel secure in your job:* Day-by-day, hour-by-hour sense of job loss. My salary was inadequate for the responsibility, the successful results, and less than my other hospital PR peers.

• *Did your supervisor handle your complaints or problems satisfactorily?* No.

• *If you could tell the president of the hospital exactly how you feel about the way the hospital is run, what would you tell him?* I have deep concerns for his welfare and for the welfare and success of Lakeshore Med employees and the institution itself. The public relations program within a hospital will be truly effective only as if the PR function is part of the administrative process. If there is no coordination with the PR director, he or she will move along, working with others without understanding the nuances of a situation, without knowledge of the thinking behind decisions; without wrestling maximum PR benefit on behalf of a stated goal.

"But before I leave, Nick, I must describe the personal and hostile conditions that I've endured since 1977. Remember when Randy and I shared that little office in the North Wing? He was your intern then and he liked and respected me for being a tolerant, accepting person so he told—or inferred—intimate details of his life experiences that I didn't need to know, especially after he became my boss. I'm sure he later feared that I might compromise him because of what he'd said and done—even to Bea and to me.

"Before he hired Bea, I was honest with him about our relationship. I was still married and he knew that she and I were lovers when he approved her being my colleague to work with me. I think he had a weird thing going for her as early as a Transactional Analysis weekend in 1973 where we were to write "stroke" messages for each person. I identified Randy's handwriting on Bea's page even without his signature, 'Dig your body. Sincerely.'

"He felt comfortable talking with me *until* he performed this sexual assault that we've never spoken about but is always between us. After Bea worked successfully with me for over two years, she hosted a farewell party for your intern.

"I stayed with Bea in her apartment as long as I could, but Randy hung around playing her damn electric piano. I had to go home. I left him alone with her when she was drunk. All of us were drinking. Even Marge said she had a hangover the next day. But that's not the deed that's hung over our heads for all these years.

"Randy sexually abused Bea when they were alone! He fucked her! A dominant act. A boss sexually assaulting an employee, especially a drunken one, transforms that woman into feeling like a prostitute. It's inherently coercive and abusive. She called me at work the next morning. 'I'm devastated, Jan,' she said, 'I can't come to work and face him. He asked me if I wanted to, and I said why not. God. I was drunk. I had to be to let him do that to me. He's our boss. I was so wiped out. And I'm so sick about what I've done. In a panic, Bea cried, 'I may have to quit my job.'"

I told her, "You can't let him fuck you over again by quitting!" And later he fired her after she admitted herself into alcoholic rehab!

"Almost every time I look at him I think of Bea and how he fucked her when she was drunk—and he never said a word to her after—completely diminishing her—and me too. And then he fired her! It costs me not only mental agony of being emotionally abused by him when he reams me out for petty flaws, it also costs me at least $10,000 a year lost in salary compared to what my peers are earning with PR agencies doing a lot of their work. And it cost my partner her job, benefits and self-esteem!"

Nick seemed stunned, but perhaps that was only my impression as I stood and turned toward the door, walking away from cruelty and injustice. I was proud and strong, cleansed, moving forward, motivated to conquer worthy and significant challenges in the future.

Bea on November 3, 1984

Someone submitted Monday's *Bay View Times* "Business News" column that simply finished off Jan's fabulous career in Lakeshore Bay: "LEAVES LAKESHORE MED: Jan Anthony, who was director of communications at Lakeshore Medical Center here, has accepted the newly-created position of public relations director at Midwest Center Medical Complex. Anthony joined Lakeshore Med in 1971; she left Friday."

<<<◇>>>

Jan's last day at Lakeshore Med had people in her office all day bringing her flowers and giving her hugs and goodbyes. But she had to see Randy to give him her keys, I.D., etc. This upset her again. She broke down when she got home. It's like getting divorced.

I didn't do much all day, just coasting, calculating and planning the options for a move to Milwaukee. I hate tearing up our house, my bones ache and everything is so frustrating. I don't want to move. I don't want to change everything. But I don't have a choice. I don't like moving my nude paintings out of the living room and hiding then in the attic. I'll miss them. It's like part of me must be hidden, as if Jan is ashamed of them and me. Our home that was so honest is no more.

I went to the mall to check out clothes for Jan whose Lakeshore Med informal pantsuit wardrobe wasn't what she could wear for a new job. I bought her two slips, several pairs of panty hose and a new curling iron. We had a wardrobe try-on session and completely organized her dress-for-success clothes with four suits and about fifteen different outfits with skirts, etc. (including the clothing I bought for the jobs I didn't want or get). After all that dressing and undressing, we put on our pajamas and lay together on the couch and held one another.

Jan on November 3, 1984

"Good luck." That's what Randy said on my last day. Did he know something I don't know? I'm sure he did.

"Good luck?" Is that what I need? No. I need courage. And as a new, one-woman PR person in this major metropolitan hospital, I need to build team support with staff already in a place to be successful in a system that I know nothing about.

Buck up! Trust your intuition! Be brave! You've been around! You will do it!

Afterward

Jan writes on July 25, 2010

Is what I have written ethical?

I've stressed positives in what we have accomplished; it's what I experienced.

Why did we write much of our lives in diaries and journals? We should have talked more about our issues than write about them. Why would we wait for the survivor, either Bea or me, to discover our volumes decades later?

Is it ethical to share them with readers?

From Mother Courage Press

Additional Books in
The Whistling Girls and Crowing Hens Series

Book 1 – *Not to be Denied* captures humorous, sad and, scary family life between 1900 and 1970: The Depression, wars and life at home, schizophrenia; tomboy girls and teen girlfriends, sexual encounters, children, husbands, and individuals' choices that shape them. Passion explodes for two women in their early '40s. Liberal religion and Transactional Analysis weekends bring them together. Their paths meld when these naïve lovers test their magnetic attraction after Jan asks, "What could it hurt if we just let it happen?" (January 2024)

Book 2—*Gullibles' Travels*, where divorced Bea tries not to be a lesbian and her lover Jan strives to keep her children, husband and Bea happy. Bea and friends test the Sexual Revolution of the '60s and '70s. Jan recalls living in Cold War Germany in the '50s and touring Greece, Leningrad and Moscow with her husband in the '70s. Jan defuses a labor/management conflict and Bea and Jan escape to Europe for a rowdy and risqué three-week escapade in '76. (April 2024)

Book 3—In *Secret Transgressions*, Jan's hospital PR job expands with Bea as her assistant. Jan's marriage turns raw. Divorce. Bea is subject to sexual harassment in the workplace, is fired, and Jan is emotionally harassed on the job. Travel helps them heal and they create Mother Courage Bookstore and Press. (July 2024)

Book 4—*Being Mother Courage* embodies a dream come true: creating a feminist bookstore and experiencing historic events and adventures in the women's movement and the gay/lesbian world.

Women's spirituality circles and lesbian support groups in Bea and Jan's home inspire and support women. Jan confronts job harassment and Bea faces the bookstore's demise. Tension turns to courageous laughter when conflicts are overcome. Bea uses her skills to pioneer Apple's Mac desktop publishing and was a guest speaker/teacher at the International Women's Booksellers Conference in Barcelona, Spain. (August 2024)

Book 5—In *Grit & Gratification*, Bea and Jan muster strength after Jan's father dies and she loses her precious Door County land. Sailor Bea successfully commands her sailing crew Jan, and together they rehab their rundown properties. Maturing offspring begin respecting their mothers' lives. Jan garners career awards. Lusty loving and travel enhances their lives and they tow their camper to experience New York City, Provincetown, America's Stonehenge and Niagara Falls. Then, as Festie Virgins, they experience their first Michigan Woman's Music Festival.

Book 6—Moving On & Up

Book 7—Closer to Fine

Book 8—Intimate Passages

For additional information on the series, contact:
Publisher Jeanne Arnold
MotherCouragePress31@gmail.com
https://www.mothercouragepress.com
**Books are on Amazon, Google Books,
and available through Ingram for libraries and bookstores.**

ABOUT JAN ANTHONY

Jan may brag about being a battled-tested warrior queen, but she's really an optimistic crone who blends truthful and imaginative words to recreate two women's audacious journey together. Their frustrated search for happiness as married women with teenage children fails. They fall in love, discover the depths of women-creative cultures and fight for successful careers while challenging socially acceptable norms. Jan's storytelling takes you into their intimate lives that enhance sensual and spiritual memories with their bodacious, risk-taking adventures.

Mother Courage Press
MotherCouragePress31@gmail.com

www.ingramcontent.com/pod-product-compliance
Lightning Source LLC
LaVergne TN
LVHW021803060526
838201LV00058B/3224